MW00987410

Praise for LARA ADRIAN

"Adrian has a gift for drawing her readers deeper and deeper into the amazing world she creates."

—Fresh Fiction

"With an Adrian novel, readers are assured of plenty of dangerous thrills and passionate chills."

—RT Book Reviews

"Nothing beats good writing and that is what ultimately makes Lara Adrian stand out amongst her peers . . . Adrian doesn't hold back with the intensity or the passion."

—Under the Covers

"Adrian has a style of writing that creates these worlds that are so realistic and believable . . . the characters are so rich and layered . . . the love stories are captivating and often gut-wrenching . . . edge of your seat stuff!"

—Scandalicious Book Reviews

"Adrian compels readers to get hooked on her storylines."

—Romance Reviews Today

Praise for Lara Adrian's books

"Adrian's strikingly original Midnight Breed series delivers an abundance of nail-biting suspenseful chills, red-hot sexy thrills, an intricately built world, and realistically complicated and conflicted protagonists, whose happily-ever-after ending proves to be all the sweeter after what they endure to get there."

—Booklist (starred review)

"(The Midnight Breed is) a well-written, action-packed series that is just getting better with age."

—Fiction Vixen

Praise for
THE 100 SERIES

"I wish I could give this more than 5 stars! Lara Adrian not only dips her toe into this genre with flair, she will take it over . . . I have found my new addiction, this series."

—The Sub Club Books

"There are twists that I want to say that I expect from a Lara Adrian book, and I say that because with any Adrian book you read, you know there's going to be a complex storyline. Adrian simply does billionaires better."

—Under the Covers

"This book had me completely addicted from page one!! There were several twists and turns throughout this super steamy read and I was surprised by how much mystery/suspense was woven in. Loved that! If you're looking for the perfect summer read, look no further than this book!"

—Steph and Chris Book Blog

"I have been searching and searching for the next book boyfriend to leave a lasting impression. You know the ones: where you own the paperbacks, eBooks and the audible versions…This is that book. For those of you who are looking for your next Fifty Fix, look no further. I know, I know—you have heard the phrase before! Except this time, it's the truth and I will bet the penthouse on it."

—Mile High Kink Book Club

"For 100 Days is a sexy, sizzling, emotion-filled delight. It completely blew me away!"

—J. Kenner, New York Times bestselling author

"For 100 Nights is an erotic delight that will have you on the edge of your seat! An instant addiction and a complete escape, with an intriguing storyline and an ending that will leave you gasping for air. This series has quickly become one of my favorites!"

"There is only one word that can adequately describe For 100 Nights: PHENOMENAL. For 100 Days was one of my favourite books of last year and this book has topped that. . . . Move over because there is a new queen of erotica on the charts and you don't want to miss her."

"If you're looking for a hot new contemporary romance along the lines of Sylvia Day's Crossfire series then you're not going to want to miss this series!"

"Lara Adrian has once again wowed me with her writing. She has created a complex erotic romance that has layers upon layers for both of her characters. Their passion for one another is romantic, sizzling, and a little bit naughty. Lara has added intrigue and suspense that keeps the reader completely involved. Each small revelation is leading to an explosive conclusion. I cannot wait for the third and final book, For 100 Reasons, to release."

Other books by Lara Adrian

Midnight Breed series

Paranormal Romance

Hunter Legacy Series
Born of Darkness
Hour of Darkness
Edge of Darkness
Guardian of Darkness

Historical Romances

Dragon Chalice Series
Heart of the Hunter
Heart of the Flame
Heart of the Dove

Warrior Trilogy
White Lion's Lady
Black Lion's Bride
Lady of Valor

Lord of Vengeance

RUN TO YOU

A 100 Series Standalone Novel

NEW YORK TIMES BESTSELLING AUTHOR

LARA ADRIAN

ISBN: 978-1-939193-40-7

RUN TO YOU
© 2019 by Lara Adrian, LLC
ISE-24-08

LaraAdrian.com

Available in ebook, trade paperback, and unabridged audiobook editions.

Run to You

1

~ Evelyn ~

I'm late.

Dammit, I'm never late. It's one of my unbreakable personal rules. Right up there with never lose control of any situation. At least, not on the outside. Yet today of all days, I'm currently eight minutes late and going nowhere fast.

As I speed through the rivers of afternoon Manhattan traffic, anxiety creeps up the back of my neck in a damp rush, making me regret that I decided to wear my dark hair up in a chignon instead of down around my shoulders in loose waves to hide the clammy sheen. I crank the A/C to full-blast, but it's not going to cool my nerves.

I haven't experienced flop-sweat like this since the first time I stepped onto a fashion runway. A long time ago. Another lifetime ago, in fact. Still, my stomach clenches at the reminder, nausea twisting inside me.

And I'm getting later by the second.

I'd already been running behind when I left my shop on Madison Avenue to make the fifteen-minute drive from L'Opale to this private client meeting across town. Rescheduling was out of the question. I've been looking forward to this appointment for several weeks. In truth, I've been busting my ass to prepare for it as if my life depends on landing this client. Maybe it does. Either way, I'm not about to let a career-making opportunity slip through my fingers.

I switch lanes to avoid a slow-moving minivan with out-of-state plates and a bumper full of tourist decals. My turn onto West 57th Street is only a couple of miles ahead. I rush to make a light, only to slam my foot on the brake an instant later, wincing as the hood of my Volvo nearly taps the yellow taxi that's veered out from the curb in front of me.

Shit. Nine minutes late now.

I can still hear Katrina, my design partner at the boutique, chiding me for insisting on driving instead of opting for the subway. And yes, as much as I hate to admit it, she was right. Never mind that I haven't set foot near those subterranean tracks even once in the past five years. To be honest, I'm not sure I can ever again. But this appointment would have been worth it to try.

Who the hell am I trying to kid? This appointment is worth *everything* to me.

God, I hope Kat was able to reach Avery Ross to let her know I'm on the way. Absently, I reach over to the passenger seat for the phone in my purse and grasp nothing but air. It's not there, of course. The vintage Chanel couture clutch—one of the few remnants of my former life—went missing sometime between my arrival at L'Opale this morning and the moment I was packing up my lingerie designs for today's private consultation.

After several minutes of panic and fruitless searching, I finally grabbed my keys from atop my desk where I tossed them and left. I'll have plenty of time to resume freaking out about losing my favorite little handbag and everything inside it when I return. At the moment, the only thing I'm focused on is getting my portfolio into the hands of my newest client who's waiting for me in the executive suite of the Baine International building.

Assuming this meeting happens at all. The only thing worse than crashing and burning in front of a celebrated artist who also happens to be the fiancée of one of the most powerful men in the city—if not the world—would be losing the chance to try.

Hope pulls me forward as I turn onto West 57th where the gleaming, dark glass tower belonging to billionaire Dominic Baine dominates the skyline and occupies easily half of the block. I'm familiar enough with the landmark building even though I've only been inside a handful of times over the years, on random occasions when I've been in the company of Baine International's chief counsel, Andrew Beckham, my starched-collared, career-driven, perfect older brother.

Andrew owns the boutique I manage, just one of many investments he's made in me since we were kids, financially and otherwise. We may only be half-siblings, sharing a handsome father who gave us our shared creamy brown skin tone and light green eyes, but Andrew has been my rock for as long as I can remember. Especially in recent years. Even when I didn't deserve him.

Since I don't have time to hunt for on-street parking or a nearby public garage—not that I can pay for either one without my purse—I take a chance and swing into the underground lot beneath the Baine Building. Punching in the access code I've seen Andrew use on the keypad outside, I wait for the metal arm to rise, then slip inside.

As luck would have it—finally a little bit of good luck today—I spot several vacant spaces, although all of them are marked *Reserved*. I take the empty one that's nearest the elevator. Killing the Volvo's engine, I unfasten my seatbelt and reach back to collect my design portfolio and laptop from behind me.

I'm still leaned into the backseat foraging around when a hard rap on the driver's side window startles me.

"Can't park here." A deep baritone, speaking in a clipped, authoritative tone.

I don't know who the voice belongs to since all I see standing outside the car when I swivel my head is an athletic-looking torso clad in a crisp white button-down shirt. A black suit jacket is open just enough for me to notice a hint of the leather shoulder holster and pistol riding beneath the pressed fabric.

The security officer's knuckles hit the glass again, before I have a chance to respond. "This space is reserved. You need to move your vehicle now, please."

Although the level tone and perfunctory "please" tacked on the end is polite enough, he talks like a man who's used to giving people orders and being obeyed without question. I'm sure the undertaker's suit and nasty-looking firearm helps in that arena, but it's the self-assured, whiskey-dark growl that really gets my attention. Not that I have time for any of it right now.

"Just a minute," I mutter from inside the car as I continue collecting my things.

With the handles of my laptop case and design portfolio gripped in one hand, I reach with my other for the handle of the door but pause when the man standing on the other side doesn't budge. Impatient, I huff as I push my face toward the window and peer up the length of his tall, obviously fit body. A silver metal pin with the Baine International logo rides the lapel of his jacket.

I still can't see his face, but I shoot a scowl up at him anyway. "Do you mind?"

He hesitates before taking a step back, allowing barely enough room to let me pop the door and swing my legs out. I plant my stiletto sandals on the concrete and stand up, smoothing the creases from my plum-colored sheath dress with my free hand before bumping my hip against the car door to close it behind me.

His gaze skims the length of me in a brief, unreadable glance that ends with a clash of our gazes. His hazel eyes are sharp and penetrating beneath the slashes of his chestnut brows. I feel the heat of those eyes like a physical touch, one that unsettles me more than I care to admit. I'm the first to break the contact, glancing away as I move the strap of my portfolio onto my shoulder.

"Excuse me. I have a meeting inside and I'm already late."

He doesn't budge. At five-foot-eleven, I usually tower over most men. Not this one.

Even though I'm in four-inch heels, my eyes hit about level with his chin. It's a strong chin, square and solid like the rest of his jaw. The bridge of his nose might have been equally rigid at one time, but it jags a degree to the right, aftermath of an obvious break. And now that I'm looking, I notice an odd dent in the cheekbone below his left eye. It's slight, but I fixate on it for a moment, wondering what happened to him, and how.

He clears his throat. "Ma'am, I said you can't stay here. This vehicle needs to move. Now."

"Ma'am. Really?" I scoff under my breath. In spite of his hard face and the assessing, serious gaze that seems to add years to his appearance, I place him somewhere near thirty, like me.

"Don't worry about my car," I tell him. "I'm only going to be here for an hour or two, and anyway, my brother won't mind that I'm in his spot." I gesture vaguely in the direction of Andrew's first initial and last name stenciled in black letters on the wall in front of my parked Volvo.

He looks skeptical. And he still hasn't moved to allow me past him. "Your brother?"

"Yes." I release an impatient sigh. "I'm Evelyn Beckham."

"I'm not aware that Mr. Beckham has a sister."

"Well, now you are."

I stare at him, awaiting the moment when this heavily-armed Boy Scout realizes his mistake. That not only am I, indeed, related to one of Baine International's chief executives, but that for a short time some eight years ago—before my spectacular fall from grace—I couldn't go anywhere without being instantly recognized as one of the most photographed, highest-paid fashion models in the world.

I was someone else back then. I've gained a few pounds and a whole lot of mileage since those runway days when it was all I could do to survive being the perpetually hungry, utterly exhausted and ruthlessly exploited twenty-two-year-old called simply, mononymously, Eve.

But the man studying me now doesn't seem to know that.

If he does know, maybe he doesn't care.

Either way, I can't deny the wash of relief that pours over me in his silence. I've spent the last five years trying to forget my time in the harsh glare of the spotlight. I've spent even longer than that trying to defend myself against opportunists and sleazeballs of all stripes who tend to see me only as a sexual conquest, or worse, an inanimate object for them to acquire as a means of bolstering their own twisted definitions of manhood or success.

The fact that this man is treating me like a normal human being—albeit a potentially suspicious one—is a welcome reprieve.

Rather, it would be, if he wasn't standing here keeping me from my meeting with Avery Ross.

"Are we done here? I think you've held me up long enough, don't you?" I sound like an epic bitch, but it doesn't seem to faze him. His coolness has the opposite effect on me. "In case I didn't mention it, Nick Baine's fiancée is waiting for me inside."

I deliberately use the nickname reserved for the billionaire's close friends and trusted colleagues. But all it earns me is a grunted acknowledgment from the Boy Scout. "I assume you have some identification?"

"Are you serious?" I gape at him, and I swear I see a trace of wry humor in the tilt of his sculpted lips.

"Just doing my job, ma'am."

Again with the ma'am. This guy's a real charmer. I barely resist the urge to roll my eyes as I prepare to show him my ID. And then I remember I don't have my purse. "Shit."

"Problem?"

"I lost my purse today." I close my eyes, giving a faint shake of my head. "My driver's license, wallet, phone . . . I don't have any of it on me right now."

"You're driving around without your license? You do know that's illegal, right?"

I glower up at him. "What are you going to do, officer, arrest me?"

"I'm not a cop," he mutters. As if he's insulted at the suggestion, his brows rankle in a scowl. He takes his phone out of his jacket pocket and touches the display. His hard gaze remains fixed on me as he brings the device to his ear. "Lily? Yeah, it's Gabe. I'm doing just fine, darlin'. How's everything on the top floor?" A grin tugs the edges of his all-too-fine mouth as a cheerful feminine voice sounds on the other end of the line. "Listen," he says, "I've got somewhere I need to be right now, but there's someone down here in the garage who says Ms. Ross is waiting to meet with her. You know anything about that?" He grunts in response, a low note that doesn't seem to carry much surprise. "No shit. Andrew Beckham's got a sister, eh?"

I tilt my head and narrow an annoyed look on him, but the arrogant Boy Scout has the audacity to wink at me while he thanks the other woman for the information, then ends the call.

"Satisfied now?" I ask as he slips the phone back into his jacket pocket.

He holds me in a stare that's closer to amused than

contrite. "Ms. Beckham, we seem to have gotten off on the wrong foot here today."

"I'll say."

A smirk flashes across his sculpted lips, arrogant and sexier than I care to acknowledge. He extends his hand to me in an apparent attempt at a truce. "So, let's start over, then. I'm Gabriel Noble, Corporate Security for Baine International. Most people call me Gabe."

Especially the women he calls "darlin'" I mentally add with no small amount of scorn.

I stare at the broad palm and strong fingers of his outstretched hand, refusing to give in to his self-assured charm. "There's no need for us to start over. And I'm still late."

He inclines his head in a slight nod. Using his open hand, he gestures toward the elevator. "If you'll come with me, I'll personally take you upstairs to the executive floor."

I readjust my portfolio and tighten my grip on my laptop bag. "That won't be necessary. Besides, I thought you said you have somewhere you need to be?"

"My job always comes before anything else."

Spoken like a true Boy Scout. I might have scoffed if he didn't sound so sincere. "Well, consider your job here done. Now, if you don't mind, I'd like to go up to my meeting."

"I can't let you do that."

"Like hell you can't." I glare at him, my anger spiking. "And if you don't get out of my way and let me go—"

He slowly shakes his head. Then he leans in, closer than I expect. Close enough that my senses immediately fill with the clean, spicy scent of him and the unsettling heat of his muscled body. "The garage elevator requires an access card. To get to the executive floors as a visitor, you also need security clearance, either from the guard on post in the lobby or by another member of the team."

"Oh."

I stare into those sharp hazel eyes, which I realize are actually an arresting combination of gray and green and brown. And right now, they're lit with a smugness that infuriates me as he continues to hold my gaze—and my body—captive in the small space between us.

"I guess it's lucky for you that we met, Ms. Beckham. Otherwise you'd be stuck down here in the garage until someone else came along."

Lucky isn't the first word that comes to mind, even though I have to admit I'm grateful for the save. Instead of giving him the satisfaction of a response, though, I squeeze past him without a word and head for the elevator.

I feel the weight of his gaze following me every step of the way. When I turn around to confirm it, I find him grinning. And fuck, he's got a great smile. A little crooked on one side and framed by a pair of boyish dimples that I imagine have charmed the panties off any number of women.

Not this one, I tell myself, clinging to my irritation for him as we reach the elevator doors. I have to cling to it. If I don't, I might be forced to acknowledge the attraction that's been smoldering between us from the moment our eyes connected.

"After you, ma'am," he says, pausing to hold the open door.

I mutter my thanks as I step inside. But I can't resist giving him an arch look as he enters the car behind me.

"As for getting off on the wrong foot, Gabe *darlin*? I'll bet that's the only one you've got."

2

~ Gabriel ~

Rush hour is in full swing by the time I make it over the Throgs Neck Bridge from Manhattan to Bayside, Queens. I should have been here an hour ago, but there's nothing I can do to fix that now.

I squeeze my black Lexus RC 350 between a pickup truck and a rusted-out Bronco in the lot behind McGilly's on Bell Boulevard, my old neighborhood. I had intended to stop by my place first and change clothes but getting held up at the Baine Building for as long as I did put the kibosh on that plan.

I know I'll catch a lot of hell inside the pub for walking in wearing a suit that costs about as much as most of these folks take home in their weekly paychecks. No telling the amount of shit they'll deal me if anyone takes note of my recently upgraded car. I bought it used, not that it would matter to anyone inside the busy watering hole. And it wouldn't be the first time I take it on the chin for being on the payroll of a man as powerful—and wealthy—as Dominic Baine.

To some people, I sold out going to work for the formidable corporate titan as part of his security team. To others, I've done a lot worse than that, turning my back on my roots to make a life for myself on the other side of the bridge. It's taken me a long time to decide I just don't fucking care anymore what anyone has to say.

I make my own decisions, always have.

I'm the only one who has to live with the consequences.

As I park my car and kill the engine, I remove the Baine International logo pin from my jacket lapel and drop it into a cup holder in the center console. That's less of a concession to the contempt it might earn me inside than it is out of respect for the privacy of my employer and friend.

Even off the clock, I don't forget for a minute how much I owe Nick Baine. He took a chance on me when no one else would, so my loyalty runs deep. There's nothing I wouldn't do for him if he asked. And that means I'm never officially off-duty.

As for my service weapon, I don't bother to stow that before I climb out of the vehicle. No one here will give the pistol a second look, so it stays holstered under my jacket as I walk to the back door of McGilly's and into the din of a gathering that's already in full swing.

A Springsteen classic rasps over the sound system. Competing for attention is tonight's big baseball game, playing on all four flat-screens mounted high on the dark wood-paneled walls. Aside from a smattering of sports fans wearing blue-and-orange jerseys in support of the favored team, the rest of the bar's regulars crowded around the tables in the small establishment are dressed in jeans and T-shirts.

This pub on Bell is as local as it gets, and unless you knew otherwise, you'd never guess the whole damn place is full of off-duty cops.

As I step farther inside, I glance toward the center of the activity in the room. A large group of men varying in age from twenty-something to seventy-ish are pounding back pitchers of beer in between hoots of laughter and shouted conversation. They've occupied most of the tables and nearly all of the floor space—an amazing turnout, and well-deserved.

Rather than spoil the mood for anyone just yet, I take a seat at the bar and nod at the squatty, dark-haired bartender I knew in high school. "Hey, Tommy. How's things?"

He glances over with a look of surprise as he places a pair of light beers in front of a couple of young women with their gazes glued to their phones. "Gabe, shit. Look at you. Civilian life's treating you real good, I see." He doesn't say it with judgment, nor does he expect a reply. "What can I get you, man?"

"Irish ale. Whatever you've got on tap."

He pours my beer and brings it over. When I put my money on the counter, he shakes his head. "It's on me. Haven't seen you in here since before you deployed. Fuck, dude, that's gotta be what—"

"Long time." I spare him from doing the math, even though I know damn well when I left for Afghanistan.

It's been seven years and a lot of road in between. Most of it littered with shrapnel and a million pieces of smoldering flesh and fragmented bone. Not all of it belonging to me.

"Yeah," Tommy says quietly, glancing at me as if he's looking for visible evidence of the injuries that got me medically discharged and ended my military career one year into my second tour. "Anyway, it's good to see you again, Gabe. Welcome home, since I haven't gotten to say that to you until now."

I nod and lift the glass to my mouth. "Thanks for the beer."

Before he decides to travel any further down memory lane, I swivel around to look at the gathering. One of the men seated at the center table stands up to deliver a long-winded toast and congratulations for the newly promoted police commander.

Through the tight cluster of bodies of all shapes and sizes, I spot the man of the hour. Tall and broad-shouldered, with a deep laugh and a crown of thick ginger hair that gleams like fire in the low yellow lights of the bar, he holds court over the rest of the room like a king.

Pride tugs at my mouth as I watch my oldest brother, Shane, soaking up his hard-earned glory. Part of me wants to just get out of here and leave, let him enjoy it. I'm the outsider at this party, anyway—never mind that many of these cops are my family.

There's a deep blue line running through five generations of Noble men. I was the first, the only one, to break the chain.

For a lot of reasons, I've never fit into the Noble mold.

That's never been more evident to me than since I came home from the desert and my entire life blew apart. I'm not sure I'll ever be able to collect all of the pieces of who I used to be.

And I sure as hell don't belong back home in Bayside anymore. Not that I ever did.

I exhale a curse under my breath and down the rest of my beer. Just as I'm about to lever myself off the barstool to make my exit from the pub, one of the guys from the party approaches from the fringes of the packed gathering.

Twin dimples that mirror mine bracket his mouth as he walks up to me smiling. "Christ, I thought I smelled Armani cologne back here. Look who finally made it."

Of all three of my older brothers, at thirty-six Jacob's the closest to me in age, even though a full nine years separate us. We're roughly the same height and build, but he's got Mom's sable hair and big brown eyes. Everything else about him is all Dad—except for the affection my brother has always shown me.

He sets his empty mug on the bar and cuffs my shoulder in a gesture that usually passes for an embrace in our family. His black T-shirt strains across his muscular chest, the short sleeves wrapped around solid biceps inked with tattoos. Even half-hidden, the body art betrays the rebellious side of him, since tats on a Noble are almost as cardinal a sin as turning one's back on the family law-and-order business.

If I have one ally among my brothers, Jake's it.

As he drops onto the stool next to mine, I smirk at him. "Armani, my ass. Unlike you, dickhead, I haven't worn cologne a day in my life. You'd think a guy aiming to make detective one day would have better skills at, you know, detecting."

He chuckles and motions to Tommy for another round of beers for both of us. "You were supposed to be here an hour ago."

"Something unexpected came up at work."

Talk about an understatement.

For what isn't the first time since I left Baine headquarters, I think about *her*. The leggy brunette with the buttery light-brown skin, silvery-green eyes, and curves that made me want to peel off her dark purple dress and run my hands over every inch of her.

I've seen a lot of beautiful women since I took the job in Manhattan, but to say Evelyn Beckham is beautiful is putting it mildly—and then some.

Maybe I pushed it too far with her, playing the inflexible cop in the garage, then insisting on riding up with her to the thirty-fourth floor. I could have taken her word that she was, indeed, who she claimed to be. There was enough family resemblance between her and Andrew Beckham to back her up, even if I've never once considered that Beck might have a sister with the face of an angel and a body that had my cock's full attention the instant she stepped out of her car.

Her fiery, confident personality only added to her appeal. If she'd bent rather than pushing back when I confronted her, I would have done my best to put her at ease. I'm not a total dick, although I'm sure she'd never believe that now. I told her I was just doing my job, but if I had been, I would have used my access card to clear her for the executive suite, then sent her on her way alone in the elevator.

The truth is, I was glad for the interruption in my day. Glad for the excuse to delay the inevitable family reunion here at McGilly's. If I didn't respect and admire my brothers so much, I wouldn't have needed any excuse to skip the festivities completely.

Our beers arrive and I pick mine up, gesturing with my chin in the direction of our eldest brother as another of his law enforcement colleagues gets up to toast his promotion. "Shane's never looked happier. Leave it to him to make Commander by the time he turned forty-two. Dad must be pleased as hell about that."

Jake glances that way and nods. "You have no idea. Mom is too. They're hosting a cookout for Shane and Lisa and the kids at the house next weekend. I think Mom invited the whole damn neighborhood."

"I wouldn't expect anything less."

"You're going to be there, right?"

I shrug and take a drink of my beer. "Depends on work, I guess. And other things."

He grunts. "Work and other things. I swear, brother, sometimes you're as elusive as that 'shadow mogul' billionaire you work for. Looks like you've even got the wardrobe."

Because the jab is good-natured and not unanticipated, I let it roll off me. I also let the tabloid-inspired nickname for Dominic Baine go without comment. Nick's reputation as a reclusive genius and ruthless corporate raider isn't totally unwarranted, but the fact is he's changed now that Avery Ross is in his life. No one who knows him would say he's been tamed or mellowed, but there is a peace about him that hadn't been there when I first met the man a little over a year ago.

His other, more private reputation—the darker one whispered about away from mainstream news headlines and business profiles—is a topic best kept between him and his fiancée.

God knows, I don't have any room to judge when it

comes to someone else's personal kinks.

"I can't stay long," I murmur, eyeing Jake over the rim of my glass. "I should head over and give Shane my congrats, then get out of here."

Jake lets out a low whistle. "Two minutes inside the door and you're already angling for the fastest way to make your escape. That's got to be some kind of record."

He's right, and I'm not going to deny it. "I came because I had to. For Shane. For Mom. Hell, even for myself. I know what this promotion means to our brother."

"And to Dad," Jake says, slanting a sober look on me. "He wants the best for all of his sons. He wants to see all of us succeed."

I scoff into my glass. "Some more than others."

I sound bitter, but damn if I can help it. Things have never been good between me and my father, but over the past couple of years, our disagreements and apparent dislike for each other has expanded into a bona fide estrangement.

My gaze strays into the pub, spotting the old man. He's seated at the table next to Shane, his meaty hand wrapped around the same mug of beer he's been holding since I arrived. He's beaming under the praise being heaped on his eldest son, chuckling at every joke, grinning as the revelry and celebration continues. From all appearances, having the time of his fucking life.

He's grown a short beard since I saw him last. Most of the whiskers have come in gray instead of the coppery hue of his thinning hair. And the beard doesn't quite disguise the leanness of his face, the thin, aging sag of his jowls.

"He's losing weight," I remark, swiveling back around to face the bar.

"You think so?" Jake frowns, throwing a quick glance in Dad's direction before looking at me again. "I guess you'd see it before any of us, considering how long it's been since you've been home." He winces as soon as the words leave his mouth. "Shit. That came out wrong. I don't mean anything by it, Gabe."

I shake my head and polish off the rest of my beer. "Don't worry about it. You're right, it's been too long. I should make a point to come around more—for Mom, if nothing else."

"She'd like that. I think he would, too, even if he doesn't say it." Jake fists his hand and knocks his knuckles into my arm. "Anyway, fuck the family drama hour. Tell me how things are going for you in the city. You doing anything interesting for Baine, or is it just a lot of standing around in pricey suits and sunglasses pretending to look useful?"

I laugh, because for the most part, he's got it nailed. And I can't deny that I'm getting to the point where I'm craving something more. "You sound jealous, bro."

He blows out a chuckle. "Yeah, maybe a little. Do you have any idea how much ass I'd be getting if I could say I was working for Dominic Baine?"

"I must've missed that item in the benefits package," I tell him with a smirk.

"Maybe you weren't looking hard enough." Jake's never been shy about his voracious appetite for women. He grins, but he's studying me now. "You know, it's going on four years since you and Tracy broke up. You're not getting any younger. Not getting any better looking, either."

"What are you trying to say?"

He shrugs, takes a swig of beer. "You need to get back out there sometime. Get back on the horse, so to speak."

"Dating advice from you?" I exhale a wry curse. "That's about as helpful as it was coming from Dad back when I was thirteen."

But Jake doesn't seem ready to let the subject go. He faces me full-on, his brown eyes careful, yet probing. "I know things haven't been easy for you since you came home. All the surgeries, the year-plus of rehab. I'm not going to act like I can relate to anything you've gone through, but don't think I won't be here to kick your ass if I think you need it."

I feel my jaw tense up at the reminder of my injury. Not that I need reminders. There are times I still wake up thinking my body's intact. Other times, I dream I'm hobbling over the scorched and bloodied dirt road where my unit's Humvee hit that IED, trying to retrieve the chunks of muscle and bone that had once been the lower portion of my left leg.

I'll never know why I survived and the other guys didn't.

It's taken years for me to stop wishing I'd died with them.

Jake drains his glass and stares at me like he's preparing for an interrogation. "When's the last time you were with a woman?"

"Singular?"

His bark of laughter says he thinks I'm joking. I'm not about to clarify, even to him. Everyone handles pain and other problems in their own way. I've definitely got mine.

Jake shakes his head. "Okay, smartass. When's the last time you took a woman on a proper date?"

Now, that is a question I don't have an answer for, not even in jest. I shrug, realizing the truth would place me somewhere around the time I enlisted. Seven years ago. The night I blurted a clumsy proposal over dinner to the girl I'd been seeing all through high school. Tracy said yes, but she was gone three months after I woke up in a bed at Walter Reed.

"That long, huh?" Jake says, as if he can tell he's making his point. "Christ, you can't be hurting for selection. The city is full of beautiful women. Have you even met anyone you'd consider dating?"

For some insane reason, my mind instantly paints a picture of Evelyn Beckham's face. I can still see her pale green eyes flashing in indignation beneath lush black lashes. I can still smell the vanilla-sweet scent of her skin when I moved in closer than I needed to just so I could fill my lungs with more of her.

I can still hear her rich, velvety voice pitched in irritation as she informed me that in her opinion the only foot I have is the wrong one. I smile to myself, amused at the irony of her remark.

"I'm not interested in dating anyone," I tell my brother. "I'm not cut out for relationships. Not that I ever was."

As for Evelyn Beckham, she'd be off-limits even if she wasn't the sister of Nick Baine's good friend and personal lawyer. I consider Andrew Beckham a friend, too, but that doesn't mean the man won't see that I'm cut loose in a minute if he hears I gave his sister a hard time.

Hell, after the way I pissed her off, I wouldn't be

surprised if she was at the Baine Building demanding her brother and Nick dismiss me right now.

And if she does, I probably can't blame her.

If I didn't think it would be a further overstep, I'd find a way to reach her and apologize. Not out of concern for my job, but because I left her upset and thinking I was an obtuse, arrogant asshole.

"You gonna call her?"

"Who?"

Jake smirks. "Whoever she is that has you scowling and gripping that beer glass so hard you're going to crush it."

I let go of the glass and shake my head, a ready denial about to roll off my tongue. But before I can say anything, I see my father heading our way.

He's still a powerful presence in his sixties, even with the slight hitch in his step and the diminished muscle tone of his once-intimidating physique. His eyes are trained on me like laser beams, disapproval in both his blue gaze and the flat line of his mouth inside the graying frame of his new beard.

I groan under my breath. "Fuck." I'm not aware I've muttered the word out loud until Jake swivels around to see who's approaching from behind him.

He gets up as the old man nears us, as if the response to stand at attention comes to him as naturally as breathing. I remain seated, refusing to give my father the satisfaction of seeing me adjust to find my balance on my prosthesis.

Jake fills the instant, heavy silence. "Hey, Pop. Great party, huh? What a turnout."

Dad's still glowering at me as he grunts a non-response. When he speaks, it's directed at my brother as if I'm not even there. "I need to go home, son. My car's parked down the block. Run and get it for me, will you?"

Christ, he sounds worse than tired. Exhausted. Depleted.

"Yeah, no problem," Jake says, taking Dad's keys. "Let me square my tab with Tommy first, then I'll bring your car around back."

"I've got the drinks," I murmur, already reaching into my jacket pocket for my wallet. I feel my father's eyes on me as I set the key fob to my Lexus on the bar, then pull a couple of twenties from the fold of larger bills in my wallet.

Jake claps me on the shoulder. "Thanks, Gabe. Be right back."

He takes off, leaving me alone with the man I looked up to more than anyone else when I was a boy. The man who probably never loved me, and now makes no secret of the fact that he despises me.

I can't think of a single word to say to him.

He must feel likewise about me. He shuffles past me in silence, then walks out the back door of the pub to wait for his son outside.

I sit there for moment, simmering in useless fury. Tommy comes over to collect the cash I laid on the bar.

"Another beer, Gabe?"

"No, thanks. I'm leaving soon." He nods and starts to walk away to get my change. "On second thought, Tommy. I'll take a shot of Jameson. Make it a double."

3

~ Evelyn ~

"These designs are amazing." Avery Ross glances up from the array of sketches and swatches of silk and lace spread out before us on the cocktail table of the executive suite's sumptuous conversation area. "Evelyn, I don't know how I'm going to narrow down my choices to just a few."

"I'm so pleased you like them."

We are seated alone in the office on a pale gray leather Chesterfield sofa. Behind us on the soaring wall of polished silver granite hangs a large Jackson Pollock original painted in monochromatic black enamel on a cream canvas. I find it fascinating how the expansive office space overlooking a prime slice of Manhattan can look slightly dark and intimidating—much like the billionaire who commands it—yet Dominic Baine's business domain somehow feels far from cold or austere.

As for his beautiful fiancée, Avery is like a splash of golden sunshine in the midst of so much gray. Her warm smile beams as she looks at me and slowly shakes her head, sending her long blonde hair sifting around her shoulders.

"No wonder L'Opale is nipping at the heels of the top bespoke lingerie shops. Everything you've shown me today is incredible."

I can't deny the surge of pride I feel at her praise. The boutique on Madison Avenue is small, but in the five years since we opened, our clientele list has grown from a handful of East Coast socialites and celebrities into an exclusive, loyal following across the country and all around the world. My staff and I have worked hard to establish our reputation for quality, and I've made it my mission to personally ensure the innovation and originality of the pieces we make for our clients.

While some of our inventory is limited-run, small-volume production based off designs Katrina and I create together, the boutique primarily caters to private clients who commission us for individual pieces or custom ensembles like the one I'm presenting to Avery today.

In all fairness, it should have been Kat in my place for a client as high-profile as Avery Ross. She's got more experience, having come to work at L'Opale around the time we first opened, after being perhaps not-so-coincidentally dropped from another luxe custom lingerie shop's design staff the week after she turned forty.

But I've developed a rapport with Avery in the past

year that she's been a L'Opale customer. She requested me specifically for this project, and I couldn't be more excited—nor more determined—to create something spectacular for her that she, and her husband-to-be, will enjoy.

She picks up one of my sketches for a frothy, pearl-accented, lace demi-bra and panties. "This one is particularly lovely." A faint, secret smile curves her lips as she studies the design concept. "And Nick does love to see me in pearls."

"That set will look gorgeous on you," I tell her, delighted by her obvious enthusiasm for the ideas I've shown her. "To be honest, I think you could walk around in cotton briefs and a sports bra and Nick would be just as dazzled as he would be seeing you in any of these designs. That man adores you. I hope you don't mind me saying that."

"Mind? Are you kidding?" She turns a shy look at me, one of the first times I've ever seen her appear uncertain. She twists the enormous diamond engagement ring on her finger. "Thank you for saying that. These past three months have been a whirlwind since Nick proposed. Now, in addition to an exhibit I'm preparing for next week, we're also renovating the Park Place penthouse and planning our engagement party. Sometimes all the decisions become so overwhelming, I'm not sure I know anything for sure."

I nod, because I understand something about pressure and how heavy it can feel on someone's shoulders. I know the kind of sabotaging self-defeat that kind of pressure can bring. "Well, take this from an outside observer. One thing you don't ever have to doubt is the fact that your man is head over heels in love with you."

If I sound a little wistful in front of her, I can't help it. Avery Ross and Dominic Baine have the kind of unabashed devotion to each other that I've long been convinced couldn't actually exist in real life. Certainly, I've never known their kind of bond. After my string of disastrous—even dangerous—choices in men, I have no intention of putting my heart on the line ever again.

To cover my momentary lapse into memories I'd rather forget, I reach for another of the designs Avery had enthused over. "This silk set can also be embellished with pearls, if you'd like me to make a few alterations and show it to you again."

"No, it's perfect just as you have it, Evelyn. I love it, in fact." She gestures vaguely at the sketches on the table. "I'll take them."

"This one and the pearl demi-bra ensemble?"

"All of them," Avery says. "I can't choose between any of your designs, so I'd like to buy them all."

It takes calling on my stage face to keep from gaping. I've presented more than a dozen original concepts, each custom creation carrying a price tag well into the thousands. I thought she'd select one or two. Hoped she might take as many as three, possibly four, if I wanted to be optimistic. But to accept them all? It's the largest order we've had since we opened our doors.

"Um . . . thank you." I swallow past the elated cry that's about to burst out of me. "Avery, really. I can't thank you enough for giving me this opportunity to design for you. I promise, I won't let you down."

"I know you won't." She places her hand briefly over the top of mine. "You were kind to me the first day we met at the boutique, and I've never forgotten that,

Evelyn. You also happen to have an amazing vision for sexy, sophisticated pieces."

"There's nothing else I want to do," I admit to her. "Designing is my escape. It saved my life, if you want to know the truth."

She nods, even though I'm certain she can't know how close to the bone that statement really cuts. Although we're friendly and Avery knows I was a model in a former life, we haven't discussed the humiliating details of my failure in that career. Or my long climb back out of the abyss.

Still, there is a note of understanding in her gentle gaze. "Painting is all I've ever wanted to do. There was a time when it was the only thing standing between me and everything awful in my life. I clung to my dreams because they were all I had left. And I never gave up— not on life or my art. Neither should you."

"Thank you." My throat is tight at her tender advice. I've never handled emotions very well, especially in front of someone else. And I'm too excited to let myself sink into self-pity, even for a moment. I collect myself and offer my newest client a professional smile as I extend my hand to her. "I'm thrilled to be working with you, Avery. I'll take everything back to the boutique and start working on them right away. Since we do the sewing in-house, we should be able to schedule a preliminary fitting for the first few pieces in a couple of weeks."

"I can't wait," she says, shaking my hand. "Thanks again for being willing to change our meeting place at the last minute today. Nick's office was a much better option, since our apartment is currently a construction zone."

"My pleasure," I say, gathering up my materials and

slipping everything back into my portfolio. "I'm sorry I kept you waiting."

She waves her hand dismissively. "It wasn't a problem at all. Katrina had already phoned to let me know you were on the way, and besides, I was still buried in phone calls and emails when Nick's assistant, Lily, came in to tell me you were downstairs."

"Ah." Lily being the sweet-voiced *darlin'* Gabriel Noble had spoken to so casually, so charmingly, after treating me like a security threat. For reasons I'd rather not dwell on, I'd been hoping to find a middle-aged librarian seated outside the executive suite. Instead I was greeted by a stunning young woman with a mane of jet-black hair and a megawatt smile when I stepped off the elevator, harried and indignant after my encounter with the aggravating man.

I suppose I have to give Gabe credit. Instead of starting my meeting with Avery amid a case of stomach-churning nerves and anxiety over the fact that I was late, I marched in energized by my fury for him. Not that I'll ever tell him he did me a favor.

And not that I'll ever see him again—if I should be so lucky.

"Well, I suppose I should let you get back to your day." I sling my portfolio strap over my shoulder as Avery rises from the sofa with me. "Like I said, I'm very excited to start working on the designs. I'll email you copies of the sketches once I get back to the boutique, so if you have any questions or ideas you can let me know."

"That sounds great."

She walks me to the door, and as we exit together, we're met by my brother and Dominic Baine, who are just arriving off the elevator. Dressed in dark suits and crisp white shirts, both men are tall, well-built, and handsome. I'm sure a more formidable pair have never ruled a boardroom. Now, at the end of a long day, Andrew's sharp maroon tie is still impeccably knotted around his creamy brown neck, while Nick's length of graphite silk is unfastened, and hanging loose along the sides of his unbuttoned collar.

I hear Avery's soft inhalation beside me as her fiancé strides toward us, his cerulean blue gaze locked on her with unbridled desire.

I get it, girl. Even though I've known him for years through my brother, sometimes I still have to remind myself to breathe whenever I see Dominic Baine. The man is a walking force of dark, vibrating energy, and it's hard not to get swept up in the powerful magnetic pull that seems to surround the attractive billionaire.

Andrew's no slouch in the good looks department, either. His high cheekbones and pale green eyes have always turned female heads wherever he goes, but his trim black goatee lends an intriguing, sinister edge to him that I imagine only broadens his appeal.

"Someone's parked in my spot," he says, grinning as he strolls up and greets me with a light kiss on the cheek.

Nick greets Avery in similar fashion, but his smile is smoldering and his sensual mouth lingers near her ear. Whatever he whispers to her sends a heated blush rising into her cheeks.

Cupping his broad palm around the back of Avery's neck in a possessive, yet tender touch, he turns his gaze on me. "Evelyn, this is a nice surprise seeing you here."

"Hello, Nick."

Avery places her hand against his chest. "I thought

it would be better to meet here while you and Beck were at the contract meeting across town."

"Of course, it's fine. Did you have a good meeting?" he asks me.

I nod. "I think it went well."

"Evelyn's being modest. She blew me away with her designs."

Nick's answering smile is wicked. "Well, I look forward to seeing the results."

I glance at my brother as the happy couple indulge in a brief, yet passionate kiss. "Sorry about taking your prime parking space. I was running late and I remembered you told me you'd be out most of today in meetings."

"No problem," he says, then quirks a brow. "You, running late? I'm shocked."

"Yeah, well . . . I got delayed at the boutique and it couldn't be helped." I haven't mentioned my missing purse to Avery, and I'm sure as hell not going to tell my overprotective brother. He already worries too much where I'm concerned, and I'd rather avoid another of his well-meaning lectures about my safety and personal well-being.

Andrew studies me for a moment. "I'm glad to hear everything worked out. I know how much you've been looking forward to presenting your work to Avery."

I nod. "I almost didn't get the chance. I thought your security detail was going have me arrested for illegal parking."

Nick's brows rankle as he looks at me. "Who are you talking about? You mean Luis down at the lobby desk this afternoon?"

"No. Gabriel Noble." It isn't the first time I've

thought about him since I arrived on the executive floor, but saying his name out loud sends an uninvited ripple of awareness through my body. I'm still annoyed with him, but my anger has mellowed from the sharp outrage I felt in the garage to a mild indignation. And none of that has had any impact on the unwanted attraction that still simmers along my nerve endings when I picture his handsome, if arrogant, face.

Andrew chuckles. "Gabe's a stickler for rules and procedure. That's part of what landed him the job here."

"It couldn't possibly be due to his charming personality," I mutter. "Does he treat everyone like a criminal, or was it just my lucky day?"

"What?" Avery chimes in, frowning. "That doesn't sound like Gabe."

Nick shakes his head in agreement. "No, it doesn't. He's a total professional, the best security person I've ever had on staff. But I'll grant you, Gabe does insist on running a tight ship."

"Probably due to his time in the military," my brother says, then glances at me to explain. "Before coming to work for us, he served in combat overseas in Afghanistan."

"A former soldier? I can't say I'm surprised," I reply. "Seems like he'd make an excellent drill sergeant."

Andrew gives me an amused look. "This coming from the girl who used to line up her Barbie dolls for outfit inspection every morning before she left for school? You've been a Type A natural-born boss from the time you could talk, Evie."

I have to admit he's right. Aside from a short period of time when we both know how deeply I lost sight of myself, I've always preferred to be the one in charge. I still do.

"As for Gabe's service record, it's stellar," Nick interjects. "Enlisted when he was twenty and deployed straight to a combat zone. From there, he rose up the ranks in record time to sergeant first class leading an infantry platoon fighting in the center of some of the worst action. He came home with a chest full of medals, including the Silver Star and a Purple Heart."

"Just to name a few," Andrew says, a sober tone creeping into his deep voice.

I tell myself I'm not impressed with Gabriel Noble's apparently heroic time in the service, even though I am. I'm curious too. But that doesn't excuse the fact that he seemed to enjoy adding to my stress today.

"Maybe you ought to send him to public relations training," I suggest, giving my brother a flat stare.

Nick smirks. Andrew starts to say something I'm sure will be a further argument for the defense, but he's interrupted by Lily's soft clearing of her throat behind him.

"Excuse me, everyone," she says, then glances not at Nick or Andrew, but at me. "Ms. Beckham, I have a call for you from L'Opale on hold at my desk."

My brother looks at me, and I can feel his shrewd gaze analyzing me in the moment before he speaks. "Why would they be calling you here instead of on your cell?"

Although I know full well, I give him a vague shrug as I step away from the group. I follow Lily back to her workstation and she hands me the phone. "Hello?"

"Hey, Evelyn. It's Megan. I'm so glad I caught you."

The perky college student is one of several front-of-the-house sales consultants who work at the boutique.

"Hi, Meg. What's up?" I take the cordless receiver and walk toward the elevator bank for a bit of privacy. "Is anything wrong at the shop?"

"No. No, everything's good here. Um, I just wanted to let you know I found your purse."

Thank God. I release a pent-up breath, relief washing over me. "Where was it?"

"Inside one of the lingerie drawers just outside the dressing rooms."

"What? That's impossible." I'm stunned. More than that, I'm confused as hell. "How on earth did it end up there?" I ask, keeping my voice quiet. "Someone must've taken it out of my office. Is this someone's idea of a joke?"

"I'm sorry, Evelyn, I don't know anything more. All I can tell you is I was straightening bras in the everyday collection to get ready for closing in another hour, and when I opened one of the drawers, there it was."

I shake my head, trying to make sense of what I'm hearing. I don't want to think that one of my coworkers could be responsible—or any of our customers who'd been in the boutique today—but I know damn well that's the only way the clutch could have ended up anywhere outside my private office.

"What about my wallet? Is it still there? Does it look like anything's missing?" I ask Megan, my mind churning as fast as my words. "What about my phone?"

"I can check for you if you'd like," she offers. "Hang on a sec."

I wait, glancing over my shoulder to where Andrew is watching me while conversing with Avery and Nick. Megan comes back on the line a moment later.

"Your wallet and phone are both here. I can't tell for

sure, but it doesn't seem like anything's been taken."

"All right. I'm heading back in a few minutes. Will you do me a favor and hold it for me until I get there?"

"Yeah, of course."

"Thanks, Meg."

My brother walks over to me while I'm handing the phone back to Lily and thanking her for intercepting the call for me. "Everything okay?"

I nod. "Everything's good." I step away from the desk and glance at my watch if only to avoid his searching gaze. "Listen, I need to take off. Meg's alone at the shop and I told her I'd swing by before we close up."

"That's too bad. The three of us were talking about going out to grab a bite. We were hoping you might like to join us."

I catch my lip on a groan, because there's nothing I'd like better than to continue the high from my meeting with Avery. "I'm sorry, I can't tonight. I really do need to get back to the boutique."

"You're putting in a lot of time at work lately."

"I know. But honestly, I don't mind all of the crazy hours because I love what I'm doing. I've never been happier."

"The shop's growing fast, Evie. I just don't want you to take on more than you can handle."

"I'm not." My reply carries an edge of defensiveness I don't intend.

"You sure about that?" His eyes hold me with concern, his deep voice taking on the serious big-brother tone that usually ends up with both of us locking horns before all is said and done. "What happened to your cell phone?"

"It's no big deal." I give him a dismissing shrug. "I left it back at L'Opale."

"You never go anywhere without your phone on you. In fact, you promised me you wouldn't."

"It's fine, Andrew. *I'm* fine." We're out of earshot from anyone, and even though I know my brother means well—even though I know I've given him plenty of reason to worry about me in the past—it rankles me to hear his over-protectiveness here, in a public space, in front of a new client. "Please, stop treating me like I'm made of glass. I'm good. You don't need to worry about me anymore. I promise."

He's silent, scowling, but I see the stress lurking behind the skepticism in his eyes. I see the cold fear that had never been there until I caused it several years ago.

"I have to go," I murmur under my breath.

I pivot away from him to say my goodbyes to Avery and Nick, then I head to the elevator and step inside alone.

Andrew's sober stare remains locked on me as the polished steel doors close between us.

4

~ Gabriel ~

I arrive at the Baine Building before six the next morning. Technically, I'm not on the clock for another hour, but I know Andrew Beckham starts his day at dawn—usually with a workout in the company fitness room before showering and heading down to his executive floor office across the hall from Dominic Baine's.

With real estate at an off-the-charts premium, few corporations provide complimentary in-house employee fitness centers. Even fewer reserve the fully windowed top floor of their company headquarters for weight training, scores of treadmills, ellipticals, and stationary bikes, plus an indoor running track—all with unmatched, 360-degree views of the city.

Beck will have been finished with his training by now, but it's still early enough to catch him before the administrative staff and other office workers show up for the day. His door is open, but I rap my knuckles on the panel anyway.

"Hey, Gabe." He looks up from a desk spread full of blueprints and stacks of contracts. "Haven't seen you in this early in a while."

I nod, still standing outside the room. "Got a minute?"

"Sure. Come on in."

As I step inside the large office, I realize we're not alone. On the other side of the room to my left, Dominic Baine is seated on a club chair. He nods from where he's working on another pile of papers and plans. "Morning, Gabe. What's going on?"

Damn. So much for any hopes of keeping my fuck-up with Evelyn Beckham on the down-low. Then again, I've never run from responsibility, and I'm not about to start now.

"Something happened yesterday that I need to make you aware of," I tell both men, keeping my attention mainly on Beck. "I was in the garage heading out for the day when I noticed someone parked in your spot down there. I went over and informed the female it was a reserved space and asked her to move her vehicle, but she was . . . uncooperative. You could say we clashed a bit. In the end, I don't think I left her with a very good impression of me."

He makes an acknowledging noise and leans back in his chair. "So I heard."

Ah, fuck. Of course, he's already heard all about it. I exhale and give a tight shake of my head. "I'm sorry, Beck. I didn't realize you had a sister. I'm sure she gave you an earful about the way I handled things with her."

His mouth quirks. "She thinks you need to work on your people skills."

I grunt. "Not the first time I've been told that. I'm sure it won't be the last. Anyway, I apologize. I didn't realize Evelyn was your sister until after I'd confronted her and asked her for ID, which she didn't have."

"What do you mean she didn't have it?" He frowns, dropping forward and resting his elbows on the desk. "Or are you saying she dug in her heels and refused to show it to you?"

For some reason, it feels like a betrayal to say anything more, but Beck is my friend. Both he and Nick are responsible not only for my livelihood but for saving my sanity as well when they hired me a year ago. Hell, they probably saved my life. I can't keep information from either one of them, especially when I'm being asked directly to provide it.

"Evelyn didn't have her purse on her. She told me she lost it yesterday."

"Lost it?" Beck looks concerned, even troubled. He and Nick exchange a glance before he blows out a short sigh and shakes his head. "Never mind, that's a conversation I'll have with her at another time."

I nod, unsure what I've missed. "At any rate, I could've handled things better than I did. You hired me to be a professional, and I am. But yesterday I stepped over the line and I need you both to know it won't happen again."

"Relax," Beck says, a wry smile on his lips. "It probably did my little sister some good to meet a man who didn't trip all over himself to impress her."

"Gabe's possibly the first." Nick strolls over to us, amusement in his eyes too. "Beck's sister would attract attention even if she hadn't once been the queen of the runways from New York to Paris."

"Queen of the what?"

I'm frowning when I glance back at Beck again. "Her career was short, but meteoric. It's been five years since she left modeling behind, but Evie still can't go anywhere without being recognized."

"Evie." And just like that, my confusion is seared away, replaced with a dawning understanding that makes me feel like an even bigger jackass. "Ah, Christ. She's your sister? That hot new supermodel everyone was talking about a few years ago . . . Eve."

"One and the same," Nick confirms.

"*Was*," Beck adds. "As in, past tense. And thank God for that."

I curse again, muttering it under my breath. "Jesus, I'm a fucking idiot. I didn't know."

What's more, I would have never guessed. Not because Evelyn Beckham isn't still a total knockout, easily the most beautiful woman I've ever laid eyes on. It's just that I wasn't paying much attention to shit like that when I was overseas. Still, you'd have to be living under a rock not to have at least heard the name Eve.

Through the haze of my surprise, I register the subtle return of Andrew Beckham's soberness where his sister is concerned. He worries about her. Part of me is intrigued to know why.

But it's not my business to wonder about Evelyn.

I came here to deliver an apology and possibly grovel to keep my job. Fortunately, the latter doesn't seem necessary, which is a damn relief because I've never been good at begging for forgiveness. God knows my father can attest to that. My ex-fiancée too.

I clear my throat. "Anyway, Evelyn mentioned she was here for a meeting with Avery. I hope it went well for her in spite of me holding her up in the garage."

Nick grunts. "I'll say it did. Last night I saw the invoice for the deposit on several pieces of custom lingerie Avery's commissioned her to design. If the down payment is that impressive, I can't wait to see the finished products."

"Evelyn's boutique, L'Opale, is in one of Nick's buildings on Madison," Beck informs me.

I nod in acknowledgment, but my thoughts are snagged on the uninvited mental image of Evelyn surrounded by corsets and G-strings and other lacy underthings. Is that what she wore beneath that body-hugging dress yesterday? I grit my teeth, trying to banish the curiosity—and the swift, hot streak of lust that ignites inside me at the same time.

When I blink and meet Beck's gaze, it's almost as if he senses the inappropriate direction of my thoughts. I can't fool myself that he doesn't. Nor can I deny the dark warning in his eyes.

She is not for you.

He doesn't have to say the words. I hear them in my own mind, in my own voice.

Even if she didn't hate me, I'd never consider laying a finger on Evelyn Beckham.

If I did, I have no doubt her brother would hate me. And with good reason.

Andrew Beckham and I met in passing a year and a half ago at a private club owned by an artist named Jared Rush. Rush's gatherings cater to an exclusive, invitation-only crowd—men and women who either require or prefer to seek their pleasures outside the boundaries of convention. BDSM. Voyeurism. Role play, group play, and everything in between. There were rumors that a certain billionaire had once been a frequent attendee at Rush's club, and while I don't exactly doubt it, I don't particularly care if it's true, either.

And as Beck stares at me now, I trust he knows that while I won't apologize for the choices I make in my life, I am disciplined enough not to drift outside of my lane where his sister is concerned.

I hold my friend's unflinching gaze. "Like I said, I know what's expected of me here, and I promise you I take it seriously."

"That's never been in doubt yet," Nick says. "In fact, I've been meaning to talk to you about something, Gabe."

"Sir?"

"Baine International has been growing this past year. With all the recent property acquisitions, it's time we take a look at upgrading and streamlining our security systems across the board. We're going to need someone in-house to lead the security teams and oversee the implementation of the new software and equipment. Ideally, someone who's already familiar with our current staffs and protocols."

"It's going to mean longer hours," Beck says. "Some field work too. You'll have to check in on the properties from time to time, help head off issues before they have a chance to become problems."

I glance between them. "Are you offering me the job?"

Nick nods. "We know you've got the leadership skills. Over the past year you've been here, you've also demonstrated you have the stamina and the experience.

The rest you'll pick up as you go. The job isn't going to be easy, though. You'll be the first point of contact on all security matters, reporting directly to me. Of course, the pay will be commensurate with your new responsibilities."

He picks up a pen and writes something on a scrap of paper from Beck's desktop. He hands it to me and I stare at the number that's just north of mid-six figures.

"That's to start," Nick adds. "There will also be quarterly bonuses for you based on the performance of the team as a whole. I estimate those could easily double that figure in time."

I can't stop staring at the number he scrawled on the paper. I feel shell-shocked. And grateful beyond words.

"If this sounds acceptable to you, Beck can draw up the necessary agreements and have them in your hands before the end of the day."

I nod. "Yeah, this sounds acceptable. Holy fucking shit."

Nick chuckles. "Don't think you aren't going to earn every dime of it."

"No, sir," I answer by rote. "I mean, yes sir. Jesus Christ . . . I don't know what to say."

I mean it too. Working for Baine International has been my lifeline this past year. Now, it's the kind of life changer I never dreamed I'd have, especially after leaving the service.

Beck comes around his desk and shakes my hand. "Congratulations. You've earned this."

"Thank you. Both of you." I clear my throat, doing my damnedest to maintain some modicum of calm. "How soon do you want me to start?"

Nick claps my shoulder. "You just did. Get some

coffee and come back up. We'll take you through the systems currently in place at our buildings around the city and you can tell us where you see immediate vulnerabilities. Then we can talk about finding someone to replace you at your former post."

"Yes, sir."

5

~ Evelyn ~

I have spent the entire day poring over fabrics and measurement notes in my office at L'Opale, and I cannot recall a time when I've ever been happier. I'm so consumed with my work, I hardly notice someone standing in the doorway until Megan quietly clears her throat.

"I hate to interrupt you," she says, her freckle-dusted face scrunched in apology. "Katrina and I are taking off now."

"Okay, thanks, Meg." Reluctantly, I pull myself away from my work, feeling the twinge of kinked muscles in my back and neck as I stand. "Come on, I'll lock up behind you."

"Staying late again?" Katrina asks when I walk out to the main sales floor of the shop. Her straight, platinum-blond bob accentuates the lean slope of her cheeks and her shrewd blue eyes that always seem a little cold, a little cynical and mistrusting. Then again, being part of the cutthroat fashion industry can do that to a person. Among other things.

"Work too many long hours and your creativity will suffer for it," she says, a trace of criticism in her voice. "I'm sure you don't want to disappoint our newest client."

It's taken a while for me to warm up to Kat, even though she's been with L'Opale from the beginning. She's mercurial and impossible to read, an intensely private person. I've never heard her mention family or a significant other—hell, even a friend—in all of the five years we've worked together.

Yet, while I've never considered us particularly chummy, we do make an excellent design team and I know her well enough that I can overlook her competitive tone now. "I should be ready to hand off a few of the designs to Jane tomorrow so she can start sewing. Avery is so enthusiastic about all of the pieces, I can't wait to have something for her to try on."

Megan's eyes light with shared excitement. "I adore the sheer boned Basque with the tiny organza flowers on it. Ooh! And the demi-bra with the pearl accents."

"Thanks. Those are two of my personal favorites too."

Katrina gives me a nod. "You did a great job on the concepts. Congrats."

"Thank you, Kat. That means a lot coming from you." I glance past her shoulder to the edge of our cashier station, where a potted miniature rosebush sits. "Where did that come from?"

Megan lightly smacks her forehead. "Oh, God, I

almost forgot. Mr. Hennings dropped it off for you earlier today. He grew it himself."

I smile at the mention of the wealthy, sixty-something gentleman who's one of L'Opale's more eccentric, but charming, clients. "What a sweet thing for him to do. It's beautiful."

"He's a romantic, that's for sure," Meg says. "I hope when I'm old and gray I've found a man like him who takes the time to tend his own roses and still woos his ladylove with pretty, handmade lingerie."

Kat scoffs. "Walter Hennings isn't buying handmade lingerie for an old lady, Meg. He's buying it for a woman in Latvia who's almost young enough to be his granddaughter."

I sigh and shake my head, even though she's right. Not that any of us have met the widowed, retired executive's girlfriend. He's sadly relayed that Ilona refuses to relocate to the States until she's able to bring her mother along with her. While Mr. Hennings wrestles with the paperwork to make that happen, he's been sending his long-distance love dozens of bespoke lingerie gifts, which I've designed to his exacting specifications—even using myself as a sizing model for our seamstress at times, since Ilona and I share a similar build.

"If you ask me, he's pathetic," Kat mutters. "I won't be the least surprised to find out she's only using him for his money. And more power to her, if she is."

Megan frowns. "Well, I think he's sweet—and apparently not yet ready to retire from the bedroom," she adds with a giggle.

Kat rolls her eyes. "That's an image none of us need in our heads. You know, he's been coming in here for the past six months and hasn't brought his mystery woman to the shop even one time. For all we know, he's wearing all of that lingerie himself."

I choke on a laugh. "Talk about an image no one needs to picture. You're awful, Kat. And there is no way in hell he could ever squeeze his portly body into anything he's purchased. Mr. Hennings may be a little odd, but he's kind and easy to work with. He's also quickly become one of our best clients."

"One of *your* best clients, you mean. That old man hardly gave me the time of day when he was in the shop yesterday. Which, for the record, is fine by me." She folds her jacket over her arm as if she's about to walk out the door, then pauses, tilting her head at me. "Why are you giving me that look?"

I catch my bottom lip between my teeth. "Because I was actually hoping I might convince you to take over his account for me, now that I'm going to be committing all of my time to Avery Ross's project these next several weeks."

Kat groans, tilting her head back on her shoulders before leveling a flat stare on me. "Go ahead, rub salt in my wounds. First, I miss out on landing a celebrity artist-slash-gazillionaire's-fiancée for a client, and now you're foisting me off on a lecherous sugar daddy. I really think I'm starting to hate you."

I lift my brows. "So, is that a yes?"

She sighs. "Do I have a choice? You're the boss."

"Thank you. I owe you, Kat."

"I know." She gives an abrupt wave of her hand. "Well, I've had enough fun for one day, so off I go. Goodnight, both of you."

"I've got to run and catch my train, too," Megan tells

49

me. "Do you need anything before I go?"

"No. I'm fine. Go on home. I won't stay long."

I walk with her to the boutique's front door, waving back at her as she hurries away on the darkened sidewalk outside. It's after seven in the evening, but Madison Avenue is still busy with its endless flow of pedestrians and street traffic. I flip our sign to CLOSED on its brass chain, then head back to my office to pick up where I left off.

I'm not sure how many hours pass before my stomach complains that I haven't eaten anything since lunchtime. Working in blissful solitude, soft music playing in the background, I am energized and could easily keep this pace all night.

But Kat had a point. Burning myself out with a manic burst of creative productivity probably won't serve me well in the long run. Not to mention the project.

And I'm liable to pass out if I don't break for something to eat now.

I get up and head into our small coffee room to grab a snack from the refrigerator, which is mostly stocked with beverages we keep on hand for entertaining our clients. As I'm digging past the cans of sparkling water and hundred-dollar bottles of champagne to hunt for my last cup of yogurt hidden in the back, I hear something that draws me upright. Just a small noise, coming from somewhere in the back of the store.

I hear it again, a faint metallic rasp that sends a current of unease through me.

Abandoning my search for food, I walk past my

office and Katrina's, toward the supply room and the rear door that opens into the small parking lot and narrow alleyway running between our building and the one behind us. The alarm is set and the door is made of steel that boasts two deadbolts, both of which are firmly seated and undisturbed.

But I could swear the sound I heard was someone testing the door handle, trying to get in.

I step silently forward and put my eye to the peephole. No one's there. Nothing in the tiny lot outside except my lone Volvo parked in the faint glow of the old floodlight mounted overhead.

I exhale a sigh. Definitely time to call it a night if my mind is starting to play tricks on me.

Still, I can't dismiss the odd prickle at the back of my neck as I turn away from the door and walk back to my office to straighten up so I can head home. I've no sooner begun than my phone rings with an incoming call. I smile when I see my friend Paige's name on the display, not only because she's one of my besties, but because at the moment I'm relieved to have the company.

"Hey, girl."

"Hi!" Paige shouts back. Loud, throbbing club music pulses in my ear, almost drowning out her voice. "You were supposed to call me this afternoon. Where are you, Boo?"

"Didn't you check your texts? I'm working late at the shop tonight." I realize I'm talking as loudly as if we both were at whatever hot nightspot she's calling from. "Can you even hear me?"

"What? Hold on, I can't hear you!"

I laugh to myself, shaking my head as she yells that

she's going to look for a quieter spot to talk to me. When she comes back on a minute later the music is muffled to a low, vibrating bass. I hear other female voices and running water, which tells me she found her way to the ladies' room. Still noisy as hell on her end, but at least Paige and I can carry on a conversation.

"Eve, you have to come check out this club. It's amazing!"

I flop into my chair and prop my bare feet on the edge of my desk. "Are you talking about that artsy weird one you like over in Brooklyn? The one with the trapeze performers and costume theme nights?"

"No," she says with a giggle. "That was my favorite a few months ago. Now I'm in love with this brand-new place called Muse. It's in the Meatpacking District, just opened last weekend. Anyway, what are you doing working this late? Get your ass over here and join me, girl!"

"Maybe another time." As much as I enjoy spending time with Paige and the rest of my friends, I'm feeling the effects of two back-to-back 16-hour workdays in the bleariness of my eyes and the kink in my neck and shoulders. "The club sounds great, but right now, all I want is a cup of hot tea and a long soak in the tub back at my apartment."

"Fine," she replies, sighing dramatically. "We're still on for lunch tomorrow with the girls, right?"

"Definitely. I wouldn't miss it. How long has it been since everyone was in the city at the same time?"

"Too long," she agrees, shouting her reply. "Hannah spends more time in Italy than she does the States now. I don't think she's been over here longer than a week or two since she and Alessandro got married."

"Well, having seen the photos of their villa in Tuscany, I can't say I blame her. She's also got a baby on the way now."

"Fair enough, I guess. How long do you think it'll be before Melanie starts talking about wedding bells and babies?"

I laugh, but it's not that I haven't wondered the same thing. "Give her time. Mel's only been dating Daniel for three months," I remind Paige.

"Yeah, but you've seen them together. She's head over heels for the guy. Honestly, it's kind of sickening how adorable and happy they seem together."

"I know, but I'm glad for her. Mel hasn't had it easy. She deserves a good man."

"I won't disagree with that," Paige says. "So, I guess that leaves just you and me, Boo. Blissfully single, right? Unless you plan to do something about that hot security guard you told me about yesterday."

I scoff. "I never said Gabriel Noble was hot."

"You didn't have to. I could hear it in your voice."

I roll my eyes. "It doesn't matter what I said or what you think you heard. He was a temporary annoyance, nothing more. I've already forgotten about him."

"Well, I haven't. Maybe you could introduce me to him. I hate to let a gorgeous hunk of prime, medal-decorated military man go to waste."

I can't help but laugh, even though it rankles something inside me to picture my beautiful, bubbly, man-magnet of a friend getting anywhere close to Gabriel Noble. "I don't know why I even mentioned him to you. Now I'll never hear the end of it."

"Probably not. And don't think I haven't noticed you're not volunteering to share."

"Consider it a favor. Believe me, you'd thank me la—"

My words cut short in my throat. Because suddenly, without any warning at all, I'm sitting in the dark.

"Eve? Are you still there?"

"Shit. I think the power just went out in the building."

"Are you serious?"

"God, it's pitch-dark in here. I'm going to check and see if anyone else on Madison lost power." I walk to the front of the shop while I'm talking. None of the other high-rises or street-level storefronts seem affected.

"I thought that swanky building belongs to Dominic Baine," Paige says. "Don't tell me he forgot to pay the light bill."

"It's probably just a blown fuse or bad circuit-breaker or something."

Because, yes, this is a Baine property, and I'm absolutely sure it has nothing to do with an unpaid electric bill. I also know from past experience that any utility blip or power outage trips an alarm at Baine's corporate headquarters. And if that alarm continues for more than eight minutes, the police will be automatically dispatched to the building to investigate.

Which means my overprotective brother will have one more reason to worry about me.

I exhale a heavy sigh. "If it is only a fuse, maybe I can reset it."

"And if it's not?" Paige makes a dubious noise on the other end of the line. "Evelyn, maybe you should get out of there."

She's nervous for me. I know because she's calling me by my given name instead of the one she's been using since we met at a fashion show during our second year in the business together.

"I'll be fine. I'm sure it's nothing."

But I keep her on the line with me as I carefully find my way back to the utility closet near the rear of the boutique. I locate the fuse box and use the illumination of my phone to check for blown switches. I'm only passingly handy when it comes to this kind of thing, but I can see that none of the fuses are offline.

"Tell me what's happening," Paige says. "Should we hang up? I can call 911 for you."

"And tell them what? Your friend could use a flashlight if they don't mind running one over to me?"

"All right, then call your brother."

"No. Definitely not." I shake my head in the pitch-darkness as I flip several of the switches on and off, hoping to jar something back to life. "It's bad enough Andrew worries I'm going to work myself into another nervous breakdown at any moment. I've spent the past five years trying to prove to him that I'm better, stronger, that I'm healthy now. I don't want him thinking I'm his responsibility, not that I ever was."

"Doesn't mean he'll ever stop caring, Eve."

The gentle reminder makes me pause. "I know."

My fingers are hovering over the fuse box switches when all at once, the lights come on.

"Oh, thank God," I murmur under my breath. "Problem solved. I have power again."

I'm fairly certain I had nothing to do with it, but I'll take the victory, nevertheless.

"Great," Paige says. "Now, will you please make me feel better and get the fuck out of there?"

"Okay, okay. I have to pack up a few things first, but

then I'll go."

"All right. Do it quick, okay? I know it takes a lot to scare you, but after what happened yesterday with your purse . . ."

"That? It was no big deal," I say, walking back to my desk. "I don't know how it ended up leaving my office or who put it in that lingerie drawer, but at least nothing was taken."

"Not unless you count that gorgeous red Dior lipstick you can't find now," she reminds me.

"I could've lost that anywhere. The point is, my wallet, ID, credit cards, my phone . . . all the important things were accounted for."

"I just think it's odd that when you found your purse, your phone had been turned off."

"Yeah, me too." As soon as I realized my clutch was missing, I'd used the shop's phone to call my cell to help locate it, but every attempt went straight to voicemail. Now, I wish I hadn't shared the whole strange incident with my friend because her paranoia was starting to make me nervous too. "I should get moving, Paige. I'll see you tomorrow for lunch, okay?"

"Can't wait," she chirps. "Text me when you get home tonight."

"I will."

We end the call and I set my phone on the edge of the desk, easily within my reach as I begin organizing my project materials and straightening up to leave. I hurry, even though I tell myself it's ridiculous to be spooked.

But I am.

I'm shaken, more than I care to admit. And I don't like the feeling. I don't like being forced to acknowledge—even to myself—that something as harmless as a misplaced purse or an unexpected power outage can make me feel anxious, off balance.

Afraid.

By the time I have my work put away and I'm ready to leave, my breath is coming in rapid pants. I can't wait to get out of the shop. My fingers fumble with the alarm pad and deadbolts on the solid back door. I free the last one and pull the panel open, prepared to step out to the lot and race to my waiting car.

But a large shape stands in my way, looming just on the other side of the door.

Shadows cloak broad, muscular shoulders and a short crown of thick, chestnut brown hair.

I hardly have time to halt the scream that climbs up my throat before I realize I know him.

"Evelyn." Gabriel Noble's strong hands steady me, firmly grasping my arms. "Is everything all right?"

6

~ Gabriel ~

"What the hell are you doing here?"

It takes her a second to speak—about as long as it takes me to realize I still have my hands on her. I let go, though not before I register the fact that Evelyn is trembling. Absolutely shaking with fear.

My own alarm spikes at seeing her visibly upset. "Are you okay?"

She exhales, some of her anxiety seeming to release along with her short breath. Her rich, husky voice sounds less distressed now. "Yeah. I'm fine."

"You here by yourself?" She gives me a faint nod. I grunt in response. "It's after ten. That's a long day."

"I could say the same to you. And you still haven't told me what you're doing here," she adds, staring at me quizzically as I step inside the shop with her.

"I was at Baine headquarters and saw that a sustained power failure alert had triggered here at the shop. Thought I'd swing by and check things out. I didn't realize anyone was still working." Primarily because L'Opale only has security cameras monitoring the sales floor, not the back offices or exterior, one of the first changes I'll recommend. And because I've spent too much time in war zones, I can't help giving the space around us a quick visual assessment as I walk farther inside to make sure there are no overt signs of trouble anywhere in the shop. "What happened with the power?"

"I don't know. I was on my cell talking with a friend when suddenly the lights went out."

As she talks, I glance into the empty offices along the short hallway. "How often do you lose power?"

"Never. And none of the other businesses on Madison seemed to be affected, just the boutique. Anyway, it's no big deal. You shouldn't have wasted the trip. Everything came back on a few minutes later."

"If it hadn't come back up, right now the cops would be here too," I tell her. I've spent the day combing over every security system and procedure put in place at the various properties under the Baine umbrella. I have things to sort out and learn, but I've already got a list of improvements I plan to propose when I meet with Nick and Beck. For reasons I assure myself are purely professional, I've just put Evelyn's boutique at the top of the priority list.

"Thank God the police weren't dispatched," she says. "That would mean my brother probably wouldn't be far behind them." At my questioning look, she adds, "Technically, L'Opale belongs to Andrew. He loaned me the money to open the shop a few years ago when I needed some . . . help."

I nod, unaware of the business arrangement she and her brother may have. Frankly, I'm surprised she's confiding in me about any of it, but she seems to be talking out of anxiety more than anything else right now. I can't imagine the confident, capable woman I met yesterday ever allowing herself to be in the position of owing something to anyone—even a family member. I also can't imagine that a few minutes without power would rattle Evelyn Beckham the way it seems to have done tonight.

I glance back and find her still standing near the exit, her arms crossed over herself. "Did something else happen here tonight? Something you're not saying?"

She stares at me, uncertainty in her gaze. "I'm sure it was nothing. I'm sure I was only imagining—"

"Evelyn. Tell me."

"I thought I heard a strange noise," she relents. "It was sometime before the lights went out."

"What kind of noise?"

"I'm not sure. It sounded like someone was at the back door. Like someone may have been trying to get in."

"Coworker?"

She shakes her head. "They'd both caught the subway home hours earlier. Normally, I'm not this paranoid but—"

I'm in motion even before she finishes saying the words. "Stay here."

Freeing the snap on my gun's holster in automatic reflex, I step outside to inspect the double-bolted steel door and look for any evidence that someone had been there before I arrived. I see nothing to give me pause, other than the cramped parking area that's too damn dark by half.

My Lexus and Evelyn's Volvo are the only vehicles there. An old floodlight mounted to the side of the building throws a thin wash of illumination onto the pavement. And outside the door to the shop, nothing but gloom and shadows. Plenty of cover for anyone to try to get in—or to wait for someone to come out alone into the dark.

I come back inside on a curse.

Evelyn stares at me. "Should I be afraid?"

"No. Not while I'm here." And I mean it. She's not part of my job, but I wouldn't hesitate for a second to protect her with my life.

Our gazes hold for a moment, long enough for me to realize she's even prettier than I recall from the first time I saw her. Pretty? Fuck. She's heart-stoppingly gorgeous. Now that I'm looking at her, I'll be damned if I can stop. My fingers itch to touch her creamy, light-brown skin and the thick, espresso waves that frame the delicate oval of her face. Her eyes are mesmerizing, a green so pale it's nearly blue, her gaze sharp and intelligent, yet soft beneath the deep black fringe of her lashes.

I mentally kick myself now that I know who she is. Or, rather, as Beck noted, who she once was. The sleek, glamorous supermodel who'd been making headlines while I was camped out in the armpit of Afghanistan, dust-caked and stinking, hunting for bad guys and trying not to lose life or limb—or my soul—in the process.

Our lives couldn't have been more different. Worlds apart, then and now.

"You need better lighting and surveillance cameras in three key locations out there," I tell her, my tone clipped because I've already counted about a dozen substantial security weaknesses in and around the boutique. And I've only been here five minutes. "I'll write up a full security plan and get the ball rolling on new equipment for you first thing tomorrow."

She doesn't seem pleased with my plan. "This is an upscale boutique. The last thing I want is for it to look like a military base."

"Duly noted," I reply, glancing away from her, unsurprised that this is yet another conversation where she and I are going to clash. I also have to wonder if the military dig was coincidental or something else. When our eyes meet again, hers are lit with challenge. "I respect where you're coming from on this, Evelyn. But Dominic Baine and your brother have put me in charge of ensuring the security of this building and all the other properties Nick owns. The last thing *I* want is to let them down."

"Always the dutiful Boy Scout, are you?"

I feel my brow furrow as I fold my arms over my chest. "The what?"

She shrugs. I'd be tempted to write her off as a gorgeous, stuck-up bitch if I didn't catch the little smile playing at the edge of her amazing mouth. "I heard all about you from Andrew yesterday," she says. "The impressive military career. Your stellar marks at Baine International. My brother and Nick obviously think very highly of you."

What else did they tell her? I wonder if she knows about my leg or the two-plus years of recovery that followed. Every inch of her is perfection. I'm scar-riddled and disfigured. Then again, none of that should matter since I'm only here in a professional capacity. A prosthetic calf and foot on my left leg won't prevent me from doing my job. Never has. It's never prevented me from making love to a woman, either.

I clear my throat. "After our introduction in the garage, I don't suppose I have to ask what you think about me."

She tilts her head, humor dancing in her eyes. "Was I that transparent?"

I chuckle, but it's only an attempt to cover for the sudden, heated jolt of lust that rockets through every cell in my body as I stand in the path of Evelyn Beckham's knockout smile. "I didn't think I'd have a job to come back to this morning, if you want to know the truth."

"Really?" Now she seems truly amused. "So, if you thought I could get you fired, why did you keep trying to piss me off?"

I shrug, leaning my shoulder against the wall. "I don't know. Maybe I like to live dangerously."

"Do you?"

"Sometimes." Which has never been more obvious to me, given the current direction of my thoughts when it comes to this woman who is completely, dangerously, off-limits. "Then again, maybe I just have a bad habit of getting off on the wrong foot."

She laughs. It's sultry, like her voice. Hearing her laugh makes me wonder what she sounds like at other times when she's having fun, when those hackles of hers aren't raised and ready for a fight. What does she sound like when she's relaxed, when she's experiencing pleasure?

What does she sound like when she comes?

Fuck. Definitely not the direction I can let my thoughts go.

I clear my throat and gesture over my shoulder with my thumb. "I'll go take a look at the front of the shop."

I pass several spacious dressing rooms on the way, each one outfitted in muted colors and soft furnishings. Evelyn follows me in silence out to the front sales room, turning on soft recessed lights and a glittering crystal chandelier that hangs from the center of the elegant boutique.

Instead of inserting some much-needed space between my boss's stunning sister and my unprofessional reaction toward her, I find myself in the middle of a room filled with things designed for seduction.

Lacy lingerie drips from silk-wrapped hangers everywhere I look. Here and there, faceless, artfully posed mannequins show off sexy, skimpy bras and corsets tied up with satin ribbons and festooned with beads or pearls or tiny flowers. There are even a few black leather options that offer an interesting contrast to the rest of the frothy confections.

It only takes my corrupted mind a few seconds to strip Evelyn bare and place her supple curves and graceful limbs into each erotic outfit. A private modeling session that I would give anything to witness in person. I banish the bad idea from my head on a stifled groan. My cock, unfortunately, is going to require more convincing.

Mirrored alcoves reflect my scowling, uncomfortable image back at me in dozens of replications as I move through the sea of feminine underthings.

I see Evelyn in the glass too. She's several paces behind me as I pull out my phone and take a few photos of optimal mount locations for surveillance cameras in the high-ceilinged, window-fronted sales room.

"So, do you always go out to personally check Baine properties in the middle of the night?"

"I do now." I slip my phone back into my jacket pocket and turn to face her. "As of today, I'm corporate security chief. That means I'm managing the teams and overseeing the security systems at all of Baine International's New York locations."

She steps closer. "Sounds like a promotion."

I nod. "It's a hell of an opportunity."

"Congratulations, Gabe." It's the first time she's said my name—or, rather, said it without any trace of disdain in her tone. And that knockout smile is back again, this time with a wry twist to it. "So, does this mean you'll be coming around asking to see my ID at my shop now?"

I smirk, despite the fact that looking at her like this is making the tightness below my belt strain toward unbearable. "I admit, I wasn't in my best form yesterday. I had to go do something I wasn't exactly looking forward to, and you caught the brunt of my bad attitude. I apologize."

"Ah," she says. "That's right, you were on your way out of the Baine Building as I was going in—trying to go in, that is. What nasty business did you have to do? Some kind of super soldier stuff?"

"Nope." I shake my head. "Family thing. One of my brothers just made commander at his precinct."

Her lips tilt. "No wonder you act like a cop. Runs in your family, I take it?"

I chuckle. "You could say that. At least, it did until I

came along. The Nobles have all the cops they need. Besides, I never would've measured up for the old man, anyway."

I'm not sure why I let the admission roll out of my mouth, but it's out there now. I wait for Evelyn to bust my balls about it, since that seems to come naturally to her and I just gave her an easy target to hit. But she doesn't make light of the pathetic blurt.

Instead, those soft green eyes study me in silence— almost longer than I can take.

"You don't get along with your dad?"

"We get along fine. So long as we don't have to see or speak to each other."

An apology lingers in her gaze, unspoken. And thank fuck for that. Last thing I want or need is someone feeling sorry for me. Especially her.

"I adore my dad," she says softly. "Andrew and I had different moms. His mother divorced our father, then Dad married my mom a couple of years later. She died when I was eight. Drunk driver hit her while she was in a crosswalk."

"That's rough," I murmur, avoiding the apology I'm tempted to give because I'm not sure if she'd welcome my sympathy either.

She lets out a sigh. "I grew up protected by two strong men. I can't convince either one to stop worrying about me all the time."

"Don't expect them to. If I had a sister, I'd worry about her too. Knowing your brother, I think it'd kill him if anything happened to you."

"I know." She glances down and goes quiet for a long moment, leaving me to wonder where her thoughts have drifted. Somewhere dark, if the haunted look in her eyes when her gaze returns to mine is any indication. Wherever she went, it clings to her. "Do you, ah . . . do you need to see anything else while you're here?"

Her distant tone erases all of my untoward thoughts and impulses. Or most of them. Either way, I chalk it up as a good thing.

"You want to show me where the electrical equipment is? Can't hurt to check it out."

She nods and starts walking away from me. I fall in line behind her, doing my best to ignore the fluid sway of her hips inside the body-hugging black pencil skirt that ends just above her knees. Her rounded backside and bare legs are firm and strong, but I can practically feel how soft she'd yield under my hands, under my mouth. Under my thrusting hips as I spread her open and push inside.

She pivots her head to look over her shoulder at me. "The circuit breakers are in here."

Shit. Fucking busted. I can't even hope to lift my gaze in time to pretend I'm not a complete barbarian. So, I glance up slowly and meet her astonished look. "All right. Thanks."

She stays outside the small closet of a room that houses the circuit and cable boxes, electrical equipment, and sundry supplies. I get right to work checking things out, basically doing anything to avoid looking at her now that she's caught me drooling.

"After the lights went out, I checked the fuses," she tells me from the relative safety of the open doorway. "I didn't see anything wrong, but this isn't really my area."

I nod. The fuses look fine. Nothing obviously out of sorts with any of the power panels or other equipment. "I'll make a few calls, have someone come out and do a thorough system inspection, just to be safe."

I feel her watching me as I carefully squat to take a closer look at the tangle of cables and other wires feeding into the boutique's internet, power, and security systems. The position is made ten times more uncomfortable for the strain it puts on my prosthesis, but it is the weight of Evelyn's studying gaze that makes me eager to wrap up and put some distance between us.

"Who's got access to the equipment in here?"

"You mean, besides the random service techs from the cable and power companies?" She shrugs. "Everyone in the shop, I guess. Me, Katrina, Megan, a handful of sales clerks who work the floor on weekdays. Occasionally, our seamstress, Jane, comes into the boutique. Baine International also sends a nighttime cleaning crew twice a week. Why?"

"Just curious." I stand up and turn to face her. "Probably a good idea to put a panel combo lock on this door too. I'll add it to my list when I talk with Nick and Beck in the morning."

"Okay."

"Nothing more to be done here tonight," I tell her, turning off the light to the electrical room as I exit and close the door behind me. "Come on. If you're ready to go, I'll walk out with you."

Evelyn's purse and a leather tote packed with papers and her laptop sit near the back door where she left them when I first came in. She picks them up and we walk out together, she pausing to lock the deadbolts while I wait.

Her high-heeled sandals click on the dark pavement of the small parking lot. I keep my head on a swivel, surreptitiously checking our surroundings as we move toward her car, one of my hands hovering near her elbow, my other loose at my side, but ready to react at the first sign of trouble.

As we approach her Volvo, she clicks the locks open with her key fob. I wait a couple of steps away, still searching the gloom and shadows as she opens the back passenger door and places her tote behind the driver's seat.

"How many years did you spend in Afghanistan?"

Her question catches me off-guard. Though not nearly as much as the realization of how close we're standing to each other in the dark. The vanilla scent of her hair drifts on the night breeze, the heat of her skin radiating in the minuscule space that separates her body from mine.

I'm shocked by the amount of control it takes for me to keep my hands at my sides, when all I want to do is reach up and smooth the dark tendril of hair off her cheek as she talks.

Even more than that, I am seized by the urge to tilt her chin and lower my mouth to hers.

I curb all those inappropriate impulses, but only barely.

"I deployed to Kandahar right out of basic," I tell her, my voice sounding rusty and unused. I'm not used to talking about my military career, let alone talking about it with a beautiful former supermodel at the tail end of a long day and a night that's doomed to end a lot sooner—and far less naked—than I would prefer. "I completed a couple of combat tours. Would've had a third under my belt, but an IED blew me home two months into it."

I hear her quiet inhalation, see the look of surprise on her face. So, she doesn't know the gory details after all. I don't know if I'm relieved or disappointed that she assumes I'm whole. All I do know is that her opinion shouldn't matter to me. Shouldn't, yet does.

"An IED." She swallows, her gaze steady and, thankfully, devoid of pity or fascination. "Andrew told me you came home with a Purple Heart."

I acknowledge with a shrug because that medal—and all the other commendations that came with it—don't mean shit to me. Each one represents a failure. To myself, my country, and, most of all, the soldiers under my command. My friends who came home in flag-draped boxes.

She reaches out, and before I realize it, her fingers light gently on my cheek. The flesh that's stretched over the metal plates serving as my cheekbone often seems a bit numb, but not now. I feel everything in that brief, tender touch.

I move out of it before I am tempted to crave any more. If there had been exterior cameras to watch us now, I never would have let that breach happen in the first place.

Or so I assure myself.

"I'll write up my proposal for new security measures when I get home," I tell her, acting as if my heart isn't throbbing like a drum in my chest, and my arousal hasn't just spiked off the charts.

It takes everything I have to resist the urge to reach for her. She nods in response to what I'm saying, playing along with my effort to pretend there's nothing happening between us.

Because there isn't. There can't be.

Not when it will mean jeopardizing my job and the trust her brother and Dominic Baine have placed in me.

But damn. It's not easy holding on to my resolve when the heat of her fingertips still lingers on my cheek. Or when the promise of her kiss simmers in her wide, expressive eyes.

I clear my throat. "In addition to motion sensor video monitoring and beefed up exterior lighting, I'm also going to recommend new locks on all doors inside and out, as well as video monitoring for all areas inside the shop."

"You really think that's going to be necessary?" She folds her arms over her breasts and sighs. "I've been working here for three years without any issues."

"And I plan to make sure that trend continues."

A smile lifts the edge of her mouth. "Now you're starting to sound like my brother."

Christ. Far from it. I take a healthy step back. "I'll be in touch tomorrow. Goodnight, Evelyn."

She turns to open the driver's door but hesitates, looking at me. "Um, Gabe?"

For one reckless moment, hearing my name spoken so softly on her lips, I imagine she's going to say something dangerous, something I won't be able to resist. An invitation. A plea.

Her forehead furrows. "Can we . . . Can we maybe not tell Andrew about any of this? The power outage. You coming out here and finding me still at work. He worries too much about me as it is. If he hears I was alone at the shop this late and then got spooked for no reason . . ."

Her words trail off because I'm already shaking my head. "I'm sorry, I can't do that."

"Right." She shrugs, releasing a heavy sigh. "Boy Scout honor, is that it?"

"If you say so," I reply, feeling anything but honorable. "You should get going."

For a moment, she neither moves nor speaks. Finally, she gives me a vague nod. "You're right. It's getting really late. Thank you for being here tonight."

"Anytime."

She extends her hand and I take it, even though the contact only makes the lick of heat swirling through me burn hotter. I wrap my fingers around her smaller hand, engulfing her in my grasp. Arousal coils inside me at the contact, but even worse, I can see the glimmer of invitation in her bold green eyes.

"To think it was only yesterday I worried that you were going to have me arrested." One of her dark brows arches playfully. "Now, look at us."

I'm looking. I'm also keeping her hand gripped in mine, even though I know damn well that looking—and touching—are two things I have no business doing. I grunt, reluctant to let go of either her gaze or her hand. "What a difference a day makes."

I want the remark to sound casual, in control. But the gravel scrape of my voice sounds anything but innocuous. I release her hand now, because whatever is smoldering to life between us is a definite no-go.

It's a *hell no*, for a hundred different reasons—including the unspoken promise I made her brother earlier this morning. Evelyn Beckham is not for me.

"Be safe," I tell her, reaching around her to open the driver's side of her vehicle.

She climbs behind the wheel and I close the door, sealing her inside before I demand she stay. She starts the engine, but wisely keeps her window closed.

With a little wave from the other side of the glass,

she backs out, leaving me standing in the dim pool of light on the darkened pavement.

7

~ Evelyn ~

After more than an hour of avid interrogation about my unexpected late-night encounter with Gabriel Noble from my friends over lunch at Vendange, one of our favorite spots in the city, seeing him in the boutique when I return almost seems like a mirage.

I enter through the front doors on Madison Avenue, having caught a taxi to the restaurant. A few customers are browsing the store, aided by the handful of sales associates who help with foot traffic during regular hours. I smile and nod, greeting them as I walk past the display tables and mannequins where just last night I'd been chatting with a man I thought I couldn't stand and doing my damnedest not to make a fool of myself by inviting him home with me.

Now, he's back at L'Opale. I catch a glimpse of

Gabe's broad shoulders, tapered waist, and much-too-fine ass in the short hallway past the dressing rooms. He's wearing his typical uniform of dark suit pants and a white shirt, but at the moment his jacket and weapon holster are off and his long sleeves are rolled up over his tanned, muscular forearms. Although he's got his back to me, he swivels a glance over his shoulder. Our eyes meet across the length of the boutique and I feel the heat of that connection lick through me like a flame.

But it's there and gone in an instant. As if I imagined it.

As if there hadn't been a volcano of attraction ignited between us last night.

With nothing more than a polite nod, he continues on down the hall.

I know I'm seriously out of practice when it comes to men and dating, but could I have read him that wrong? The pang of confusion—of a deeper disappointment than I care to admit—lingers as Megan rushes to me across the sales floor, wide-eyed and smiling.

"We have company."

"I see that."

She's a little breathless, a little flushed in the face, as if being around Gabriel Noble has addled her brain as much as it apparently did mine last night.

"I didn't realize we were getting new security equipment installed today," she whispers.

"Neither did I."

Meg follows alongside me as I head for the hallway to investigate. I hear Gabe's deep voice coming from the back of the shop. And Katrina's, pitched in a light, breathy tone she never uses with Megan and me. My whole body tenses when I enter the small space and see her leaning over Gabe's shoulder as he taps something onto the keypad of an electronic panel, newly installed near the rear exit.

"So, as of today our keys no longer work on this door?"

"Right," he says, without looking up from his work. "Everyone will have their own four-digit code for the alarm panels on both points of entry into the boutique. It's more secure than having keys floating around, and it also means we'll have an ongoing record of traffic and access. If you know what you want to use for your code, you can set it right now."

"All right," she replies in that feminine rasp that's setting my molars on edge. Kat may be fifteen years older than me, but she doesn't look it, and she's working everything she's got on Gabe. She leans in to him even closer and taps her red-lacquered nail on the pad, reciting the numbers as she types them. "Six, nine, six, nine."

I clear my throat. "Kat, could you help out front for a while, please?"

She pivots toward me, her smile a little guilty, yet challenging at the same time. It takes her a second to answer. "Sure. I'd be happy to."

We have ample sales staff on the floor, and while I'm certain she knows that, too, she isn't going to argue with a direct request from me. Nevertheless, she takes her time sashaying up the hallway.

Gabe is turned around now, and I wait to see his gaze follow her out, but his hazel eyes stay rooted on me.

I fold my arms. "You certainly move fast. I thought you were only writing up a report today."

Before he offers an answer, I hear my brother's voice

coming from behind me.

"No reason to delay putting in some new locks and cameras," Andrew says as he walks out of the electrical room and pauses to give me a light kiss on the cheek. "Especially if you think someone was messing around with the back door last night."

I blow out a sigh at his sober look. "I shouldn't have mentioned it at all. I'm sure it was nothing."

"I hope you're right. In the meantime, Gabe's made some solid recommendations for upgraded security measures."

A clipboard rests on a table next to some opened equipment boxes and tools. I walk over and flip through the first few pages of schematics and handwritten notes, scrawled in an aggressive, confident print that I find just about as sexy as the man who wrote it. "No plans for razor wire or surface-to-air missile defense systems?" I arch my brows at Gabe. "That's a relief."

A smirk plays at the edge of his mouth while my brother scoffs, unaware of our inside joke from last night.

"I realize you think I overreact," Andrew says. "But believe me, I know the kind of animals who live in this city. I want you to be safe."

I tilt my head at him. "You always overreact, but at least you're consistent."

"Very funny." He frowns and lowers his voice, looking so much like our father I can't help but smile. "Cut me a break here, okay? It's not like you never had to deal with a stalker or two over the years, Eve."

My breath freezes in my lungs at his use of my old nickname, especially in front of Gabe. I don't like flashing my former career around. In fact, I'd bury it if I could.

But when I glance at Gabe, there is no surprise in his expression. No confusion.

The first day we met, he had no idea who I was. He definitely didn't recognize me from my runway days. But he knows now. He knows because Andrew has told him, I have no doubt.

And from the way he averts his eyes as I stare at him, I'm betting he knew before our brief, but enjoyable conversation last night.

What else might my brother have told Baine's new security chief about that awful part of my life?

I feel suddenly exposed and vulnerable. I hate the feeling.

I hate that I'm standing here wondering if the connection I felt between Gabe and me last night really was an illusion. Maybe the charm I believed was authentic was only him changing course from the arrogant bastard I met in the garage to a smooth tactician looking to get into my good graces—or into my bed— after realizing who I was . . . who I used to be.

He wouldn't be the first to try.

Except Gabe had been the one to turn me away.

When I touched his broken, brutally handsome face, he'd stepped out of my reach like he'd been burned. Now, he seems unwilling to look at me at all.

I glance at my brother, forcing a flat edge into my voice. "It's been a long time since I've been in the public eye. And besides, no one's ever gotten close enough to hurt me."

No, I did the worst damage to myself.

Thankfully, Andrew doesn't say the words I know we're both thinking. If he did that in front of Gabe right now, I don't know if I could forgive him.

In the lengthening silence between us, Gabe exhales a breath. "I'm going out to check the motion sensor on the parking lot floods."

Andrew nods, waiting for him to leave before he speaks again. "Tell me something, Evie. If Gabe hadn't responded to the shop last night because of the power outage, would you have told me you were working late and thought you heard someone trying to break in?"

"Break in? That's an exaggeration."

"We can't be sure." Andrew's voice is stern. "The question is, would you have told me?"

"Probably not. Like I said, nothing happened, and I don't want to give you any more reasons to worry—"

"I'm your brother, damn it," he reminds me, his black brows furrowing over his flashing green eyes. "If you don't want me to worry, you should've been born into a different family."

As tight as we've always been, I know when my growly big brother is reaching the limits of his patience. I try not to push him past that line, but there are times— like now—when all we seem to do is cross swords.

His broad mouth flattens with his scowl. "Gabe told me you lost your purse the other day, along with your phone and wallet."

"Of course, he told you." I scoff, shaking my head. "I wish he hadn't. It wasn't his place to tell you that. And for the record, I didn't lose anything. My purse was here in the shop the whole time." A slight stretch of the facts, but I'm not feeling particularly charitable with them at the moment.

Andrew gives me an exasperated look. "You're pushing yourself too much again, Evie. The boutique is taking off faster than anyone could've expected. I'm proud of everything you've accomplished, and I have no doubt this is only the beginning for you. But I don't want to see you take on more than you can handle. I don't want to see you burn out. And I'm saying that not only as your brother who loves you, but as your partner in this business."

"I'm going to pay you back, Andrew."

"Not the point." He shakes his head. "I'm not worried about the money. This shop is yours."

"No." I lift my chin. "I owe you, and I'm going to pay you back as soon as possible."

"Fuck the money." He curses under his breath. "It's always been my job to protect you. I failed you once. I won't stand by and let it happen again."

"No, Andrew. It's never been your job." Even though I know he's coming from a place of love, his doubt scares me. I pull away from him, my pulse pounding in my ears. "I am not your problem to solve. And dammit, I'm not a child, either."

The back door opens and Gabe steps back inside. There's no masking the awkwardness of my argument with my brother, so I don't even try. Leaving them both in my wake, I head into my office and close the door.

I work for several minutes in the solitude before a knock sounds. "Yes?"

I'm expecting one of my coworkers, or maybe my brother refusing to let go of a case he doesn't yet consider closed. Instead, I glance up from my desk to find Gabe filling the space of the open doorway. "Beck was called away on other business, so I'm wrapping things up now and then I'll be heading out. I took the liberty of programming a back door access code for you."

He steps in and places a sticky note with the four-digit number on my desk. "Okay. Thanks."

"The panel controls the new electronic deadbolts," he says, speaking in a calm, businesslike demeanor that only agitates me further. "As for the interior cameras and motion sensors I've recommended, those are on order and should be here soon. We'll have an electrician come in next week to take a look at the utility room before we start implementing the new equipment and install the full security system."

"Why are you telling me all of this? You report to my brother, right, Boy Scout?"

As intended, that irks him. I see the flare of irritation disrupt some of his maddening control. Scowling, he steps farther inside my office. I can't help but notice he doesn't ask for permission, just invades my space as if he belongs here. As if he knows I won't turn him away.

"What's going on, Evelyn? Have I done something to upset you?"

I lean back in my chair. I'm not sure I want to have this conversation, but for some reason having clarity means more to me than my dignity. "Last night. Why didn't you mention that you knew about my modeling career?"

He shrugs. "It didn't seem relevant to anything we discussed."

I study him for a moment, looking for cracks. Looking for signs that he is anything other than what I see—a strong, stoic man. A man who's comforting and sexy. Trustworthy.

"What else has my brother told you about me?" God, I hate how anxious my voice sounds. I dread that he might have heard about the self-harm or the addictions, or about the months I spent in recovery from both, alternating between fighting to get better and wanting to die.

Gabe closes the door behind him and slowly shakes his head. "Beck didn't say anything else. Only that he cares about you."

"Was that before or after you told him I'm so incompetent and overworked that I lost my purse?"

"I didn't say that." His square jaw tenses as he looks at me. "I didn't intend to betray any confidence in mentioning what you said in the garage. For that, I apologize."

"My life is none of your business."

"Agreed."

I want to hold on to my anger, but it's not easy. Not when Gabe seems so steady in his calm. And I cannot deny that seeing him again is wreaking havoc on my senses. He approaches me around the other side of my desk, his presence consuming space and oxygen, making me lightheaded and breathless with every step that brings him closer.

My heart pounds in my breast as he stops only a few paces from me. I should feel trapped. Instead I stare up at him in silent anticipation, my blood racing, my skin tingling everywhere his gaze lands on me.

"You're pissed at me," he states flatly, but the low tenor of his voice is anything but emotionless. "Right now, I don't think your anger has anything to do with your brother or anything he might have told me. You're not even pissed at me because of anything I may have told him while doing my job."

"And you're this insightful about my feelings having

only spoken to me a couple of times?"

"Yes."

I scoff, but it only makes him smile. His dimples flash momentarily, drawing my gaze to his mouth. Big mistake, because now I can barely look away.

He makes a noise in the back of his throat, deep and knowing. Arrogantly male.

"I think you're pissed because I didn't kiss you last night."

Indignation launches me out of my seat. "And I think you should leave now."

He nods, unfazed. "Yeah. So do I. But not until we clear something up."

We are facing each other, only a few inches separating our bodies in the privacy of my closed office. I could back away if I want. The other side of my desk provides an easy escape.

But that's not what I want.

He knows it as well as I do.

"I don't care about what happened in your past. Who you were. Why it ended. I'm not going to go digging anywhere to find out, so if you want me to know, you'll have to tell me yourself."

He won't uncover anything, even if he tried. Other than an internet rumor or two when my troubles first began, Andrew has taken great strides—and gone to significant expense—to make sure the ugliest photos and tabloid stories have been buried. I've held on to some of the worst pictures myself, if only to remind me of all that I've overcome to get where I am now.

Gabe shakes his head on an uttered curse. "You think I don't have a past? You think I haven't spent years trying to carve some semblance of a new life for myself after everything that happened to me over in that desert, or in the years that came before that? Think again."

His gaze sears me as it travels every inch of my face. This man is steady and strong, but he burns hot. I can feel the intensity of his arousal in the heat that fills the space between us. I can see how tightly reined he manages his control, but he is on the verge of losing it.

He reaches out, stroking his thumb along my jawline. His fingers splay against my cheek and a moan builds in my throat. He shakes his head, whether in warning to me or himself, I can't be certain.

"Do I want you, Evelyn? Hell, yes. You're all I thought about after I got home last night. And today, I couldn't get here fast enough, just to see you again."

"Stop." The word gusts out of me on a sigh. "Stop saying all the right things."

"I'm just being honest."

"Maybe you're just saying what you know I want to hear. Maybe you're just looking to put a notch in your bedpost. Another conquest to brag about."

"Do I strike you as the kind of man who would do any of those things?"

"No . . . I don't know." God help me, I've never known a man who could strip away my defenses like Gabriel Noble is doing now. I cling to my indignation, but it's a wall made of sand.

He lifts my chin on the edge of his knuckles. "Well, I'm not that kind of man. And if I were, you would've already been naked beneath me—either in one of our beds, or right up against your car in the parking lot last night." When my eyes widen in shock, he pins me with a carnal look. "Tell me that's not what you wanted me to do. In case you forgot, you were the one who touched me first."

"Did you also put that in your report to my brother and Nick today?" My heart is pounding as I say it, every cell in my body feeling electric under the intensity of Gabe's stare.

He doesn't react to my jab, just holds my gaze in abject seriousness. "No, they don't know any of this. They never will. But I can't let this happen between us, Evelyn. That's what you need to understand. Your brother trusts me as a friend, as a colleague. Nick does too. I won't risk that, not for anything. No matter how much I want you."

"No. Of course, not," I reply, before I can stop myself. "After all, you don't want to tarnish that Boy Scout honor of yours."

His scowl deepens, turning almost savage. Yet his voice is utter calm. "Is that really what you think?"

He doesn't wait for my answer. He steps forward, his muscled frame consuming the space that separates us while his hands reach out to me, both palms curving around the back of my neck, taking me into a hold that is possessive and hungered. His mouth claims mine—no permission, no apology. Only raw, consuming need.

A moan builds in my breast. When I part my lips to let it free, Gabe's tongue sweeps into my mouth. His kiss is wild, hot. Obliterating everything in its path. Including my anger and doubts. I melt into the firmness of his body pressed against me. The hard ridge of his arousal makes the fire smoldering inside me erupt into a desire I'm not at all sure I can contain.

All I know is that I want more.

More of this kiss . . . and more of this man.

He growls against my lips, then breaks contact on a

jagged curse. His hands slide away from my neck. As if he's not yet ready to let me go, one thumb brushes over my wet bottom lip as he stares at me through darkened, stormy hazel eyes.

"Fuck." He grits the word out harshly, drawing back and raking a hand through his short brown hair.

I stare helplessly, shocked with the depth and intensity of my need.

Gabe takes another step away from me, his face rigid, jaw clenched. Then he turns, his long stride carrying him to my closed office door. He pauses there, swiveling to give me one last look.

"Do us both a favor," he tells me in a roughened voice as he grabs the handle. "Don't ever talk to me about honor again."

8

~ Gabriel ~

Two days later, as I sit in my office writing up notes from a security walk-through of a Baine property in SoHo, the memory of that kiss still smolders on my lips. And that's nothing compared to the other parts of my anatomy that continue to crave Evelyn Beckham to the point of maddening distraction.

I can't say I didn't know the kiss was a mistake. I knew damn well it was, even as I reached for her and crushed my mouth against hers. Now, neither of us should have any doubt.

Honor, she said?

Christ.

I thought I had a little before I met her, but all it took to incinerate it was the feel of her hand against my cheek in the dark outside the boutique. Her tender, yet uninhibited, touch that night awakened more than the blunted nerve endings in my shrapnel-shattered face.

I tried to deny it—to myself, at least. But that lie blew apart as I stood in my shower that same night, stroking my cock under the hot spray while remembering the soft warmth of Evelyn's fingertips on my skin, her bold green eyes conveying the invitation she didn't seem quite ready to speak aloud.

And thank God for that.

If she had said anything—if she had tested me with anything more than that gentle touch—I would have made good on the threat I issued in her office the next day. The two of us, naked and sweaty, in the nearest location we had to go to make that happen.

The hell of it is, I still want that.

I want her like I haven't wanted anyone in a long damn time.

Not simply lust. That much I could handle. That much I could extinguish elsewhere, with any of the nameless, faceless women who've served to numb me from all of my various pains since I returned home from the war.

Evelyn's touch—and, now, that stupid, stolen kiss—has aroused a yearning in me that goes deeper than physical. And that makes her dangerous. Not only to the job that demands my attention and discipline, but to the friends whose trust I cannot—and will not—fail.

Since I've proven to myself that I can't rely on honor, or even duty, to steer me in the right direction where she's concerned, I've decided the best tactic is avoidance. Although I'm struggling with that too. I've avoided the urge to turn the internet inside out looking for intel on Evelyn's life in the spotlight, if barely. But fortunately, no one other than me is privy to the number of times I've checked L'Opale's parking lot video feeds to look for her vehicle. I've lost count of how often I've reviewed the recorded footage, watching to confirm that she's arrived and left safely from the shop.

Purely from a security monitoring standpoint, of course.

Fuck, the last person I'm going to convince of that is myself.

I shake my head and put my focus back where it belongs, on the report I want to have in Nick and Beck's hands before the end of the day. I've been busting my ass, working a lot of overtime this week, trying to wrap my arms around my new role and responsibilities. Part of the job has been hiring added staff to the team here at Baine International's headquarters.

One of those new recruits, a fellow veteran I met last year in physical therapy, knocks her left hand on my open door.

"Pardon the interruption, sir."

"What's up, O'Connor?" I glance at the petite strawberry-blond who'd served in Iraq as an army MP around the same time I was in Afghanistan. Kelsey O'Connor might have come home and joined a police unit Stateside after her recovery, but the loss of her right arm from hand to elbow and most of her right leg limited her job options. She was elated with my offer of a spot on the Baine security team. "And you can stop calling me sir. I'm Gabe, same as I've been since those months we spent together in PT at Walter Reed."

She gives me a crisp nod. "Thanks, Gabe. I just wanted to make sure it was okay if some of us head out for a quick bite for lunch?"

"That time already?" I stand up from my desk and

walk around it. "Yeah, go on. You mind bringing something back for me? Any kind of sandwich would be great."

"Sure, no problem." I hand her some money for my food and she glances at me as we walk out of my office, heading for the spacious lobby of the sleek Baine tower. "Are you coming to tomorrow's game?"

If there's a wheelchair basketball game tomorrow night at the veterans center, that means today must be Friday. I'm taken aback to realize how fast the week has gone. And now I'm reminded of a different weekend obligation I'd give anything to avoid. "Gonna have to miss the game. I've got a cookout at my folks' place tomorrow. Big party for Shane's promotion to commander."

She smiles, aware of some of the strife that exists between me and my old man. "I'm glad to hear you're going to spend a little time with your family. Broken fences shouldn't stay that way forever. Sooner or later, someone's got to be willing to mend them."

I grunt. "That some kind of home improvement show life logic you're hitting me with, O'Connor?"

She laughs. "Hey, don't knock my guilty pleasures. Everyone has a vice or two."

Don't I know it. If I'm not careful, I'll have to add the name Evelyn Beckham to my list.

O'Connor walks beside me in silence for a beat. "So, is Jake going to be at the cookout too?"

"I have no doubt." I swivel a questioning look at her. "Why?"

"No reason, really. Just wondering."

If we weren't already in the lobby, I'd probe for a better answer than that. Although O'Connor's slight blush tells me all I need to know. No way. The last thing I want to think about is my older brother, the unapologetic player, getting within striking distance of a sweet girl like Kelsey O'Connor.

As she and I approach the desk we find the two other fresh hires waiting there, chatting with Luis, whom I've promoted to my old post full-time. As O'Connor and I approach, Nick's limousine rolls up to the curb outside and he exits the backseat of the black vehicle along with Beck.

"Holy shit," one of the new guys murmurs beside me. "Dude, that's Dominic Baine."

I smile at the unvarnished awe in that simple statement. I get it, even though I've gotten accustomed to breathing the same air as the almost legendary corporate titan I call a friend. I glance at O'Connor and the others who've only been on board for a couple of days. "Look sharp. You're about to meet the boss."

Nick and Beck stroll into the lobby, wrapping up a conversation that has both of them chuckling. I stand with the new members of my team and give the two executives a nod in greeting.

"Afternoon, everyone," Nick says, his sharp blue eyes traveling from me to the group all standing at attention. "These must be the latest additions to Baine's security team, Gabe?"

I incline my head. "Dominic Baine, Andrew Beckham, I'd like to introduce Kelsey O'Connor, Joe Rodriguez, and Mitch Hawkins."

"Welcome to Baine International," Nick says, smoothly shaking O'Connor's prosthetic hand first, then moving on to greet the others.

Beck follows suit, and for a couple of minutes the

two men engage the new hires in easy conversation about their first days on the job and offer them suggestions for the best lunch places nearby.

After O'Connor and the others head out to eat, Nick claps me on the shoulder. "Great work on the security assessments this week, Gabe. Damn, I wish I'd had you on the team years ago."

"Thanks," I reply. "I'm just glad to be part of the team now. I'm happy to be of use any way I can."

Beck gives me a wry grin. "You may have spoken too soon."

"We've just returned from the youth recreation center in Chelsea," Nick says.

I nod. "I know the one."

It's a new property under the Baine umbrella of real estate holdings in the city, a spacious community campus that Nick conceived of and built for a neighborhood without a lot of resources. Not with any intent to turn a profit, but because it gave him personal satisfaction. He created the rec center because it was a good thing to do, the right thing to do. And I know from talking with him that the Chelsea center is only the first of many he plans to build.

"The security system for Chelsea is top-notch," I remark. "I didn't note a single element in need of improvement. Unless you're about to tell me I missed something."

"No, your report covering the center was spot-on," Nick says, then a smile tugs at the edge of his mouth. "How do you feel about zoos?"

I stare at them both. "I'm sorry, I don't follow."

Beck chuckles. "Lions, tigers, bears. You know, the usual. Plus, a bouncy house and a couple hundred screaming kids along with their parents."

"Still clear as mud," I reply, obviously missing the joke here.

Nick rubs his hand over his beard-shadowed jaw. "The rec center was supposed to be hosting its first family picnic tomorrow at one of the kiddie amusement parks in Brooklyn. We've had the whole place reserved for months, but now there's some rain in the morning forecast and that means most of the rides will be closed."

"Not good news for the kids."

"No," Beck agrees. "But the park is within the terms of their contract with us. Actually, they could shut the entire park down for the day if weather is a concern."

"Right," Nick says. "So, rather than risk any disappointment, we're moving the whole event to a new venue instead. I managed to persuade the Bronx Zoo to take us on short notice."

I give a low whistle. "I'll bet that didn't come easy."

"Or cheap," Beck adds.

Nick shrugs. "It'll be worth it to every one of those kids. But that means a lot of scrambling to get provisions in place on less than twenty-four hours' notice. I've pulled a few favors from friends to provide catering and entertainment, so we're covered on that front. There are still a few things left to arrange."

"How can I help?"

He slants me an apologetic look. "I hate to chew into your weekend, especially considering all of the hours you've already put in this week—"

"You need me, I'm there." I don't need anything more. My offer is sincere, and it's not even about wanting an excuse to skip the family cookout in Bayside. I know how much the rec center and the kids mean to

Nick, so if he wants me to lend a hand in some way, it's the least I can do.

"Think you can round up half a dozen security team members to work the event tomorrow? It'll be paid overtime, of course. Plus a bonus for everyone in appreciation for the last-minute assist."

"Consider it done." I nod, already forming the list of names in my head.

"No suits or visible holsters, Gabe. I want plain clothes on everyone, and service weapons concealed. You and the rest of your team need to blend in. These kids see enough law enforcement patrolling around their homes and schools. Tomorrow is all about showing them a good time in a safe, comfortable environment."

"Sounds like a plan. What time would you like us to be there?"

"Setup will start first thing in the morning, but security won't need to be in place until about an hour before the families are scheduled to arrive. If you can see that everyone is at the venue by ten o'clock, that would be great."

"All right. We'll see you then."

"Thanks, man." Nick reaches for my hand and clasps it the way he might over beers at a bar, not as my employer. "I know it's a big favor to ask, and I really appreciate that you always have my back."

"Anytime. It's no problem at all."

I say that with total conviction, even though it does pose something of a problem for me. A personal one. Because now I have the dubious obligation of calling my mother and Shane to let them know I won't be making the family gathering.

I can almost hear my old man's scorn already. But,

hey, what the hell? He's always looking for another reason to despise me. Why should I let the son of a bitch down now?

9

~ Evelyn ~

"What do you think of the fit?" I place the final pin, then step off the dais in one of the private, mirrored dressing rooms at L'Opale to allow Avery Ross to see herself for the first time in the balconette bra and panties I designed for her.

For a long moment, she doesn't speak. I send an anxious glance at my seamstress, Jane. The stocky, gray-haired woman is a master at her craft, and until this second I didn't have a single doubt that our newest client was going to love this preliminary look at the romantic, yet utterly sexy, ensemble. Now, I hardly know what to make of her prolonged silence.

"The antique-pink Leavers lace is handmade in a little shop near Calais, France," I tell her. "The silk ribbon is only tacked on for now. Jane will adjust everything to your measurements today, so if there is anything you'd like to change or revisit at another fitting before we finish this set—"

"No." Avery's voice is soft, almost a whisper. She slowly shakes her head, her long blond hair sifting around her bare shoulders and the delicate, pleated straps of the bra. "Evelyn, Jane . . . it's absolutely perfect. Please, don't change a single stitch on either piece."

Oh, thank God. "I'm so glad you're happy with them."

She turns away from the mirrored walls, her smile beaming as she looks at Jane and me. "I feel like a princess. Your work—both of you—is amazing. Every woman should be able to feel this beautiful and sexy at least one time in her life."

I can't help but agree. Every time I design an expensive, bespoke piece of lingerie like the ones Avery is wearing, I wish I had the means to create this kind of magic for every woman. And I can't deny that so often, I wish my designs weren't reserved exclusively for flawless bodies and limitless bank accounts.

But right now, nothing can diminish the satisfaction I feel at seeing Avery so openly delighted with what I've created for her.

She glances at the mirrors once more, smoothing her palm over the sheer floral lace and the delicate cups that lift her breasts like bonbons. "Nick's going to lose his mind when he sees me in this. I can't wait to see his reaction."

I smile. "If you like this one, I think you're really going to love all of the other sets we're working on."

"I'm sure I will." She turns to let me carefully unhook the bra for her, then she steps off the dais and enters the changing stall. From behind the closed door, she asks, "How long before I can take this one home with me?"

I glance at Jane in question.

Lips pursed, she gives a small wave of her hand. "The original measurements I took were nearly perfect," she says, without a trace of humility, something I've come to expect and appreciate from the older woman. "So, to finish the work shouldn't take me long. If I start immediately, I'm sure I can have it ready in the morning."

"Thanks, Jane. If you like, Avery, I would be happy to swing by tomorrow and hand deliver the finished pieces to you at your home."

"No, I couldn't ask that of you." Soft rustles sound as she takes off the lingerie and puts on her own undergarments and clothing. "Besides, I'll be at an event in the Bronx all day with Nick. We're hosting a big outing for the kids and families who are part of the youth recreation center in Chelsea."

I'm familiar with the project she mentions. While Dominic Baine had eschewed a lot of the publicity surrounding his generous gift to the community in the months since it opened, the rec center hit the press with a splash. Success stories about the kids it serves and the people who have benefitted from Nick's generosity continue to run on local news and internet articles on a regular basis.

"The original plan for tomorrow was bumper cars and Ferris wheels at an amusement park," Avery says. "Nick just informed me about an hour ago that he had to change the venue. So, now we'll be hosting the party at the zoo instead."

"That sounds even better to me. I used to love going

to the zoo when I was a kid."

"Would you like to come?" She walks out of the dressing room wearing jeans and heels and a gray silk blouse. The bra and panties are folded neatly in her hands. She thanks Jane as the seamstress takes the pieces and shuffles out of the room. "A few of my friends are going to be there too. Why don't you join us, if you don't have other plans?"

"I don't have plans," I admit, and after a stressful week—topped off by a kiss that's left me breathless and utterly confused even two days after Gabriel Noble stalked out of my office—the thought of spending a Saturday afternoon in one of my favorite childhood places seems like exactly the kind of escape I need. "All right. I'd love to come."

"Great," Avery says. "The event starts at eleven, but we'll be there early, so stop by the park anytime. You can text me when you arrive and I'll make sure you can find me."

"Okay. Shall I bring the finished lingerie with me?"

She grins. "You'd better not. If Nick realizes what it is, he won't stop until he's got me in it, no matter where we happen to be. And then he'll be unbearable until he gets me out of it."

I smile. "Isn't that the ultimate point of beautiful lingerie?"

"Yes, but I'd rather imagine the kids getting an education in animal husbandry from the actual animals tomorrow, not from my insatiable and utterly shameless, hot husband-to-be."

I laugh, but hearing her talk about the passion she has with Nick makes me relive the smoldering possessiveness I felt in those brief, searing moments that

Gabe's mouth came crushing down on mine. I've been telling myself I'm glad he hasn't come back, that I am thankful I haven't been asked to return to the Baine Building to meet again with Avery and risk running into Gabe in the process.

I've spent the past two days trying to convince myself that this man and his kiss hasn't cracked something open inside me, that it should be easy to banish the memory of his lips on mine with the same disregard he seems to have for me.

Yet, meanwhile, for all of these past two days, he's continued to invade my thoughts.

And at night, he invades my dreams.

Avery studies me now, as she collects her purse from the velvet-upholstered settee near where we stand. "I understand Gabe is overseeing some security enhancements here at L'Opale."

"Yes, he is." My bitterness toward him is still ripe enough that it slips out of me on a short scoff. "Lucky me."

I'm not sure how she could tell I'd been thinking about Gabriel Noble, but there's no mistaking the curious gleam in her eyes now that she's mentioned his name and caught my reaction.

"Don't tell me you two are still locking horns?"

Among other things. As the fiancée of the man Gabe works for, Avery doesn't need to be burdened with the details of my last encounter with him. But she doesn't seem inclined to let it go. She studies me with the kind of look Paige or my other friends tend to give me when I'm trying to be evasive.

"If I'm pressing, please tell me. But . . . is something going on between you and Gabe?"

I groan. "No, there's nothing going on. At the moment, I don't think we're even speaking to each other."

"Do you want to tell me what happened?" She makes a circling motion with her finger. "Consider this room our cone of silence. Anything you say won't leave here, I promise."

I release a sigh, and before I can stop them, the words tumble out of my mouth. "When Gabe came here to install a bunch of cameras, electronic locks, and other security measures I'm not sure are necessary, we ended up arguing. I said some things that upset him, then he said some things that only upset me even more, and then . . . I kissed him."

Avery's eyes go wide. "You kissed him?"

"Technically, he kissed me. The point is, it happened. And trust me, neither one of us is happy about it, either. But now it's been two days since he stormed out of here, and I can't decide if I'm relieved or furious as hell that I haven't seen or heard from him."

"Maybe some of both," Avery suggests gently, and I sense she knows something about this feeling herself. "He's a good man, Evelyn. I don't think he's without his own demons, but then how many of us can say we are? Some people are worth all the effort it takes to love them, or to show them that they're worth loving."

I mentally reel back. "I'm talking about a couple of arguments and an angry kiss. Love is the furthest thing from my mind. Or his, I'm sure."

She smiles, giving a faint lift of her shoulder. There is something sly in her gaze now, and in the faint tilt of her lips. "Anyway, Gabe won't be able to avoid you forever. Especially if you and I start spending more time together working on lingerie designs."

"It won't be a problem," I assure her. "You're my client, Avery, and I promise none of this will impact my work or the quality of my time spent with you. I've actually cleared my other clients to devote myself completely to this project. I won't disappoint you."

She shakes her head. "I know you won't, and that's not what I meant. What I'm trying to say is that I want to expand the scope of our agreement, Evelyn. I'd like you to design all of the lingerie for my wedding and honeymoon. If you're interested, that is."

I'm gaping, but I can't help it. "Avery." I reach out and squeeze her hand, but then my gratitude and excitement overcomes me and I can't resist giving her a hug. "Thank you. I would be honored."

"I can't imagine trusting it to anyone else," she says, smiling as I release her. "We can talk some more about it next week."

"I look forward to it."

"Me too," she says. "Now, I'd better run. I have a hundred things to do before tomorrow, but this was by far the best part of my day."

We leave the dressing room together and walk out to the front of the boutique. There are a few customers browsing the shop, but it is the gray-haired gentleman in the prim suit seated in one of our consultation areas that draws my attention.

"See you tomorrow afternoon," Avery says, giving me a quick hug before heading for the front door.

I wave to her, then step behind the cashier counter where Megan is eyeing me uncertainly. "What's Mr. Hennings doing here today?"

"He says he had an appointment with Kat."

"I thought she was off today."

"She is. But apparently she forgot to tell Mr. Hennings." Meg taps the computer screen to bring up the shop calendar. "He's right here on her schedule, Evelyn. Anyway, he asked to wait for you."

"All right. I'll handle it." Suppressing my disappointment in Kat for this uncharacteristic slip, I paste a smile on my face and walk over to greet the kindly older man. He stands up as I approach, inclining his balding head. "Mr. Hennings, good afternoon."

"Ah, Miss Beckham. Hello, my dear." He takes my offered hand in his grasp, his palm soft and a little humid.

I draw mine back and fold my arms. "I just heard there was a scheduling problem on our end today. I apologize for the mix-up. I know Katrina will feel terrible about this too."

"It's no trouble at all," he assures me. "Mistakes happen. I hope you don't mind that I'm intruding on your day. I see your talents are very in demand lately."

A guilty pang jabs me at the remark, especially considering my work with Avery has limited the time I used to spend on his account. "First of all, you're not intruding. I'm just sorry you came all this way and Katrina's not here. Is there something I can help you with?"

"If you don't mind, I was hoping to check on the progress of that delightful little negligee we discussed a couple of weeks ago. The one that's almost the precise color of your pretty eyes."

I know Kat would groan at the old man's feeble attempts to flirt, but I've learned to take it in stride. I invite him back to my office and he follows, pausing to thank Megan for the tea she brought him while he waited for me to finish with Avery.

His round face lights up in a smile as soon as he enters my office and sees his rosebush situated on the edge of my desk. "You found the perfect spot for it."

"Thank you again for your lovely gift, Mr. Hennings. It really wasn't necessary."

He gives me a dismissive wave of his hand. "You create such beautiful things, I wanted to make something beautiful for you."

I smile and motion for him to take the guest chair. "Please have a seat. I'll be right back with your project files and we can review them together."

10

~ Evelyn ~

The shrill cry of a monkey echoes through the thick green jungle habitats that lay just ten miles from the urban chaos of Times Square.

"Looks like the zoo is a huge hit," I say as I approach the picnic table where Avery directed me to meet her and a couple of her friends when I arrived.

"I'm so happy you made it, Evelyn." She greets me with a hug and a bright smile. "Who needs amusement park rides when you have animals and all this space for kids to run?"

All around us, happy families stroll here and there along the paths while hundreds of excited, chattering children race from one exhibit to another in the large section of the zoo that's been closed for the community center's private party.

Avery gestures to the pair of attractive women sitting

at the table with her. "These are my friends Tasha Lopez and Lita Frasier."

I smile at the petite, visibly pregnant Latina mom who's holding a sleeping toddler girl in her lap, and the curvy, tattooed woman with bright teal hair seated across from them. "Nice to meet you both, Tasha and Lita. I'm Evelyn Beckham."

They offer me warm smiles and friendly welcomes as I join them. Tasha adds in a whisper, "This little hellion is Zoe. You're catching her in a rare moment of recharge. Normally, you can't get her to slow down for anything."

"Just like her mama," Avery says, then glances at me. "Tasha and I used to work together at a restaurant on Madison. It's not far from your boutique, in fact."

"Really? Which restaurant?"

"Vendange. Do you know it?"

I laugh. "That happens to be one of my favorites in all of the city. My friends and I must end up there for lunch or dinner at least once a month."

Tasha nods, tilting her head and studying me. "You look really familiar. I'm sure I've seen you there a few times. Or maybe somewhere else . . ."

"Tasha's been managing Vendange for about a year and a half," Avery interjects. "Before that, she and I tended bar there."

"Yeah, we bonded over our shared misery of working for the misogynist jerk who used to manage the place," her friend says, her brown eyes continuing to watch me over the top of her sleeping child's head. "Then Ave met Nick, he bought the restaurant, canned our old boss, and put me in charge."

Avery nods. "If you ask me, one of the best business

decisions Nick's ever made."

Seated beside me on the picnic table bench, Lita grins, making the diamond stud in her nose twinkle. "I'd say he's done all right in the art appreciation department too. After all, Nick spotted your talent before anyone else was smart enough to realize what a gifted artist you are."

"Look who's talking about having a gift," Avery replies, then glances at me again. "Lita and I, along with another friend, Matt, have been sharing studio space in East Harlem for about as long as I've been with Nick. I still can't paint worth a damn anywhere else but next to her."

Lita bats her lashes like a vixen, an odd juxtaposition with her heavily inked skin and multiple piercings. "What can I say? I am clearly a great and powerful muse."

I laugh, finding it easy to get swept into the camaraderie between the three women. "What kind of art do you do, Lita?"

"Metal and mixed media sculpture. I've dabbled with paint, too, but I'd much rather smash things with a hammer or bend them to my will using a blow torch. My shrink used to tell me I had anger management issues." She exchanges a private look with Avery. "I wonder what she'd say now."

As Lita talks, I'm reminded of a local business article I read a few months ago about a Brooklyn technology firm that had commissioned an original metal art sculpture for their corporate flagship's lobby. I didn't recall the female artist's name, but the company's billionaire CEO, Derek Kingston, is a perennial hot topic for the press, given that the handsome, very eligible bachelor made his first fortune with a string of hit songs and sold-out rock concerts all over the world.

"Are you the sculptor who's creating the piece for DekTech's new headquarters?"

Lita's face seems to blanch a bit. "Not anymore. I tore up the contract."

"Oh." I sense it's a touchy subject, and since I've only just met her, the last thing I want to do is make Lita uncomfortable. "I'm sorry. I hope everything is okay with that."

She gives a subdued shrug that speaks volumes. "It'll be fine. I always land on my feet somehow."

An awkward silence begins to fall over Avery and her friend. Tasha's the first to break it. "Am I the only one who's starving right now? Ever since we sat down, I've been smelling something amazing cooking on a grill somewhere."

"That's our catering," Avery says. "I don't think I mentioned it to anyone yet, but Nick managed to persuade Gavin Castille to cook for our party today."

"You've got to be kidding," Tasha says, laughing. "Leave it your fiancé to hire a celebrity chef on zero notice. I'm surprised the zoo didn't insist on supplying the food."

Avery winces. "I don't think Nick gave them the chance to argue. As for Gavin, since he's a good friend and he donates time at the rec center, too, he was more than willing to come to our rescue today."

"Speak of the devil," Lita murmurs.

I glance across the area where we're seated and see the tall, beachy-blond Australian striding toward us carrying a plate of food and a stack of napkins. Gavin Castille is built like an athlete, long limbs and a trim body that doesn't seem to carry an ounce of fat in spite of the decadent dishes he's famous for, both in the media and in his signature restaurants all around the world. His latest place, GC, has a reputation for months-long reservation lists and a menu to die for.

His fluid, cowboy swagger and movie-star handsome face would have made him famous even if he wasn't an incredibly talented chef. Certainly, he's never had a shortage of beautiful women on his arm at any given moment.

As he nears us, the aromas of grilled meat and savory vegetables and sauces practically make me moan in anticipation.

If I wasn't still fuming about a certain aggravating Baine security chief, I might also be tempted to moan over the sheer male perfection of the man now giving us all a dazzling, dimpled smile.

"Afternoon, ladies." His deep voice and accent are as dangerous as the rest of him, and from the wicked gleam in his eyes, I'm guessing he knows how to use his charm to its fullest advantage. He leans down and gives Avery a brief kiss on the cheek before setting the plate down on the table between all of us. "I thought you might like to sample a few things before the chow bell rings to summon the throng."

Tasha peers at the offering. "Barbequed chicken, grilled veggies, and potato salad? I didn't realize you had it in you to be so basic. Color me shocked."

Obviously, they know each other. Which shouldn't come as a surprise, given that Nick and Avery are evidently close to Castille.

"Nice to see you, too, Tasha." He winks at her, then places a gentle hand on sleeping Zoe's head for a moment. "Where's my buddy Tony?"

"He's around here somewhere. Probably acting a bigger fool than most of the kids, if I know him. I'll bring him by later to say hello. I know he'll be eager to bend your ear about his latest obsession."

"Another home brew experiment?"

"No, much worse. He's discovered the joys of pressure-cooking."

"Ah, Christ." Castille chuckles. "My sympathies."

He glances at Lita and me, and Avery makes introductions for us. He's friendly and warm, and for a few minutes, while we all pick at the plate of food he brought, he and Tasha entertain us with good-natured banter about their restaurants' ongoing kitchen rivalry.

Tasha pulls off a piece of grilled chicken and pops it in her mouth. "I'm just saying, this new chef we hired is outstanding. Since we brought her on, we've nearly tripled our weekend dinner receipts."

"And where did you say she trained again?"

"I didn't. But since you asked, she's homegrown. She got her start as a line cook right here in the city and worked her way up one kitchen at a time."

He grunts, hardly hiding his skepticism. "I guess I'll have to come in sometime and see what's cooking."

Avery laughs. "Tasha, you'd better watch your back. I know Gavin, and he's either going to recon your menu or try to steal your new chef out from under you."

Castille holds up his hands. "Vicious lies. I just like checking out the competition. I didn't get this far without paying attention to who might be breathing down my neck and looking to unseat me one day."

As everyone talks, I notice that Lita has gone quiet next to me. I glance at her and find her face a little pale, tiny beads of perspiration gathering above her upper lip. She seems to sway a bit, her hand moving up to her mouth.

"Are you okay?"

She nods. "Yeah. I'm fine." But she swallows hard, and a look of discomfort washes over her face. "I think I just . . . need to . . . get some air or something."

"I'll help you," Avery says, popping off the bench and moving to her friend's side. To the rest of us, she adds, "It does seem awfully humid today after this morning's rain. We're just going to take a little walk."

I glance at Tasha, who looks as concerned as me. "Well," she says, "I should probably go waddle off to find my husband and let him know there's food to eat. Everything's great, Gavin. You know I just have to bust your balls."

He nods. "Always a pleasure, Tasha. Tell Tony I'll watch for him at the catering station."

With her sleeping daughter slumped over her shoulder, Tasha waves and heads off across the open space.

"And then, there were two," Castille says.

I smile, feeling instantly at ease with him, even though I would have guessed by his reputation that he'd be an insufferable egomaniac. But I know he has work to do, and I figure I'll wander the grounds on my own for a little while before heading home.

"Thanks for the snack, Gavin. It was delicious." I stand up, wiping my mouth and fingers on the napkin. "Nice meeting you."

He tilts his head. "Actually, we met about seven years ago in Sydney. One of those fashion event after-parties, as I recall."

"Oh." I feel my smile falter a little as I struggle to place him in the blur of my runway days. "Those things were always so hectic and it was a long time ago. I'm sorry, Gavin, I don't . . ."

"Hey, no worries. It's cool if you don't remember. We only spoke briefly." He doesn't seem put off or judgmental, just the same easy smile and relaxed demeanor he's shown since he came over to the table. "It's all right, you were the one making the big impressions that night."

"I'm sorry. I really don't recall much about that trip."

But I do remember one thing. Because the Sydney trip was the first time I landed in the hospital, fatigued to the point of exhaustion. My brother flew to Australia and brought me home. Andrew was horrified at my condition, and insisted I rest up for a while. My agent had other plans. By the end of that same week, he had me back to work and booked for another show, propping me up with cocaine during the day and sleeping pills at night.

"Listen, I've got to get back to work," Gavin says, picking up the plate and used napkins. "Where're you off to now?"

I shake my head. "Nowhere specific. I'm just here to hang out and enjoy the time outdoors."

"You wanna lend a hand feeding some two-legged animals?" He grins. "I'm about to unleash the kraken over at the catering station. My staff's got everything covered, but you're welcome to help sling plates in the serving line, if you're up for it."

I shrug, finding his energy irresistible. "Sure. I'd love to."

I follow him back to the area that's been set up for

the picnic, and he introduces me to his coworkers, then outfits me in an apron and puts me behind one of the long serving station tables near the grills. Before long, we are overrun with ravenous kids and grateful parents, all of whom descend on Gavin's fantastic cooking in a happy swarm.

I'm having such a great time being part of it all that I almost look past the tall man with broad shoulders and a thick crown of short chestnut brown hair standing just twenty-some yards away. But once I see Gabe, everything else fades to the background.

Everything except the attractive woman he's talking with under the shade of the large trees on the walking path across the way.

They're dressed casually, Gabe in jeans, sneakers, and a black T-shirt that showcases his powerful arms and clings almost indecently to the slabs of firm muscles on his chest and abdomen. His pretty, strawberry-blonde companion is also in jeans, paired with a summery, sheer short-sleeved blouse buttoned over the top of a camisole. Her arms are down at her sides, and I notice that her right forearm and hand is a prosthesis.

It's obvious that she and Gabe are more than passingly familiar with each other. They're relaxed and friendly, almost intimately so. She says something that makes him laugh, and I am stung with a sharp and ridiculous stab of jealousy.

Are they here together on a date?

God, if he is involved with someone, I feel even stupider for the way I acted in my office with him. I didn't even consider that he might not be single. Then again, that kiss sure as hell didn't feel like he belonged to another woman.

Whether I have any right to feel it or not, resentment simmers inside me as they walk off together. At least, this might explain Gabe's obvious avoidance of me. Doesn't make my disappointment hurt any less, though.

I tear my gaze away from them as they depart, forcing a bright smile onto my face as I continue greeting the kids and families streaming through my catering line.

11

~ Gabriel ~

It takes me about twenty minutes to find her, after a not-so-casual patrol of the zoo grounds.

I'd first spotted Evelyn hours ago, when she'd been sitting with Avery Ross and a couple other women near the private party's picnic area. I hadn't realized she would be here today and seeing her again was a gut punch I wasn't prepared for. Once I laid eyes on her, it was all I could do to keep my focus on my job as my team and I covered the event.

Even O'Connor sensed my mind was somewhere else. Hell, how could she not have sensed it? Each security circuit we ran together through the park seemed to bring us right back to wherever Evelyn was. I finally had to send my friend off to pair up with another teammate, just to put a stop to her relentless questions.

Now, I can't even pretend I've found Evelyn by

accident. With a couple of hours left before the outing ends, I've ditched the rest of my team to walk the grounds on my own.

Even though I've had time to get used to the idea that she's here, seeing Evelyn halts my steps and sends an uninvited lick of heat into my veins. The sexual attraction is only natural. It's the other response I feel, the strange mix of longing and regret, that twists my lips into a scowl.

I'm not used to holding back on anything I want, yet now I stand in the shadows off to the side of the jungle path to watch her. She's chatting with a group of kids at the observation area near one of the animal habitats. Alone with the half dozen boys and girls, she stands behind the safety railing overlooking the grassy enclosure for a herd of petite Thomson's gazelles.

"If you look really hard, you'll see it." I catch the velvet sound of Evelyn's voice as she squats down to the children's level and points to direct their gazes at the animals. "There's a baby gazelle sitting in the tall grass just to the left of that big boulder. Do you see her?"

"I see!" One little girl in a pink dress gasps in awe. "It's so cute! Look, you guys, it's right there!"

The rest of the kids jockey and bob excitedly for positions at the barrier. Evelyn rises, smiling as she watches them enjoy the discovery. She is relaxed and open with the kids, a stark contrast to the wary, mistrusting woman who faced off with me in her office a couple of days ago.

With her long dark hair swept up in a bouncy ponytail, she's wearing casual beige slacks and running shoes, paired with a simple white V-neck top that hugs the fullness of her breasts and plays up the warm toffee color of her smooth skin. As gorgeous as Evelyn is in professional attire and high heels, the only way I've seen her so far, this relaxed, natural side of her is even sexier.

So is her easy laughter, which shuts off abruptly as soon as she turns her head and spots me.

She doesn't move, not even when the pack of giggling children race off, prompted by the shout and summoning wave of a nearby parent.

Part of me expects her to run after them.

Part of me hopes like hell she will.

But Evelyn stands firm as I approach, her lovely face unreadable, but watching me. Her posture is graceful, yet guarded, as if she's trying to decide whether to brace for a fight or ready herself for a desperate flight, like the herd of skittish prey animals currently tearing from one end of their artificial plain to the other in the habitat behind her.

"I didn't expect to see you here," I say, walking up beside her at the railing.

She stares at me for a moment, long enough for me to recognize that I was wrong about one thing. There is nothing in this woman that's prepared to back down. "I didn't expect to see you, either."

Something in her tone tells me if she'd known our paths might cross, she wouldn't have come at all. Her gaze flicks past me, and I wonder if she's concerned that her brother or someone else from Baine International might walk by and catch us talking.

I should be concerned, too, but being around this woman has the unfortunate tendency to make me reckless. She draws my attention away from things that should matter—things that *do* matter, and will, long after I force myself past this inconvenient infatuation.

That's what part of my seeking her out right now is about. I need to close the door on this feeling I have toward her. I need to lock it up tight and walk the fuck away before I do something idiotic like kissing her again.

I've been telling myself it's my job I want to protect. That I need to preserve the trust I've earned with Beck and Nick. But staring into her challenging green eyes leaves me no room to deny that pushing her away is in the interest of my own survival too.

Especially when all I want to do is pull her into my arms and claim another taste of her sexy, silky mouth.

"You're good with the kids," I tell her, watching her wave to the little girl in pink who shouts goodbye to Evelyn as her mother leads her up the path.

"I hardly remember being that young," she says, more to herself than me, it seems. When she glances my way again, a frown rides her brow. "What are you doing here, Gabe?"

"The event only has a couple more hours to go. I was taking one last walk through the park and saw you here. I was hoping you and I could speak privately." I pause for a moment, trying to determine the best way through this. When she doesn't give me any indication that she even wants to see me, much less talk to me, I curse under my breath. Might as well plow straight in. "After my conduct the other day, Evelyn, I feel I owe you an apology."

She doesn't hide her skepticism. Her lips press flat, and the look she gives me is somewhere close to contempt. "Or maybe you're just worried I might say something that could make things awkward for you today."

Her venom shocks me. "I guess I deserve that." I

shake my head, deciding here and now that she's got every right to be angry, even vengeful. "I stepped way over the line when I kissed you, Evelyn. It won't happen again. If you feel you need to tell your brother or Nick what I did—hell, if you want to demand my job for it—I'm not going to fault you."

She scoffs. "Actually, I expected you to be more concerned that I might say something to your date."

"My what?"

Folding her arms, she pins me with a cold look. "I saw you, Gabe. You and the pretty blonde you're here with. I saw you chatting and laughing with her over by the picnic area."

I frown, as confused by her assumption as I am amused by the fact that she seems to be stewing in jealousy. "O'Connor's not my date. She's a friend. As of this week, she's also reporting to me on the Baine security team. We're working this event today."

Her lips part and some of the chill leaves her expression. "Well, it doesn't matter to me, anyway."

But it did matter when she thought there was something between O'Connor and me. I refrain from pointing it out to her, because as pleased as I am by her possessiveness, that's not why I'm here.

It can't be, no matter how much I'd like to chase that stung look off her lovely face with another kiss.

One that would leave no doubt in her mind about just how powerfully I want her.

Instead, I let her denial stand and opt for a less thorny subject. "Were you recruited to help out today, too? I couldn't help noticing that the surfer dude in the kitchen uniform kept you busy for hours behind the catering station."

"So, you did know I was here," she says, sounding smug and eyeing me with raised brows. "That 'surfer dude' is a world-renowned celebrity chef, by the way. His restaurants here in the city are booked solid months in advance. Don't tell me you've never heard of Gavin Castille."

I shrug. "Heard of him, sure. But I'm not really impressed by that kind of stuff. Maybe I've spent too much time camping out in desert war zones. Basic meat and potatoes is as close to gourmet as I'll ever need."

And even if I did have more than a vague idea of who the guy was or why I should care, I'm not about to reinforce Evelyn's apparent favorable regard for him. I'd cruised by the catering area more than once after I spotted her there, checking to see if the good-looking Aussie seemed anything less than professional with Evelyn. He'd passed all of my investigatory fly-bys, but that didn't mean I had to like him.

"Is that where you met your friend O'Connor?" Evelyn asks. "Were you in Afghanistan together?"

"No. She served in Iraq. We didn't meet until after we both came home."

I know why she's asking. I know if she's seen O'Connor's prosthetic arm and hand, it's not that great a leap to assume Kelsey is a veteran like me. What Evelyn doesn't understand is that time in service isn't the only bond O'Connor and I share.

"We met at Walter Reed, actually. In the amputee physical therapy center."

For reasons I haven't stopped to analyze, I haven't let on to Evelyn that I am anything but whole. I don't know why. It's not like me to hide my injury. I'm not ashamed of it and never was. It's just something that happened to me, something I survived.

My injury was something I couldn't control, no matter how well-trained and confident I'd been leading that routine patrol that claimed the rest of my platoon and nearly killed me too.

Yet as I watch Evelyn absorb what I'm telling her, I realize that I do know why I've kept it from her. I haven't wanted to see her shock or horror. I haven't wanted to see her pity.

I haven't wanted her to view me as any less of a man. But fuck all that.

She is not mine, and unless I want to lose my job and my friendship with her brother, she never can be.

I lift the pant leg of my jeans, revealing the lightweight carbon-and-titanium prosthesis that extends out of my left shoe. "The stump starts below my knee. It's called a transtibial amputation."

I hear Evelyn's quiet inhalation and that small sound kills something inside me. I don't know what I expected her reaction to be, but I'd hoped for something else. I meet her gaze, hardening myself to whatever I'm going to see in her eyes.

I'm not prepared to see mortification, even humor. "I'm such an idiot."

"What are you talking about?"

"In the garage," she says, wincing and shaking her head. "The day we met, that stupid thing I said to you—"

I chuckle, remembering. "You mean the crack about me only having the wrong foot?"

"Yes! Oh, my God." She groans and covers her face in her hands before laughing with me. "You probably thought I was a bitch *and* a complete moron. Not that you didn't have it coming."

I'm still laughing, both in relief that she's not treating me any differently and because the irony of what she said that day is even better now that we can share it.

I lift my other pant leg. "As you can see, no wrong foot here. It's the right one all day, every day, baby."

"Stop!" She makes a face and smacks her palm lightly against my chest. "Why didn't you tell me?"

I shrug, not ready to go there yet. Not that we'll ever get there, not if I can help it. "Why didn't you tell me about being famous once upon a time?"

Her expression relaxes into one of quiet solemnity. "Because I don't like people making judgments before they see me for who I really am."

"Ditto," I reply, arching my brows.

She nods, a silent acknowledgment of our common ground. Then she glances away for a moment, pensive. "I don't volunteer anything about that part of my life because I don't ever want to feel I'm being used for what someone thinks I am, or what they think I should be."

"That seems fair."

"It's the only way I know how to live. It's the only way I got through a lot of bad times, by putting that part of my life in a box and never opening it again."

"I'm no psychologist, but that doesn't sound like dealing with it. How are you going to come to terms with something that hurts, if you only let it fester in a locked box somewhere?"

"What about you? It can't have been easy fighting in the war, but I don't imagine it was easy coming home realizing you would never go back, either."

"No. It wasn't."

"How did you get through? How did you cope?"

"I don't know. I'm still trying."

It's a glib reply, yet there is a lot of truth in it too. I could leave it at that, and I probably should. But talking to Evelyn is easier than I thought it could be. Maybe it's because I have no reason to try to impress her. Or maybe it's because I sense we're both fighting similar demons in some ways. Both of us still trying to claw our way into the light, onto safe and solid ground.

"I was engaged when I deployed for Afghanistan," I tell her. "My high school girlfriend, Tracy. I was young and stupid. I guess we both were."

"Did you love her?"

I nod, then it turns into a shrug. "I thought I did. I wanted to know I had someone back home who gave a shit about me, other than my mom and my brothers. I wasn't thinking about what I was truly asking from her. When I woke up in the military hospital and saw her face, I knew she wouldn't stay. I'd been gone half as long as we'd been together. We hardly knew each other by that time. I was looking at long months of recovery and rehab. She wasn't prepared to travel that road with me, and it wouldn't have been fair for me to expect it of her. I was still living at Walter Reed in Bethesda when she moved out of our place three months later."

Evelyn's brows pinch. "I'm sorry. That must've been very hard."

"It was better, easier, not having to worry about Tracy while I was recovering. I focused on my rehab, threw myself into it because it was all I had left."

"And your family?" she asks cautiously. "Were they there for you?"

"My brothers were, especially Jake. I'm the youngest of us four. He's next, nine years ahead of me." I blow out a breath, my lungs feeling heavy when I talk about my brother who's always been my best, tightest friend. "I don't even recall how many times he came down to the amputee ward at the hospital to be with me. He used up all of his vacation time and sick days at the precinct—time he could've been doing anything else other than helping me clean and work with my stump or propping me up while I learned to walk again."

"He sounds pretty great." Her green eyes search my face for a moment. "What about your parents? I know you told me things aren't the best with your dad."

Shit. I didn't intend to wade this far into my own head or my pathetic home life, but it's hard to push Evelyn out now that I've opened the door. I glance away, watching a pair of male gazelles knocking their antlered heads together in the field. "Mom visited a few times with Jake or one of my other brothers, Shane and Ethan. I know she wanted to be there more, but she struggled seeing me like that."

"And your dad?"

"The old man never came. Not once." I state it matter-of-factly, because that's all it is now. Fact. But for those first few months, I kept waiting to see him. Expecting it. Hoping. "He never wanted anything to do with me, even when I was whole. See, I'm the classic mistake, the kid who came along just when things were going south in my parents' marriage. They patched it up, but sometimes I think he's holding me responsible for making him stay."

"I'm sorry, Gabe. If that's true, it's terribly unfair of him. And cruel."

"Yeah, it sucks, but whatever. I'm long past needing any father-and-son bonding. If you want to know the truth, I only made it out of Bethesda thanks to a steady flow of pain meds and Jake's regular ass-kickings, something that he's perfected from the time I was a kid. Working with O'Connor in PT helped as well."

In my peripheral, I see her looking at me with gentle understanding. "I think you can also take some of the credit for where you are. No one else could do the work for you. You had to be willing to step up, to fight back and heal. You're the only one with the power to take control of your life."

I slant her a wry glance. "Who says I've done that?"

She smiles. "Being a work-in-progress counts for something."

"Speaking from experience?"

"Maybe." That sweet curve of her lips doesn't mask the guardedness in her eyes. "I thought we were talking about you."

"Until a second ago, so did I." I lean toward her, bumping her shoulder with mine. "I told you, if you want me to know anything about you, you've got to tell me yourself. Nothing's going to make me think less of you or judge you. And I'm not going to put it in a report to your brother. Scout's honor."

She laughs at that, and I see some of her reticence fade away. "You think I'm that easy?"

"Lady, I don't think anything about you is easy." As soon as I say it, I shake my head. "No, that's not true. Looking at you is easy. Talking to you, that's easy too."

When she swivels her head to look at me, I swear it's all I can do to keep from reaching out to touch her face. I want to do more than merely touch. I want to kiss her. Claim her. Possess her in every way.

I must be out of my fucking mind, either from the

stifling humidity or from treading into the uncharted territory of having a real conversation with a woman who isn't a comrade or a colleague. Because more than anything, I want to be the man Evelyn trusts with all her secrets and pains.

And her pleasures.

I inhale deeply, which is only a mistake that fills my lungs with the warm vanilla scent of her. I let it go on a gusted sigh and turn my gaze back out to the animals in the habitat.

"Never mind," I say abruptly. "You don't have to tell me anything. Not my place to ask."

She's quiet for a moment. About the time I'm thinking I should check in with my team and go back to earning my paycheck, she finally replies.

"I started modeling in high school. Local print ads, department store promotions, that kind of thing. I didn't land my first national runway spot until I was twenty-one. Everything started moving really fast after that. I had an agent and a contract, and suddenly I was on the road every week, booked in one show after another." She goes silent, and when I glance at her, I can tell her thoughts are miles and years away. "I was making more money than I'd ever imagined. But I was exhausted and lonely. I was scared and hungry and so very tired. I found ways to cope with the fatigue and anxiety. My agent helped there, arranging access to physicians and psychologists who knew just what to prescribe. When those weren't enough, he had other contacts who were eager to provide whatever he thought I needed."

"Narcotics?" I guess, and I don't need to see her nod to imagine the scenario.

"The cocaine had the added benefit of suppressing

my appetite, and as my weight decreased, my bookings began to explode. Pretty soon, the cocaine wasn't enough, so I started purging too. It was a vicious cycle, one I didn't even realize was happening until one morning I collapsed on the verge of cardiac arrest in my hotel room in Paris."

"Jesus Christ." I can't curb my shock, or my fury at her agent and everyone else in her orbit at the time who'd allowed her health to spiral that far down—or, hell, encouraged it because of their greed. If I'd been there, I would have killed the ones responsible for her decline. "What about your brother? Did Beck know any of this?"

She shakes her head. "He knew I was working too hard. Early on, he tried to intervene, but things weren't so bad then. I thought he was just trying to hold me back. Later, as my career took off, I hid the truth from him for as long as I could. Paris was the end of everything. The paramedics revived me, and Andrew was on a plane from the States as soon as he was notified. He brought me home, then he and my father checked me into rehab, where they made sure I stayed for the next eleven months until I was healthy and sober."

"And you never went back to modeling?"

"No. If I had, it would have killed me. Even I could see that. Andrew paid to bury all of the photos and gossip pieces that might have come out after what happened in Paris, or my rehabilitation afterward. So, as far as anyone else was concerned, 'Eve' had simply retired. No one knew I was fighting for my life. Some days, I didn't think I had the strength, or the will, to make it. Some days, even after I was out of rehab, I didn't want to make it at all."

"But you did," I point out. Gently, because even though she's strong, I can feel the pain still radiating from her. I can feel the undercurrent of doubt still living inside her, despite the confidence with which she carries herself.

I angle toward her, and this time I can't keep my hand from reaching out. With my palm cupping the side of her face, I stroke my thumb over the velvet-soft skin near her mouth. "I'm glad you're here, Evelyn."

She nods, her gaze dusky now, those gorgeous green eyes drinking me in. "I'm glad you're here, too."

Standing here with her like this, it's impossible to deny how much I desire her. With her lips parted on a soft exhalation, her eyes locked on mine, all of the denials I'd girded myself with when I first approached her crumble away.

My head dips toward hers, without a thought for honor or duty anywhere in my reach.

Until, from somewhere behind me, I hear the jarring sound of someone clearing their throat.

"Ah, excuse me . . . Gabe?"

O'Connor's voice is tentative and quiet, but I swing around as if I just heard a gunshot. "Yeah. What's up?"

"I'm sorry to interrupt your, ah, conversation," she blurts, her gaze darting from me to Evelyn, before finally remaining glued on my face in a look somewhere between apology and utter shock. "The, um, catering service is about to start packing up, so the other guys on the team and I were wondering if you wanted to grab some chow with us."

"No, thanks." Ordinarily, I'd be tempted to joke with my buddy about her bottomless pit of a stomach, but I can't even fake that. I sound guilty as fuck, and there's no covering up what my friend and teammate just walked up on. And while I know she won't mention my indiscretion to anyone else on the team or otherwise, that doesn't make the whole thing any less awkward. "Go on without me. I'll head that way in a few."

She takes off without another word.

"I should go, too," Evelyn says.

It's probably a good idea, considering I can't seem to keep my hands off her, even in full view of the public, not to mention risking being seen by anyone else from the company. I turn toward her and nod. "How'd you get here? Subway?"

"No." Something dark, almost haunted, flickers in her expression. "No, I . . . I never take the subway. My car's parked at the River lot."

I know where it is, since that's the same lot where I met up with my team when we arrived at the event this morning. "Come on, I'll walk you there."

"You sure? I don't really need an escort if you have things you need to do."

"Let's go."

It's a decent hike from where we are, and although my leg will feel it later, I'm not about to let Evelyn make the trip alone. We walk most of the way in companionable silence, even though the air around us still crackles with the awareness of our intensifying attraction and the kiss that would have happened if not for O'Connor's timely interruption.

"Why don't you like taking the subway?" I ask as we near the crowded parking lot situated between the Bronx River and the Parkway.

"I just don't." She gives me a nonchalant shrug, but

her expression is too carefully schooled for me to believe. I can also sense that the openness she shared with me back inside the zoo is behind us now, so I don't press.

If she were mine, I wouldn't rest until she laid all her demons out for me to slay.

I'd slay them all now, even though she'll never belong to me.

We reach her Volvo and I stand back, near the front bumper while she takes out her remote and clicks the unlock button. If I get any closer, I'm not certain I can trust myself to let her go.

It isn't until she opens the door and starts to climb in that I notice something's off with the tilt of the vehicle. I glance down and immediately see the cause.

"Evelyn, wait." She looks at me in question as I hunker down near the front wheel on the driver's side. "You can't drive this car anywhere right now. The tire's flat."

And the closer I look, I realize the tire hasn't just gone flat.

It's been deliberately punctured.

I run my fingertips over the deep, inch-long slit in the rubber that's been made near the rim and the hair at the back of my neck rises.

A knife caused this hole. And whoever wielded the blade in broad daylight, chose to make the puncture in a way that wouldn't be readily detected. But who—and why—someone chose to disable Evelyn's vehicle out of all the other cars in the lot is a question that begs a fucking answer.

And this seemingly random incident on top of the recent peculiarities at L'Opale makes my combat instincts prickle with foreboding, even dread.

"What happened to my tire?" Evelyn steps around the open driver's door to see what I'm looking at.

Since I don't want to alarm her before I have more facts—and definitely not before I have a chance to alert Beck to my suspicion that something is very wrong here—I stand up and insert myself between her and a clear view of the tire.

"I'm not sure yet, but it looks like it's in bad shape. You're going to need a new one."

She frowns. "There's a donut spare in the back."

I shake my head. "You're not going to drive home on that. Don't worry about it. I'll take care of the tire. But first, I'm giving you a lift home."

I step away from Evelyn and call O'Connor. "Yeah, it's me. I need you to do me a favor."

"Anything," she says, no hesitation at all.

"Cover for me for about an hour. Andrew Beckham's sister's got some car trouble, so I'm going to run her home. Anything comes up in the meantime, call me."

"No problem, Gabe. You got it."

I end the call and slip my phone into the pocket of my jeans. I can't help giving the lot a surreptitious visual sweep as I settle my hand on the small of Evelyn's back. "Let's get you out of here now."

12

~ Evelyn ~

The drive from the Bronx to my apartment building on the Upper East Side takes about half an hour. Riding next to Gabe in his Lexus almost feels like we're coming back from a date, especially after the electrically charged moments we shared back at the zoo.

I still feel the current of awareness rolling off him as he smoothly changes lanes ahead of the traffic light at my block of East 86th. It still lives inside me too. I glance out the passenger window and bring my fingers to my lips on a silent sigh. If his friend O'Connor hadn't walked up when she did, I have no doubt Gabe would have kissed me right there in front of the Thomson's gazelles and anyone else who happened to look our way.

It stuns me how much I wish he had. How much I still want him to, even though he's gone from tender and sexy to all-business in the time since he discovered my flat tire. Maybe he's relieved to have an excuse to avoid talking about what almost happened between us. Then again, he doesn't strike me as a man who requires an excuse for anything he does or doesn't do.

Right now, his focus seems rooted solely on getting me home and getting back to his job. Since we've been in the car, he's kept our conversation limited to directions to my place and a brief update on equipment and installation timelines for L'Opale's new security system next week.

"After I drop you at your apartment, I'll head back to your car and take care of it for you," he tells me, his eyes hidden behind sunglasses and glued to the road ahead of us. "Do you have anywhere you need to be between now and Monday?"

"No. I'm going out tomorrow night with some friends, but I'm not driving. My friends are picking me up."

He grunts, still not looking at me. "Where are you going?"

"Some new club in the Meatpacking District. It's only been open for a couple of weekends. Melanie and I have never been, but our other friend, Paige, can't stop raving over it. The club's in a converted warehouse, so it's got a massive dance floor and the top deejays in the city. Supposedly, there's also a VIP room with a twenty-grand cover fee, unless you're accompanying a member as their guest. Anyway, I don't care about any of that. I'm really just going so I can hang out and have fun with my friends."

He nods, jaw tense, but I can't tell if he's actually listening. I'm sure my plans for a girls' night at a noisy dance club makes for riveting conversation in his opinion, but he *did* ask.

Rounding the corner onto my street, he says, "I should be able to have your car back in your hands before Monday. I've got a cousin who owns a garage in the Bronx. The flat shouldn't take him more than an hour or so to replace, then I'll see about having the car brought out here to you once it's fixed."

"You mean delivered?"

He shrugs. "Len owes me a favor. But he's family, so he'll do it just because I asked."

"You really don't have to go to the trouble, you know. I'm capable of arranging my own vehicle repairs."

"Never said you weren't." He glances at me, a grin at the edge of his lips. "Nothing I can do if you need a doctor or a lawyer, but if it's a job for a cop or a mechanic or a first responder, ask a Noble and we've got you covered."

Even though he says it like a joke, I can hear the family pride in his voice and it makes me smile. "Well, in that case, thank you."

"No problem." His attention returns to the traffic as we approach my block and the nineteen-story tower where my apartment is located. "Which building is yours?"

"The tall light-gray one between the two brick buildings."

"Nice."

It's an understatement that's not lost on me. The neighborhood is one of the best in Manhattan, and in this building even one-bedroom units start around seven figures. My two-story, three-bedroom on the tenth and eleventh floors is one of the most coveted spaces in the building, if not the entire block.

"I bought my apartment as soon as my modeling started paying really well," I explain. "Now, it's all I've got left to show for my former career."

"Looks like a good investment," Gabe says as we roll to a stop at the curb. He takes off his sunglasses and drops them into the cup holder in the console where I've given him my Volvo's key fob. "Parking?"

I glance at him in question. "You could just drop me off here."

"I said I was seeing you home. In my book, that means seeing you all the way to your door."

His expression is solemn, not that I really want to argue. No, what I want to do is lean across the seats and take the kiss his friend robbed me of. I can't keep my gaze from straying to his stern mouth, and when I finally do, I see the stormy gleam of hunger in his darkened hazel eyes.

"Tell me where we're going, beautiful."

God, I wish I knew. If I didn't think he would push me away, I would tell him where I'm really hoping we might go. Up to my bedroom. Into the backseat of his car. Anywhere that will mean feeling his hands on me, his mouth on mine, our bodies unclothed and moving together.

I've never been meek about sex, in spite of my current, lengthy drought in that area and my seemingly endless single status. I'm not shy, but I am choosy. And right now, everything female in me has chosen Gabe.

A tendon jumps in his jaw before he turns his head away from me to look out the windshield. "Is that the entrance for the garage?"

"Yes. It's underground, just past the lobby doors."

I point and he drives past the doorman on duty, taking us down to the gate at basement level. I give him my access code for the panel, then show him where my reserved space is.

"I'll get your door," he says, turning off the engine and not waiting for me to tell him that gallant gesture isn't necessary, either. He's at the passenger side in no time, holding his hand out to me as I exit the car.

The elevator lets us off in my private vestibule on the tenth floor. Gabe pauses behind me, waiting as I retrieve my apartment keys from my purse. "Would you like to come in?"

"For a minute," he says, his voice a deep growl. "I'm curious to check things out."

He enters my home and it's as if I'm seeing it for the first time too. I watch Gabe take in the blond hardwood foyer and the large, neutral living room into which it opens. It's airy and bright inside, with pale gray and cream furnishings, and two-story windows that draw in light and the multimillion-dollar views of the city.

To the left of my spacious living area and green space terrace outside is the entrance to the formal dining room and chef's kitchen. To the right, my office and a library, plus a pair of guest rooms down the hall. Overlooking the two-story living area is open loft, accessed by an elegant, curving staircase that provides windowed views all the way up to the palatial master bedroom suite.

Gabe is silent as he strolls farther inside, his head on a swivel, his shrewd eyes drinking in every detail, searching every corner of the enormous space.

"You have a lot of windows." He walks up to the tall glass, staring out at the buildings across the street before tilting his head down to watch the activity on the ground below. "No privacy blinds?"

I touch a switch panel on the wall and built-in, semi-opaque louvers pivot closed between the double-paned glass. "I prefer natural light. Plus, I never get tired of the view."

"I can see why," he says, pivoting to walk toward me now. He chuckles. "If you like light and views, you'll never want to see my place. I rent an overpriced, undersized second-floor walk-up. One of my windows looks right into my neighbor's kitchen. Another one has an unobstructed view of the dumpsters out back."

I laugh. "I'm sure it's not that bad."

"No, it is." He grins, pausing in front of me in the living room. "With my new promotion, I plan to get into a bigger place eventually. Something closer to headquarters, if I can swing it."

"You must really like working at Baine International."

"I love it."

"What were you doing before?"

He shrugs. "Private security. Events. Some occasional bodyguard work here and there. I honestly don't know what I would've done if Beck hadn't given me the opportunity to come in and meet Nick."

I tilt my head. "I didn't realize my brother helped you get the job." I'm taken aback, although it's obvious to me that Andrew and Gabe have developed a friendship that extends beyond work. Gabe and Nick too. "How did you and Andrew meet?"

He gives me a vague shake of his head. "Like I said, I was doing a lot of random temp jobs. They all start blending together after a while. I think I was working the door at some private club when I ran into Beck."

"My stiff, workaholic brother at a club? I'd pay to see that."

Gabe clears his throat and drifts away from me, heading toward the kitchen. "You must like to cook?"

"Sometimes." I follow him into the gleaming, modern kitchen that was my favorite feature in the place when I bought it. "I only know how to cook big meals, like my mom used to make. Cooking for one just doesn't seem to be part of my DNA."

"You and my mom would get along great."

"Yeah?"

He glances at me. "Yeah. She'd love you."

His steady gaze seems to reach inside me, as warm and enticing as a caress. A soft yearning that goes beyond the physical unfurls within me as our eyes linger on each other. I want to know more about this man. I want to know who he is outside the boundaries of his work for Nick and my brother. I want to know everything there is to learn about him.

In a small, private corner of my heart, I realize that I want him to let me into that other part of his life.

He walks around the large island in the center of the kitchen, back toward the bolted emergency door that leads to the interior stairwell fire escape. "Who's got keys to this door?"

"Just me and the building maintenance manager." I arch a brow at him. "Would you like to inspect my entire apartment, officer?"

He slants me a sheepish smile. "Sorry. Bad habit. I should probably get back on the road."

I follow him out of the kitchen and back toward the living area. As he passes a narrow table situated behind one of the sofas, I see his gaze pause on my collection of framed photographs that sit there. I have pictures of my friends and places I've traveled all around the world, but it's the candid snapshot of my parents that Gabe reaches for.

"Your mom and dad," he says, more statement than question. "They look happy."

"They were." I move in beside him, looking at their smiling faces. My mom is seated on weathered white porch steps in rolled-up denim overalls and a baggy T-shirt, peeling a bright red apple. Her chocolate-brown hair is gathered in a messy bun, her fair, freckle-spattered face flushed, either from the day in the sun or warmed from the fact that my dad is sitting behind her, his strong brown arms wrapped around her waist, his squared chin resting on her shoulder.

I can still see the love in their eyes as they stare out from the glass-covered image. My heart breaks a little for them, too, knowing that this captured moment in time was one of only a precious few they had left before a drunk driver in town would steal my mom away from us.

"I took this photo not long after I turned eight years old. It was such a wonderful day. We had just come in from the orchard with a bushel of apples, and Mom and I were going to make a bunch of pies. They looked so happy sitting outside on our veranda, I ran into the house and got my new camera to take their picture."

"This was taken when you were eight?" Gabe remarks quietly, and I know he remembers that I told him about losing my mom at that age. His eyes are tender when he looks at me. "I'm glad you have this memory of them."

"Yeah. Me too."

He carefully sets the photo back down. "So, you

didn't grow up in the city?"

I shake my head. "Not at all. We lived upstate on fifty acres of apple orchard that belonged to my mom's family. My dad's still there."

Gabe smiles. "I figured you for a city girl."

"I love the city. I love the energy of it, the culture, the endless opportunities you can't get anywhere else." I pivot around to face him, resting my hip against the edge of the table. "I'm glad I grew up where I did, but this is home."

"I know the feeling. My family's all in Bayside, going back several generations. I like it well enough there, but that wasn't the life I wanted."

"Is that why you joined the military? To get out of the hometown and see more of the world?"

"At the time, that's what I told myself." He considers his words in silence for a moment before speaking. "The truth is, I enlisted because I knew if I stayed, sooner or later, the old man and I were going to hit a wall neither one of us could move past without coming to blows. I didn't want to do that to my mother. Or to my brothers. So, I left."

I place my hand lightly on his forearm, because I can't hear that bitter edge of pain in his voice and not offer some measure of comfort—whether he wants it from me or not. He doesn't withdraw from my touch.

He glances down where my fingers gently caress his lighter skin. A slow breath escapes through his flared nostrils. When he lifts his eyes to mine, they are fierce with desire.

Tormented with it.

"Eve," he rasps, the first he's ever called me that name. And while it's been a source of pain and bad memories for me for these past many years, hearing Gabe say it with such raw need inflames me like nothing else can.

He grabs hold of me, his hands warm and strong on either side of my face as he takes my mouth in a fevered, possessive kiss that burns through every cell in my body. I was melting before he touched me, but now I'm on fire.

He catches my moan in his mouth, his tongue pushing past my parted lips. My sex clenches in answer to each wet stroke and lick and thrust. Our bodies crush against each other where we stand, Gabe's muscled arms pulling me into the hardness of his arousal.

He reaches down and cups my ass in both hands as the demand of his mouth renders me boneless and aching, so ready for him I can hardly breathe.

His mouth is open on mine, our kiss mutually hungered. Our desire is dangerously close to exploding out of control.

It's what I want. What I crave more than anything right now.

This man. This kiss. This white-hot attraction that's been smoldering between us from the day we first met.

With one hand buried in the silkiness of his short hair, I use the other to explore the hard slabs and planes of his chest. It's not enough. I tug the hem of his T-shirt loose from his jeans and slip my hand inside. His skin is hot and velvety soft, even in the places where I feel the ridges of several scars. His abs are rippled beneath my fingertips, a delicious eight-pack, punctuated by a line of crisp hair trailing down to his groin where the steely ridge of his erection proves more than I can resist.

He hisses against my mouth when my palm slides

over the top of his zipper. His hips buck, rocking into my caress. He growls my name in a ragged tone, somewhere between a warning and a plea.

He releases one hand from my backside, dragging his fingers around the side of my thigh. He finds the loose edge of my top and lifts it, moving his hand beneath the fabric and up to the swell of my breast. His grasp is bold, dominating. As he kneads and caresses me, his tongue invades my mouth once more, owning every breath and gasp and moan that leaks out of my throat.

I am wet for him, beyond ready for anywhere he wants to take me. Despite the fact that we're both fully clothed, I teeter at the edge of a pleasure I haven't felt in a very long time—and never as intensely as this.

"Fuck," Gabe snarls, shuddering as I continue to stroke him. He draws back from my mouth on a harsh curse, panting hard. *"Fuck."*

He's shaking with barely controlled arousal. I know, because I feel the same powerful need vibrating inside me. I lick my kiss-bruised lips. I stare up into his stormy gaze, hating the anguish I see there. I skim my fingers over the furrowed crease of his brow.

"If you'd like a tour of the rest of the apartment, my bedroom is just up those stairs."

It's a lame attempt to defuse some of the torment I see in him, but his faces relaxes a fraction. He groans, clamping his molars tight behind the flat line of his mouth when he should be kissing me some more. "I'd better not."

We're not talking about a house tour, and I can't pretend I'm not aching desperately for him to stay. "Do you want to, though?"

"More than you can possibly know," he says, his

voice rough and jagged.

But he's still moving away from me. Another inch back now, with a deepening scowl and a curse ripe on his lips as he stares at me.

"If I go down this path with you right now, there's no coming back. Hell, I've already gone too far. Every minute I'm with you, I'm betraying your brother's trust. Nick's too."

"They don't have anything to do with this. They're not here."

He shakes his head slowly, his hazel eyes scorching me as they drink me in. "I can't do this with you, Evelyn. It wouldn't be fair. I don't do this. And don't do relationships, either. I've tried before. I'm not any good at it."

"I don't recall asking for you for that."

"You should." His reply is sharp, even uttered low under his breath. "Christ, you should demand it. You deserve something more than this."

"More than this," I ask hesitantly, "or more than you?"

"Both."

He says the word with finality. Another step carries him out of my reach, and I know his control is stronger than my wish to keep him here. He wants me, there's no question about that. I see it in his handsome, rigidly held face. I see it in the thickness of his erection, straining against the confines of his dark jeans.

"I have to go."

I nod mutely, then watch as he walks out the door.

13

~ Gabriel ~

"It was a knife, all right." My cousin has taken the flat tire off Evelyn's car in the zoo parking lot and rolls it over to where I stand with Beck and Nick. He sticks the end of a flathead screwdriver into the gash in the rubber, showing us the severity of the puncture. "I can probably patch it but based on where the hole is and the size of it, I'd recommend a replacement."

Beck nods tightly. "Sure. Do whatever you think is best. I'll handle the bill. Thanks, Len."

"No problem, Mr. Beckham. Take care, Mr. Baine."

I follow Len to the flatbed tow truck where he's already loaded Evelyn's Volvo. He tosses the bad tire behind the driver's seat before hopping into the cab. "I'll personally run the car back to the owner for you, Gabe. She should have it later tonight."

"I appreciate it, man." We shake hands, then he drives off with a salute, diesel engine rumbling as he rolls out of the empty lot.

Beck gives me a concerned look as I turn back to him. "You haven't said as much, but I'm guessing you don't think this was random."

"No. I don't." The feeling has been gnawing at me since the moment I saw the blade-sized cut in the tire. "Someone zeroed in on Evelyn's vehicle, out of all the other cars left in the lot all day. The way I see it, that someone either tailed her to the event, or knew she'd be here."

Someone who had decided to make a bold move, whether to scare her or to disable her means of leaving, I'm not sure. But either scenario puts a cold fury in my veins.

I don't have any right to feel personally protective of her, let alone possessive. But that doesn't diminish the rage simmering beneath the surface of my outward calm.

"And the zoo security staff?" Nick asks. "They weren't any help?"

The park security office was my first stop when I returned from taking Evelyn home. I knew that would be the place to start asking questions, but I also needed the extra time to regroup and get my head screwed on straight before I had to look Evelyn's brother or my boss in the eye after pawing her like an animal back at her place.

Not that she had complained.

And not that I wouldn't be tempted to do it all over again, given half a chance.

Christ. Just thinking about her in my arms makes me start to go hard all over again. The feel of her against me, her soft curves pressed to all of the hard places I ached for her, her sweet mouth open and yielding to mine . . . her whispered invitation to take her up to her bedroom and fuck her the way I've been wanting to ever since I first set eyes on her.

It's all fuel to a spark I cannot allow to catch fire. Not without the risk of it consuming everything in its path.

I clear my throat. "The security staff tried to help with my questions. They showed me the security camera feeds from the lot today, but unfortunately, there's nothing to go on. The cameras here are meant to monitor the gate traffic in and out of the zoo, more so than the vehicles parked outside."

Nick grunts. "That's fucking great," he says, in a tone that conveys both his frustration over not having control of the situation, as well as his impatience to get to the bottom of any problem.

I can relate. I also share the urgency of both men to determine if Evelyn is in actual danger, and, if so, mitigate it by whatever means necessary.

I rub a hand over my jaw as I consider the slashed tire and the other unsettling things that have happened over the past week. "This feels deliberate. It feels targeted. And now I'm beginning to think it's neither random nor the first incident where Evelyn's concerned."

Beck's expression goes grim. "You're talking about a few nights ago at L'Opale? The strange power outage, and the possibility that someone was trying to get into the shop that night."

"You mentioned that Evelyn's had some problems with stalkers in the past."

He exhales a tight sigh, his nod sober. "Aside from the typical parade of losers sending her lewd messages and dick pics over social media back when she was modeling, there was a nutjob or two at some of her runway shows. One asshole in Milan managed to get backstage before security bounced him hard enough to put him in the hospital for a few days."

My jaw clenches at the mere idea of anyone getting that close to Evelyn. If I'd been there, the son of a bitch would have had bigger problems than a hospital stay. "What about now? She's been out of the spotlight for several years. Has she mentioned any recent problems? People who might still be interested in her career? Ex-boyfriends?"

"No. Not that I'm aware of. As for ex-boyfriends, I wouldn't know. Evie keeps her personal life private."

I can't deny my sense of relief over that revelation, considering I had my tongue down her throat just a short while ago. Still, the lack of information doesn't help assuage my concern for her safety. "What about her coworkers?"

"What about them?"

"Has she made any enemies at the boutique? Former employees, current colleagues who might have a beef with her—either real or imagined?"

Beck shakes his head. "I don't know. Shit. You're serious. You really think she's in some kind of danger."

I hold his stark gaze. "I think it would be foolish to assume she's not. Right now, though, the only basis I have for that is my gut."

He blows out a slow breath, concern rankling his brow. "Your gut is good enough for me."

Nick gives a nod of agreement. "Good enough for

me too."

"All right," I say, starting to put a plan together in my head. "I can tap one of my brothers to put a cop on her. It can't hurt to put one on the shop for a while too."

Beck scoffs. "Christ, no. She'll never go for that. It's bad enough that she thinks I'm an overbearing pain in the ass. If I put a babysitter on her, she'll only push back harder than ever. It might be enough to lose her for good, and I can't risk that."

"She wouldn't need to know. It could be totally covert, just another pair of eyes to make sure she's protected."

Nick's dark head bobs as I speak. "He's right, Beck. And I agree with you that bringing in law enforcement when all we've got is a hunch would either scare Evelyn or make her rebel. If we're going to keep a covert eye on her, it needs to be someone she trusts. Someone we trust explicitly too." That shrewd blue gaze that has helped Nick negotiate impossible deals all over the world now levels meaningfully on me. "The only question is, are you up for the job?"

"Me?" Ah, fuck. It wasn't my intention to enlist for this job.

I glance at Beck, hoping to see the same misgiving I'm feeling. But all I see in his face is hope, even desperation. I see a determination that's not going to take no for an answer, even if I were inclined to turn down his request.

"I realize it's asking a lot, Gabe. But there's no one else I'd trust to keep her safe."

My denial is perched on the end of my tongue. Hell, I've got plenty of reasons to decline, not the least of which being the eager way my cock responds to the idea of spending more time around Evelyn.

I know I can keep her safe better than anyone else. That's not a brag; it's a fact. A promise I've already made to myself, if not her brother.

I know I can protect Evelyn from any threat—even if it means protecting her to my dying breath.

What I'm not sure of is how I'm going to accomplish any of that without ending up in her bed.

14

~ Evelyn ~

Dance music pounds so hard in Club Muse, I feel it vibrating through every bone in my body.

Even for a Sunday night, the massive converted warehouse in the Meatpacking District is stuffed to the rafters, with a line of people snaking around the block. If not for Paige knowing the bouncer from another club she used to frequent in Brooklyn, she and Melanie and I might still be waiting outside instead of staking our claim on a tall cocktail table near the dance floor.

With her choppy black pixie haircut, knockout body, and stunning face, Paige's magazine-perfect looks alone have always opened doors wherever she goes. Tonight, my fellow former model has wrapped all her assets in a black leather miniskirt and backless silver top that's been turning heads ever since we arrived about an hour ago.

I opted for black too. My dress is sleeveless and simple, hitting just above my knees with a zipper running down the front of it. Mel's the only spot of color in our little group. Her fiery red hair gleams like copper in the swirling lights and strobes of the club, her pale blue silk blouse and skinny white jeans seeming almost innocent amid the sea of black and flashy metallics. Although she's never stepped foot on a runway or in front of a fashion photographer's lens, Mel's got a fresh-faced, girl-next-door beauty that belies the terrible hardships of her upbringing.

Paige downs the dregs of her fourth Cosmo, dancing where she stands. "Isn't this place amazing?"

Melanie and I nod, both of us having almost given up on talking over the din of the music and the crush of bodies all around us. The energy is infectious, though, and it's hard not to get swept up in the throbbing dance beats and the dizzying spectacle of the lights and special effects.

Muse is a feast for the senses, and an unapologetically erotic one at that. Nearly every wall is a mirror, from the ground level to the gallery overlooking the dance floor below. The effect makes the club seem to stretch on toward infinity, replication after replication of dancing bodies and sparking, colorful lights.

Intermittently, in varying places around the club, the mirrors flash with a backlight, silhouetting moving shapes of human bodies that seem to live behind the reflective glass. Some of the shapes are dancing, some of them are engaged in BDSM and sex acts. It's impossible to catch more than a glimpse of any one vignette before it's gone, the light doused and the mirror reflecting back on the rest of the pulsing club.

"Do you think it's real?" I ask Melanie, leaning toward her as Paige turns away from us, losing herself in the rhythm of the deejay's latest track.

Mel shakes her head, chewing on the straw that came in her soda. "Can't be real, right?"

Since she started back at university last year, Melanie doesn't drink. Tonight, I'm glad for that, because Paige has been making sure the drinks have been nonstop since we sat down. She raises her voice to be heard over the din of the music and conversation all around us. "I mean the name of the club is Muse, so maybe that's just part of the game. Erotic illusions meant to inspire a sense of freedom and abandon. Or to tempt with the possibility of it existing just outside the grasp of us mere mortals on the wrong side of the glass."

I grin at her, more than a little tipsy, and take the final swig of my martini. "You and your big sexy brain, Mel. I hope Daniel appreciates that you're not only gorgeous but smart as hell too."

She smiles, rolling her eyes. "Well, I could be wrong. Those could be actual people behind those mirrors having actual sex all around us."

"Who's having sex?" Paige swings back to the table, an eager look in her eyes. "Eve, are you holding out on me? If you got naked with your hunky Baine security chief without telling me I'm going to be seriously pissed."

"You're already seriously pissed," I tell her, moving the empty glass out of the way of her hands. "And, no, I haven't gotten naked with anyone."

"But you want to." She sing-songs the words, wagging her finger and giggling.

It's true, I did want to. Still want to.

But unlike Paige I'm not so free-spirited and lacking in inhibitions that I'm going to throw myself at a man. I've come close enough to that as it is with Gabe. And he still said no.

I can't deny that when the doorman called up to tell me someone had delivered my Volvo, I'd been hoping I might find Gabe waiting for me in the lobby. His cousin Len seemed nice enough, but I'm sure my disappointment was obvious when I went down to thank him.

And while I'm enjoying spending time with my friends tonight, I can't pretend I'm the least bit interested in meeting someone here at the club. Unfortunately, being in a meat market like Muse means dealing with a lot of unsolicited advances. The three of us have shooed away several men and even a couple of women since we arrived, but the flybys have been steady and persistent.

Paige handles them all like she's directing air traffic at JFK. She's been back and forth from the dance floor dozens of times, apparently discarding each prospect in turn, and for reasons I can only guess at. She's got her standards, loose as they are.

"All right, ladies. I'm going on the hunt." She pulls a small scrap of red lace from the pocket of her skirt and twirls it on her index finger.

Melanie gapes. "Are those your—"

"My calling card," she interjects, smiling shamelessly. "He doesn't know it yet, but one lucky son of a bitch on that dance floor is going home tonight with a smile on his face and these panties in his pocket."

I practically choke. "You're crazy."

She laughs, unrepentant as she dances away from our

table. "You should try it sometime, Boo."

Paige melts into the crowd, and I glance back at Mel. "I worry about her."

"Yeah. Me too." She goes quiet for a moment, using the chewed end of her straw to chase some of the ice around in her glass.

"I'm really glad you came tonight, Mel."

She looks up at me and smiles. "God knows Paige needs a DD. Not to mention a chaperone."

I laugh, but Mel's being with us means more than just her sobriety and willingness to drive. "How are things with Daniel?"

"Good. Great." She nods enthusiastically. "He's such an amazing man. So talented and ambitious. And he's good to me."

"I'm glad, Mel." I reach over and squeeze her hand. "He'd better be good to you, or he'll be answering to both me and Paige."

Her smile seems fleeting, as does her gaze. "I know that."

"Where is he tonight, anyway?"

"Las Vegas."

I frown. "I thought you guys just came back from a Vegas trip."

"We did. But Daniel's got business there." She abandons her straw and leans back on her stool, arms folded over her breasts. "He had to go back and take care of some things."

"New building project or something?"

She nods. "I guess so. He doesn't like to talk about the specifics of his work."

I want to ask why the hell not, but before I get the chance someone taps me on the shoulder. I swivel my head and find a blond man with sloped shoulders and an inebriated grin on his face. He's wearing dress slacks and a button-down designer shirt with monogrammed cuffs. In his hand is a brown longneck beer, which he uses to point with at me. "Have we met somewhere?"

"I don't think so." I look away, hoping it's enough to discourage him.

It isn't. "You sure? Because, damn, you look so fucking familiar. You a trader too? Maybe I've seen you around at Goldman's or somewhere?"

"No. You haven't." My answer is firmer this time, and so is my glare. "Do you mind? I'm trying to have a conversation with my friend."

"I wanna dance with you."

"I'm not interested," I tell him, getting exasperated.

Mel slides her hand across the table, weaving her fingers through mine. "Actually, we're together. As in, a couple. In fact, I was about to ask this sweet girl to marry me before you walked up and ruined what was going to be a very romantic moment."

"It's true," I tell him, deadpan. "We're very much in love."

He stares at us for a second through drunken eyes, then mutters something under his breath and lumbers off. As soon as he's gone, we both start laughing.

Mel wiggles her brows at me. "Want to dance, sweetheart?"

"Sure. I thought you'd never ask."

15

~ Gabriel ~

I didn't have to ask Evelyn the name of the hot new nightclub she and her friends were planning to go tonight. There is only one place drawing record crowds in the Meatpacking District on a Sunday night, and after bypassing the line of people stretching nearly two blocks to get into Muse, I walk up to the bald behemoth standing at the door and flash my ID, along with the murmured name I know will grant me instant access.

The bouncer eyes me for a moment, sizing me up in my dark suit. If he wanted to be a dick and pat me down, he'd find I'm carrying. But he's not worried that I'll be a problem for anyone inside. And I'm certain if he was, there are easily a dozen guys on the other side of the door, similarly armed and ready to take me out.

Touching his earpiece and speaks into the mic in a

low tone. At his nod, I head inside the packed club.

Dance music throbs and pulses, accompanied by the swirl of colored laser lights and strobes. There is hardly a square foot of breathing room to be had, nothing but bobbing, gyrating bodies filling the dance floor and spilling out to the rest of the club as well. The old warehouse space is enormous, made to appear even larger by the mirrored walls that reflect back at the crowds from all directions.

But that's not the only purpose of the mirrors. I realize it an instant later, as a flash to my left briefly illuminates the vague silhouette of a man and woman having sex on the other side of the glass. Her hands are braced over her head while the man fucks her vigorously from behind. The shocking glimpse is there and gone in a beat, but the image was unmistakable.

And erotic enough to make my cock stir behind the zipper of my slacks.

As I push deeper into the club, all around me I see more sparks of illumination behind the mirrors, more voyeuristic, profane flashes of activity, no doubt intended to speed the pulses and incinerate the inhibitions of everyone in the place. From the way the whole building seems to vibrate with sexual energy, it seems to be working.

I spot the circular bar and head that way, figuring the central location will be the best place to search the mass of clubgoers for the only one of interest to me. The one whom, as of yesterday, it's my paid duty to protect.

My covert duty, I remind myself with no small amount of misgiving.

Evelyn's the sole reason I'm here tonight, and as much as I want to believe I'm just doing my job, my determination to find her—to see her, even if I have to stealthily observe from the fringes of a packed dance club—feels far from professionally motivated.

I wasn't happy to hear her say she was planning to be at Muse tonight. Now, I've got half a mind to drag her out of here as soon as I find her.

At the bar I order a beer I have no intention of drinking, then send my gaze into the crowd to search for Evelyn while I wait. She's hard to miss, even dressed in black like ninety-nine percent of the rest of the club.

Dancing with another young woman, an attractive redhead in white jeans and a pale blue top, Evelyn seems lost in the sensual beat of the music. Eyes closed, she sways and undulates, her hips and arms moving in fluid rhythm. Each pivot and roll of her body triggers a bolt of pure lust in me. I stare, hungry and possessive, unable to look away even for a second.

It's crazy how much I want her. Worse than crazy; it's negligent as hell, especially now that her life is my hands. If I am to protect her, I damn well can't do it from between her legs.

And if there really is someone aiming to do her harm, I need to be firing on all cylinders. Vigilant, not distracted by the thought of having Evelyn beneath me.

Caught up in her own bliss, she is mesmerizing, sexy as hell. Unless I miss my guess, she also seems a little tipsy, which makes my guardian instincts rise to attention as swiftly as my baser instincts.

The bartender returns with my beer, and I as reach for some cash to pay for it, a hand comes to rest on my shoulder from behind me.

"Drink's on the house."

I swivel at the familiar, slightly Southern drawl of

Jared Rush's smoky voice. Standing as tall as me, Rush has a beefy build, a mane of sandy brown hair just past his shoulders and a trimmed beard framing his square jaw. Tonight, he's dressed in a black shirt and pants, but he still carries a laid-back, rebel look that seems more suited for the rodeo circuit than the edgy, avant-garde art world where he's made a staggering fortune on his provocative, profane, often disturbing, paintings.

Anyone who knows the mysterious artist—and that's a small, private list, to be sure—doesn't have to guess where he gets his inspiration. The only thing more notorious than his work is his voracious appetite for beautiful women and the ultra-exclusive, ultra-expensive gatherings he hosts at his various residences and private sex clubs.

Muse is a departure for Rush, his first foray into a public venue.

"Good to see you, Gabe." He grins, clasping my hand in greeting. "Heard you dropped my name at the door."

I shrug. "What good are connections if you never use them? Nice place, by the way. I didn't realize you'd already opened."

"You like it?" He gestures with both arms open, unabashedly proud of his latest creation. "The dance club is succeeding beyond expectations, but it's the VIP suites that really make Muse special. You should come back and have a look."

I grunt, giving him a smirk. "I think I've already caught the previews."

I nod in the direction of the mirrored walls and Rush smiles. "I'm going to have to put a time limit on the mirror suites or double the fee. You should try one—no charge to you, man. Hell, I'll even stake you in one of the game rooms, if poker's more your speed tonight."

"Thanks, but no," I say, shocked to realize I'm not even remotely tempted. "Maybe another time."

As reluctant as I am to let on that I'm here for a specific reason—a specific person—I can't keep from glancing back out to the dance floor to find Evelyn. She's still dancing with the same woman, both of them laughing under the swirling prisms of the strobes.

Rush's shrewd brown gaze doesn't miss a damn thing. And it lingers on Evelyn and her friend longer than expected. "They're lovely. And since you work for my old friend, Dominic Baine, I'm sure you're well aware that one of those beautiful girls is Andrew Beckham's sister."

"I know." My answer is clipped, and when I look at Jared Rush, I hope he sees the warning in my eyes. "She's under my protection now."

"Your protection?" His brows lift in curiosity. "You mean personal security, or . . ."

"She's mine."

"All right." He raises his hands, chuckling. "Fair enough, man. I never poach in a friend's backyard. Now, as for my enemies? That's a whole other thing."

There is a current of danger in that statement that's not lost on me. And I can't help but notice when his gaze slides back in the direction of the dance floor. Back to Evelyn.

Or is it her pretty companion who's captured his attention?

When he looks back at me, his expression is bland, unreadable. "I should get back to my guests. Good to see you, Gabe. Enjoy your night."

I nod, watching Jared Rush prowl away from me, cutting a path through the throng as he makes his way through the center of his domain.

The instant he's gone, I turn back to search for Evelyn.

It takes me a moment to locate her. She and her friend have moved to the far right edge of the dance floor now, where a slick blond douchebag in a sweat-blotched dress shirt is attempting to chat Evelyn up. He's swaying as he talks, gesturing sloppily with a brown longneck bottle of beer.

On a growl, I step away from the bar and head briskly in their direction.

As I near them, I catch the slurred tail end of what he's saying to her. "Why you so stuggup? I knew I saw your face somewhere before. You're her, right? C'monn, Eve, I'm juss tryna be frennly!"

I walk up behind the drunken idiot and drop my hand down on his shoulder. "Get lost."

He jumps, and I don't know who looks more surprised—the asshole who apparently won't take Evelyn's "no" for an answer, or her and her friend, both gaping at me mutely.

The asshole is the first one to speak. "The fuck? Who're you, her dad?"

I give him a cold smile. "I'm the guy who's going to ram that longneck down your throat if you don't leave these women alone. And I mean now, motherfucker."

16

~ Evelyn ~

I'm sure my shock must show on my face as I watch Gabe insert himself between me and the persistent Wall Street drunk who's been annoying Mel and me for the past half hour or more.

Not only did I never expect to see Gabe here, I can't believe he's managed to end up in front of me just in time to assist with an uncomfortable situation.

"Thanks," I say, blinking up at him in a mix of astonishment and relief as the other man staggers away. Then I shake my head because I'm still not sure I'm actually seeing him or if it's the night's four martinis playing tricks on me. "What . . . what are you doing here?"

"Someone told me about this hot new club that just opened," he says, only the barest trace of wry humor in his deep voice. "I thought I'd come check things out."

"Is that right?" I tilt my head, unable to keep the big grin off my face.

Definitely blaming *that* on the martinis, because if I were even a little more sober, I'd be holding my cards a lot closer to my chest. Instead, I feel ridiculously thrilled to be staring at Gabe's handsome face under the spinning lights of the club.

"After what happened between us yesterday at my place, I didn't think I'd ever see you again," I admit, my unfiltered thoughts slipping right off my tongue.

I see Gabe's gaze slide to my left, where Mel is still standing in mute confusion beside me.

"Oh. Sorry. This is my friend Melanie Laurent," I explain. "Mel, this is Gabriel Noble."

"This is him?" Her eyes go wide when I glance at her. "Oh. Um, hi. Nice to meet you."

"Hello, Melanie." He nods at her, but he's already looking at me again. His brow is slightly furrowed, his hazel eyes dark and serious. "You okay?"

It takes me a second to realize he's not asking about my state of sobriety, or the fact that I can't seem to stop staring at him. "Yeah, I'm fine. Thanks for getting rid of that guy."

"Who was he?"

I give a vague, dismissive wave of my hand. "No one."

"You don't know him?"

"No."

"Have you seen him before?"

I shake my head, feeling more satisfied than I should to be on the receiving end of Gabe's stern, almost possessive, interrogation. "He's just some rando who recognized me and refused to go away. At least, until you showed up."

Gabe grunts, his expression schooled, yet radiating an unmistakable menace as he flicks his gaze into the crush of people. Although I've never seen Gabe in uniform, I can imagine how formidable he must have looked garbed for war and armed to the teeth with heavy weapons. Because right now, even dressed in his dark suit and graphite-gray buttoned shirt, there is no mistaking the fact that he is a dangerous man, a skilled and lethal warrior.

God help me, I've never wanted him more.

A heated, heavy silence pulses between us as he looks at me. If I'd been doubting that he wanted me yesterday, it's hard to think it now.

Even Mel seems to pick up on the tension that smolders in our silence. She rests her hand against my upper arm and awkwardly clears her throat. "You two probably want to, ah, catch up. I'm sure I saw Paige across the way just a minute ago. I should go find her."

I think I say something in reply before Melanie takes off, but I can't be sure.

I can't be sure of anything so long as Gabe holds me trapped in the hooded intensity of his dark eyes.

"Did you really only come here tonight to check out the club?" I ask him. "Or did you come here to look for me?"

"What do you think?"

I reach for his hand, lacing my fingers between his. "I think I want you to ask me to dance."

He makes a low sound in the back of this throat. "That's probably not a good idea."

"I think it's an excellent idea. One of my better ones, in fact."

A slow grin spreads over his sensual mouth, making the quick flutter in my stomach kick into a steady, warming pound in my core. But he still shakes his head in slow denial. "I don't dance. I'll only step on your toes."

I smile. "You've been stepping on them since we met, Boy Scout. Why stop now?"

I don't wait for him to refuse again. Still holding on to his hand, I swivel and sway to the tempo of the current track's bass-heavy beat. Gabe's feet stay rooted to the floor, but his eyes follow my every move. They are hooded and unblinking, searingly hungry.

I let myself go, sinking into the music. I only intended to tease him a little, maybe cajole the stiff soldier into having a little fun, but it doesn't take more than a minute for the playfulness of my intentions to give way to something deeper. I hear his low growl as I move my free hand into my loose hair, then bring my fingers down along the silver line of the zipper that runs the length of my dress. His jaw is rigid as he watches me, his body radiating a palpable heat in the scant inches that separates us.

Knowing he's watching me, knowing he wants me, strips away any inhibition not already erased by the martinis I've consumed. I guide his hand to my hip and hold it there as I continue his private dance, slowly moving closer to him, until there is no more room between our bodies. I dance against him now, shameless in my desire for him.

And while his need is held on a tighter leash than mine, I can see that he is close to breaking. I want him to. God, I want to smash that iron control of his into a million jagged pieces.

Impulsively, I reach up and take hold of his scowling face.

I kiss him, slow and deep and desperately.

He kisses me, too, searing me with the heat and power of his answering desire. But then his strong hands are on my arms, his grasp tight and unrelenting. He growls, and the dark, furious rumble of it vibrates through me, all the way to my marrow.

I've pushed too hard this time.

The scorching truth of it is written all over Gabe's thunderous expression, and in the low curse that boils out of him as he stares at me now.

Yet he is infinitely gentle as he sets me away from him.

It takes a moment before he speaks. When he does, his voice is as rough as gravel.

"Tell your friends you're leaving now. I'm taking you home."

17

~ Gabriel ~

She doesn't speak a single word to me for the duration of the drive from Muse to her apartment building on the Upper East Side.

Maybe she senses the volatility in me. She damn well should. I am caught in a vise of dark emotions, beginning with the unspent fury that's been riding me since I first glimpsed that drunken jackass accosting her at the club.

Nothing would have given me more satisfaction than planting my fist in his leering face—or in that of any of the other men who'd been circling Evelyn like sharks on the dance floor before I approached her.

As the man who's now personally responsible for her well-being, I'd have been justified taking her out of there based on concerns for her safety alone.

But it's not her safety that's foremost on my mind as we enter the elevator from the garage where I've parked next to her repaired Volvo.

It's not duty I'm thinking about as the elevator doors close behind us and I reach for Evelyn's hand.

And it's not fury that makes me drag her against me, although it is something dangerously close to it. A rough curse explodes out of me as I crush her mouth beneath mine.

She moans, going instantly pliant in my arms. It's not enough for me that she's willing. I need her to know that this time, there is no turning back.

Not tonight.

Not for either one of us.

I am a goddamn powder keg, and she is the open flame that's going to obliterate me.

Christ, she already has.

If I thought I could deny it before, that private slow dance she performed for me back at Muse, and the kiss she'd ended it with, has burned all of my resolve to ash.

This woman has torched every last scrap of my reason and my dubious honor, too, because right now I'd trade everything—including my other leg—just to be inside her.

Somewhere in the back of my mind, I realize she and I have been heading toward this moment from the beginning. I try to rationalize now that maybe the only way to put out this fire is to get in front of it. Let it burn itself out tonight, and maybe then we can both go back to our lives as they were before.

It's a flimsy plan, but I'm willing to grasp for anything. Especially anything that will allow me to justify the arousal that's raking me as I hold Evelyn against me now.

A shocked sound escapes her as I clutch the rounded

swells of her behind and grind her hips into my erection. I push my tongue past her parted lips, invading, taking, demanding.

The elevator walls are mirrored, and I can't help thinking about the one-way glass of Muse's VIP rooms. If I were any less a man—if Evelyn Beckham were any other woman in the world—I'd have her naked and bound, spread out beneath me in one of those voyeuristic playrooms right now.

The thought alone makes my cock even harder. But I don't want to share her with anyone. Not even the hapless building security personnel at the lobby desk who's probably monitoring the elevator feed at this very moment.

As soon as the doors slide open, I stalk out to the vestibule outside her apartment, holding Evelyn by the hand. My lungs are heaving, my voice nothing more than a rasp. "Give me your keys. I'll get the door."

She fishes them out of her small crossbody purse, positioning herself in front of me as I hastily work the locks. Her hands rove across my chest and up along my neck, driving me past the point of distraction. We barely make it inside before she attacks my mouth in a fevered kiss.

Fuck. I'm a man who prefers control when it comes to sex—hell, I require it—but it won't take much for me to lose my grasp now. I'm too raw, too hungry for this woman who seems to trigger every base craving that lives inside me.

I slam the door closed and pivot her against it, our lips joined and hot on each other. I'd assumed all of the blood in my brain had already vacated to points south, but as I pin Evelyn's soft curves beneath me against the door, my arousal surges past agony to rampant, urgent need.

She moans into my open mouth, her body meeting mine as I move against her, punctuating each thrust of my tongue with a hard roll of my hips. She wraps one long leg around my ass, opening herself even more, teasing me with the promise of what we both need. The release that waits for both of us beneath the barrier of our clothing.

"Gabe," she sighs, panting between kisses. "Please, Gabe . . ."

"I know, baby." It's all she has to say. We're both too far gone to slow down, let alone pause to think this through.

I reach up for the zipper of her black dress and pull it down. A faint metallic scrape of sound as the tiny teeth let go, inch by delectable inch. Evelyn's shuddery exhalation as I peel the curve-hugging fabric away from her buttery light-brown skin. It all combines to drive me fucking wild.

I lower my head to taste the velvety smoothness of her collarbone, then the delicate dip at the base of her elegant throat. The mounds of her breasts ride high on her chest, firm and buoyant, held aloft in the pretty black lace cups of her bra. I bend further, trailing my mouth over both lovely swells, cleaving my tongue into the sweet valley between them.

"This is beautiful," I murmur, tracing the edge of the black lace with my thumb. "One of your designs?"

She nods, her bottom lip caught under her teeth. I grunt and rip the lace open.

At her startled gasp, I arch a brow. "Did you think I was going to play nice after the way you teased me tonight?"

Whatever she means to say in reply dissolves into a shuddery groan as I lift one of her perfect breasts in my hand and bring it up to meet my mouth. Her dusky brown nipple is as tight as a pebble on my tongue, her skin as sweet as sugar. I suck her deep, grazing her with my teeth while I caress and knead her with fevered hands.

Her fingers toy with my hair, wrapping tightly as her body quivers under my assault. I tear my mouth away from her on a low curse.

"Jesus, what you do to me. You had me so hard in that club, you're lucky I didn't lift your skirt and fuck you right there in front of everyone."

Her eyes widen, but there's no fear in her shocked gaze. "You should've tried. What makes you think I would have stopped you?"

Holy hell. A wordless growl rumbles in my throat. It's all I've got, lust rendering me incapable of speech now. I swoop back to her mouth, taking it with another hard, hungered kiss.

I push her dress and bra off her shoulders, leaving the clothing to pool at our feet. She's so exquisite it almost hurts to look at her. Every inch of her is perfection. Flawless beauty, dressed only in strappy black sandals and minuscule black lace panties that match the pretty bra I've ruined.

I want to apologize for that, but I can't when she's looking at me with such open need. I step in close again, wedging myself between her legs as I catch her face in my hands and kiss her until we're both out of breath, both vibrating with the force of our need.

I'm fully clothed, with my service weapon still

171

holstered across my chest beneath my jacket. I want to be naked against her, but the desire I see in her face won't wait for that. My own desire won't wait for the time it would take me to free my leg from the prosthesis and undress so I can make love to her the way I want to, the way she deserves.

Her head falls back against the door as I leave her mouth to have another taste of her breasts. With one hand still caught behind her neck, I send my other over her breasts again, then down the smooth planes of her torso, until my fingers graze the top edge of her panties.

My cock jerks when I reach beneath the lace and find her smooth and bare. "Ah, Christ." My fingertips slip into the silky, wet cleft of her pussy and my answering groan sounds raw, animalistic. "You're so soft here, Eve. So fucking hot."

"Gabriel . . ."

Hearing my name slip off her tongue like a prayer decimates what little control I have left where she's concerned. I want to hear it again. I want to hear her scream it and know that I'm the only man she wants right now. The only man she needs.

Rubbing the firm bud of her clit with my thumb, I cover her mouth with mine and sink my fingers into her slick, silken folds. "You're so tight," I mutter against her lips. "I can feel your little muscles working all along my fingers."

She moans, moving in time with my strokes, her teeth grazing my tongue and lower lip. I thrust deep, into her mouth and into her sex. She shudders, her body soft and melting against me, her tiny muscles rippling against my fingers.

She's teetering on the edge of climax, but I'm not

ready to take her there just yet. Not with my hand.

"I need to taste you, baby. I want to feel you come against my tongue."

She stares at me through desire-drenched eyes, then trembles as I move away from her mouth and begin to kiss my way down the gorgeous length of her body.

I sink to a crouch between her parted legs, pausing along the way to tongue the hollow of her navel and the tender skin above the lace of her panties. I slide them down her thighs, then guide her to step out of them.

The honeyed scent of her hits my senses like a gunshot. Her pussy glistens, dark pink and slick with her juices. I move in like a thirsting man in need of water, pushing my face between her thighs.

She staggers back on her high heels, her spine thumping against the door. "Oh, God."

Her fingers spear into my hair as I lick and lap at her, feasting on the molten sweetness of her. She shudders on my face, a tight cry curling out of her as I suck her clit into my mouth.

"Gabe," she gasps. "Oh, God."

I growl in praise of her response, wondering if she's ever felt this depth of need with anyone else. I know I haven't, and it staggers me to think that I have found it now, with her. The one woman I shouldn't want and have no right to take.

But there's no use for second thoughts now. No room for regrets, not that I can muster either when Evelyn is about to shatter on my mouth.

I thrust two fingers inside her heat as I increase the tempo of my tongue's worship of her clit. Her hands tighten in my hair, fists clenching as her thighs tense around me and her hips convulse in time with my strokes. My cock is rock hard. I'm on the verge of exploding, but I hold it together, if barely.

Not a moment too soon, Eve's pleasure erupts on a broken shout. "Oh, shit, Gabriel. Oh, fuck yes."

She shatters against my mouth, tremors rippling over her body and vibrating on my tongue. I keep fucking her with my fingers, drawing out her climax, savoring every nuance of her release.

Holy Christ. I knew this moment would taste sweet, but as she unravels in my arms, I realize the true depth of my mistake here.

Because this need I feel for Eve isn't the end of what I want from her.

It is only the beginning.

I rise, looping her arms around my neck as I come to stand in front of her again. I kiss her slack mouth, brushing some of the damp hair from her face.

"Wrap your legs around my waist." She frowns in confusion but complies without a sound. "As I recall, you offered me a tour of the second floor last time I was here."

She nods, resting her head on my shoulder. With my hands under her bare thighs, I carry her toward the winding staircase that leads to her bedroom.

18

~ Evelyn ~

I feel boneless and weightless in Gabe's arms, my senses still thrumming with the force of my orgasm.

I don't know how he manages to carry me up all of the steps and into my bedroom as if I'm no more than a feather. I don't know how he manages to make me burn like no other man before him, but he does. He has from the very beginning.

He makes me feel safe in his strong arms, protected—though from what, I don't even know.

All I know is that I like this feeling I have with him.

I like it too much. Because I fear it is my heart that will be in need of saving when it comes to this man.

I cling to him, my head resting on his shoulder as he walks to my empty king-sized bed and sits on the edge of it with me in the semidarkness of the room. I am seated astride his lap, naked against the fine fabric of his suit and dress shirt. My thighs are spread wide open, my sex nestling the hard bulge of his erection. Maybe I should feel exposed or vulnerable like this, but the only thing I feel is keenly, unabashedly aroused. I've never felt more alive than I do in Gabe's embrace.

His hands spear into my unbound hair, dragging me to his mouth for a fevered kiss.

I can't help wriggling closer to him, craving his firmness against the ache that still throbs in my core. Each lick and thrust of his tongue makes my arousal coil tighter, reigniting the fire that was merely banked by my climax, but far from extinguished.

I moan, breaking away from his lips on a shallow pant. "I'm getting you all wet."

His hands move down to my bare ass, gathering me deeper into his lap. "You hear me complaining?"

"No," I say, managing a laugh. "But I think we should get you out of those clothes."

He smiles, his eyes smoldering. "I like the way you think."

I begin undressing him, starting with his jacket. I push it off his muscled biceps, my gaze flicking to his when I realize he's wearing a shoulder holster and firearm strapped over his dark gray shirt. The black leather strap is thin and discreet, but the pistol snapped into the sheath is deadly serious.

"Are you always on duty, Boy Scout?"

A grimness seeps into his expression. "Always."

He removes the holster, reaching around me to carefully set it and the weapon away from us on the floor beside the bed. I can hardly wait to attack the buttons on his shirt. His skin is tan and smooth beneath the crisp fabric. And scarred.

I hadn't realized it the last time he was in my apartment, when I'd run my hands under his T-shirt. All along his left side, dozens of silvery, healed shrapnel wounds—some worse than others—pepper his chest and shoulders. The same side where he lost his leg. I want to know more, I want to understand everything he's been through, but not now. Right now, I just want to be with him.

I open his shirt further, pushing it off his arms and then leaning down to kiss the center of his chest. His skin is hot beneath my lips, like velvet beneath my tongue. I kiss each scar I find, from his throat to his shoulders then down onto the ridges and valleys of his muscular abdomen. I revel in the controlled power of him, in the battle-tested beauty of his body.

His hands are in my hair, caressing my scalp as I move over him, kissing and licking my way back up to his mouth. When our lips join, his tongue invades, hot and hungry. Splaying his hand against my spine, he presses me against his bare chest. My nipples brush the smooth warmth of his skin and I moan into his mouth as arousal spirals through me.

"I need you, Gabe." I rock into his embrace, needing the contact even more than I need my next breath. "I want my hands on you."

I reach down between us, hastily unfastening his belt. It jangles softly, the only other sound except for the rush of our combined panting. I open the button of his dress slacks then tug down his zipper. His erection juts upward, the thick length straining the fabric of his dark boxer briefs. My mouth waters, and a surge of hot need floods me.

I slip my fingers inside the waistband and he groans,

his stomach flexing sharply at the contact. His cock fills my grasp, overflows it. The girth and length and weight combine to make the hunger inside me roar into a wordless sound of pure need. With greedy hands I free his erection from the confining aggravation of his briefs. He helps me, pushing his pants down off his hips. The movement makes his shaft surge in my hold. He makes a strangled noise, pumping restlessly now.

I scoot back on his thighs to get a better look as I run my hands all over him. His spine arches as I stroke him, his powerful body rigid and taut as a bowstring.

"You're beautiful, Gabriel." I mean it sincerely, but he chuckles wryly, as if he takes my praise as a joke. I glance up at him. "What's funny about that?"

"A woman who's utter fucking perfection tells me I'm beautiful." He scoffs, slowly shaking his head. "You haven't seen the worst of me."

His voice is low, almost a warning. I'm not sure he's talking about physical flaws, not when I can see there is a storm brewing in his eyes. He's trying to keep it shuttered from me, but it's hard to hide wounds from someone who also bears her own.

I reach up with one hand and cup the back of his skull, compelling him to look inside me too. "I want to see all of you. I need to know that what I'm holding onto is real."

"Don't I feel real?" His mouth quirks, wicked and sensual, at the same time he thrusts deeply into my grasp on the hard length of his erection.

He's evading and I know it, putting up a wall I don't feel equipped to climb. Not now, when my desire for him is still swamping me.

"Come here," he growls. Cupping my face in his

warm palms, he draws me into his kiss.

His mouth is fierce on mine, leaving no room for my doubts. There is no room for anything but pleasure and sensation when my breasts are crushed to Gabe's naked chest, our bodies melding together as he deepens our kiss into a breath-stealing conquest of my lips.

He's even harder now, and the feel of so much power in my hand makes my desire twist into something ravenous. Panting, I break our kiss on a moan and slide off his lap, easing down onto the floor on my knees in front of his bent legs.

I tug his pants and briefs off his hips, captivated by the sight of his cock as it springs free, jutting high against his taut abdomen. I lick my lips in anticipation, swamped in carnal need of this man. His eyes are hungry on me too. But I detect the firming of his jaw, the fractional halting of his breath, as I pull his clothing farther down his thighs and uncover the top of the prosthesis on his left leg. A cushioned sleeve starts halfway up his thigh, covering the sturdy plastic cup that's attached to the metal calf, ankle, and artificial foot below it.

Letting his pants fall off his knees and down around his ankles, I run my hands over the soft bristly hair on his bare thighs, sliding my fingers back up to stroke the length of his arousal all the way to its crown. I spread his knees with my body, turning my head to drag a kiss along the inner portion of one thigh, then the other.

I draw back, drinking in every scarred and beautiful inch of him as my hands make another slow trek along his legs. I keep going, sliding my caress over both his knees, the one that's bare, warm flesh and the other that's encased in the cool sleeve and plastic socket of the prosthesis.

"Does it turn you off?"

His voice is low and flat, emotionless. I glance up and find his gaze rooted on me, his handsome face schooled into a bland expression that I would never mistake for anything close to casual. I press my mouth to the inside of his left thigh, just above the edge of the sleeve.

"Nothing about you turns me off."

His skin tenses beneath my lips and my tongue, and I hear the ragged breath he inhales through gritted teeth. I rise up on my knees, kissing my way back to his cock. He groans when I take him deep into my mouth, his hips bucking as I move atop him, my tongue teasing the underside of his shaft.

On a guttural curse, he arches up, pulling me off him and dragging me onto his lap again.

I swipe my tongue over my wet lips, frowning at him. "I wasn't through with you."

"No, baby," he says, taking me in a raw kiss. "We're just getting started."

I moan against his mouth, delirious with desire. "Your pants," I murmur. "Don't you want to take them off?"

He gives a faint shake of his head. "The leg would have to come off first. It's a process."

"I can be patient," I say in between kisses. "The wait'll be worth it so I can have my wicked way with you."

His answering chuckle vibrates against me. "You might have patience for that, but who says I do?"

He reaches for something in his discarded suit jacket and I raise my brows when I hear the faint crackle of a condom package. "You come prepared."

"You're the one who likes to call me a Boy Scout." He gives me an adorably unrepentant smirk as he tears open the packet and suits up.

"Just how often do you go home with random women you pick up in dance clubs? Or maybe I don't want to know."

"You're not random," he says, dead serious. "*This* is not random. It wasn't supposed to happen—you and me. I knew where to find you tonight. I should've stayed away, but—"

"But what?" I ask, suddenly afraid of his answer.

He shakes his head, lips pressed flat. "If I could have convinced myself to take any other woman in that place home tonight, believe me, I would have. But it's only you I want, Evelyn." He curses, a tight, violent hiss. "Fuck. What I want is this."

I nod, bereft of words. All I have is need.

I shift on Gabe's lap, positioning myself over him until he is seated at the mouth of my sex. I sink down on him, taking his length slowly, gasping as the girth and power of him fills me. Completes me. Breaks me wide open.

"Oh, God," I moan, moving atop him.

He holds onto my hips, meeting every wet slide of my sheath with a strong thrust. I knew it would feel good to have him inside me, but I was wrong. It's heaven. It's more pleasure than I can bear.

Our tempo turns frenzied. Gabe's arms cage me against his heat and strength as he drives deeper and deeper. My climax builds quickly, a tide I neither slow down nor escape. I close my eyes against the overwhelming pleasure of it, catching my lip on a broken moan.

"Let me see you, baby." Gabe's harsh whisper commands me. "Let me see you come for me."

His rhythm is masterful, merciless, pushing me right over the edge. A cry rips from my throat as sensation explodes through me, sharp and white and jagged.

"So beautiful," he snarls against my parted, panting lips. "Ah, Christ. You feel so fucking good wrapped around my cock."

A low roar boils out of him as he pounds into me from his seated position on the bed. My legs are all but useless now, my head resting in the curve of his bulky shoulder, my body still caught in the aftershocks of my orgasm. Gabe does all of the work, his hands clutching my ass, his hips driving hard and tireless.

I can sense the moment when it all becomes too much for him. His muscles tense under my hands, every inch of him feeling like granite against me, while inside me, his strokes are tight and deep, hard shudders striking a place in me that's so sensitive it nearly makes me weep. Then he bites off a sharp curse and I feel him erupt inside me.

And still he keeps rocking into me.

The friction is delicious. I can't help myself from moving along with it, desperate to hold the pleasure close. The pleasure, and the man delivering it.

"How many condoms do you have, Boy Scout?"

His chuckle sounds a little breathless against my ear. "Enough."

"You sure?" I angle into him, taking each upward thrust as deep as I can. Each withdrawing slide is met with the protesting squeeze of my inner walls, striving to keep him inside.

He moans, his cock jerking inside me and still as hard

as when we began. "You're not going to make this easy on me, are you?"

I lift my head and meet his dusky, heavy lidded gaze. "Nothing about me is easy. Didn't you say so yourself just the other day?"

"So I did," he admits, a devilish grin curving his mouth. "And just so we're clear, I never back down from a challenge."

19

~ Evelyn ~

I wake in the darkness, sometime before dawn. I'm drowsy and sated, aching in all the right places.

Gabe is not in bed with me, but when I sit up I notice that his suit jacket and shirt are folded with military precision on the bench at the end of the mattress, along with his holstered weapon. I don't see his pants or his prosthesis, which he removed sometime last night before we depleted his condom supply.

I smile at the memory of how vigorously and thoroughly we pleasured each other.

And that's all it takes for arousal to unfurl inside me all over again. I groan, clamping my thighs together against the rising ache I still have for him.

So much for my sexual drought. Gabriel Noble not only opened the dam last night but obliterated it.

I slip out of bed and follow the sliver of light coming

from the connected master bathroom, pausing to grab a short kimono from my large walk-in closet as I go.

Gabe is freshly showered and seated on the marble edge of the big soaking tub, a white guest towel wrapped around his hips. His broad, muscled back is bent forward as he scrubs a hand over the top of his damp, tousled brown hair.

"Good morning," I murmur, leaning against the doorjamb.

"Hey," he says, glancing up. His voice is low and rough, like it was last night when he whispered so many delicious, dirty things to me. "I hope you don't mind that I used your shower."

"Of course, I don't mind." I let myself soak in the sight of him, finding it difficult to calm the flutter in my stomach as my gaze travels from his handsome face to his thick shoulders and the solid planes of his chest and lean abdomen. His prosthesis is propped against the bathroom wall near him. I don't want to stare at his legs, but I don't avoid looking, either.

After last night, I can't look at him enough. I've explored every inch of his gorgeous body, and I'd love nothing more than to start all over again today.

I step inside the bathroom and seat myself beside him. "What time is it?"

"Almost five. I didn't mean to wake you."

"It's okay." God, he smells good. And the droplets of water on his golden skin only make me want to lick him dry. "You're leaving early."

I sound disappointed because I am. He was so tender and giving in bed, I can't deny that I was looking forward to waking up in his arms.

"It's Monday morning," he says. "My day starts early,

so I have to get going."

I lean toward him, pressing a kiss to his bare shoulder. "You sure there isn't anything you want before you go?"

The corner of his mouth quirks. "I can think of several things. Unfortunately, I'm already late and I need to swing by my place and change clothes. I wasn't planning to stay over."

"I'm glad you did."

He nods, reaching up to stroke the side of my cheek. When I turn my face into his open hand and kiss the center of his palm, he groans. "You start that and I'm going to want to finish it."

"I don't see a problem with that."

"My team will. I've got a meeting with them this morning at headquarters."

"Call in sick. I will too. We can go out for breakfast and some more condoms."

He chuckles. "Tempting, but I can't. After the meeting, I'll be with Nick and Beck reviewing the new security system installation for your boutique later this week."

"Tell them you're playing hooky with me. Or I'll tell them. My brother will understand."

The look he gives me is so stark it makes my breath catch. "No. He won't understand, Evelyn." He glances away then, muttering a harsh curse. "Your brother will fucking kill me if he finds out what I've done to you. And for good damn reason."

"What you've done to me?" I laugh, but he only grows soberer. Distant. I swear he flinches when I place my hand on his back. "Hey. I was only kidding about saying anything to Andrew. I won't. My sex life is none of his business, just like his is none of mine. Not that he has a sex life. I'm pretty sure my big brother is a monk."

This attempt at humor falls flat too. Gabe swears again, low under his breath. "I gotta go."

He reaches for his prosthesis and his slacks that lay on the edge of the tub at his other side. Afraid to say anything else that might worsen the gap that seems to have opened up between us so quickly, I get up and brush my teeth at one of the sinks as he hastily puts on his boxer briefs, then grabs the sleeve that fits onto the stump of his left leg.

He struggles with it, his hands moving hurriedly. He peels it off and starts over. When he does it a third time, the curse that explodes out of him makes me jump.

"Can I help?"

"No." Another curse, more vivid this time. Then he blows out a sharp breath. "Do you have any alcohol?"

"Um . . ."

"Rubbing alcohol," he clarifies. "It'll help lubricate the sleeve."

"Sure. I think I have some." I check the cabinets and find a bottle near the back. "What else do you need?"

"Just that."

I bring it to him and stand back while he pours some into his hands, then smooths it onto the silicone sheath. He sets the open bottle down and starts aligning the rounded cup of the sleeve at the bottom of his stump. I can see the sides catching again, friction tugging against it instead of allowing the sleeve to roll smoothly over his knee and onto his thigh.

"Do you need some more?"

He nods tightly. "Just a bit, right here."

I kneel down in front of him, then pour the alcohol

in my palms and rub it onto the silicone where he indicated. His skin is warm beneath the sleeve, his thigh muscles taut and strong. The silicone covering slides easily under his hands now, and he finishes adjusting it into place.

He gives me a rueful glance. "Bet you think I'm real fucking sexy now, right?"

"Just real," I tell him. "And that's okay. More than okay."

He scoffs quietly, his lips pressed flat as he reaches for the prosthesis. "I hate that you're seeing me like this. That's why I don't do this kind of shit."

"Stay over at a woman's place, you mean?"

"Relationships," he says. I hear the anger in his voice, but it's the deeper wounds that open up an ache in my breast. It's the fear I see in his gaze now that moves me. "I don't do this. I haven't been with anyone like this— like you—since I got out of the hospital. Hell, I wasn't very good at relationships even before I got injured."

"I don't do this, either, Gabe. I haven't wanted to let anyone in for a long time." I rub my hand along his covered thigh, caressing him, drawing on his strength. "After I left modeling, I spent a long time in hospitals too. Emergency rooms. Rehab programs. I even checked myself into a mental institution for a few months."

"Christ," he whispers, reaching up to engulf my hand in his.

I force a laugh. "Real sexy, right?"

"Just real," he says, returning my answer in a voice that's so tender it nearly breaks me. "What happened? You mentioned eating disorders and the drug addiction, the physical exhaustion. But I know there's more."

I nod. "There's more."

"The subway?"

I swallow, unsure I'm ready to admit out loud just how weak I'd once been. No one knows the depth of my self-destructive impulses because I haven't dared speak them out loud. Not then, and not in all the time since. But Gabe's hazel eyes hold me gently, a tether I feel myself reaching for even through my fear and shame.

"It was about a year before L'Opale opened. I had finally come through everything. I'd gotten better . . . so I thought. I was clean and sober. My weight had rebounded. Anyone looking at me would think I was completely healthy." I shake my head, glancing down as the memories swamp me. "I'd fought my way back. I'd survived something that should have killed me." The words clog in my throat. "I should have been happy. Why couldn't I have just been happy?"

"Baby." Gabe curses, bitter and sharp. He gathers me up, lifting me onto the edge of the tub beside him and swinging my bare legs over his so that I'm halfway on his lap. He pivots toward me, caressing my face, his brow furrowed. "It's okay. I've got you."

"I should have been grateful simply to be alive, but instead—"

"All you wanted to do was die."

"Yes." I'm astonished that he knows how I felt, that he understands. And yet I shouldn't be. Because I can see a similar pain in his handsome face, in those haunted eyes that have seemed to reach deep inside me from the moment our gazes first met.

"I bought groceries that morning," I tell him. "There is this great farmers market in Inwood, at the northern tip of Manhattan."

"I know the place," he remarks. "I don't live far from there."

"I took the subway to the market," I say, as his comforting touch and patient, concerned gaze encourages me to continue. "I always took the subway around the city before that day. And I'm not sure what was different on that morning, but as I was returning home, I just felt lost. I felt so empty and afraid. I remember standing on the platform, waiting for the train. My foot kept inching forward, onto the yellow line . . . then over it. I felt the vibration of the oncoming train as it started rolling into the station. I remember I closed my eyes as I inched farther forward."

"Jesus Christ."

I can't hold Gabe's bleak stare as I let the rest of the words spill out. I glance down, ashamed. Terrified of what he'll think of me. "I remember feeling nothing but air beneath my right foot. Then the sudden gust of hot, exhaust-tinged wind. Less than an instant later, I was violently yanked back. I stumbled on my heels and landed on my ass on the concrete platform. I don't know who saved me. The crush of people crowding on and off the train was like a stampede. All I saw were legs and moving bodies. I left my groceries scattered everywhere on the ground and I ran back up to the street. I ran for blocks and blocks before I finally collected myself enough to hail a taxi home."

"And you've never stepped foot in the subway again."

I shake my head, swallowing hard. "I can't. I'm afraid it could happen again."

"Not if you don't let it." He caresses my cheek, then leans forward and kisses me softly on the lips. "And it won't ever happen again while I have anything to say about it. Scout's honor."

I smile in spite of the cold weight that's settled inside me. But that weight is lessening. It's lifting, the longer I stare into Gabe's eyes.

I want to believe him. I want to trust that what I'm feeling is real.

He kisses me again, his strong hands cupping my face. When he releases me and settles back, he sighs heavily. For several long moments, he doesn't speak. I'm not even sure he's breathing. But then his hand covers mine, his thumb idly brushing my fingers.

"The day of my injury, my platoon was coming in from a routine sweep for IEDs. We'd spent eight hours combing a stretch of godforsaken, hot desert dirt road. It had been a good day, as far as good days went in Kandahar. We were heading back to base on a road we'd been on a hundred times before when the explosion hit. Our vehicle went airborne. It slammed down on its side, smoke and flying shrapnel everywhere. Fire burning inside and out. My ears were ringing from the detonation, but I could still hear my friend Norris choking on his own blood beside me. His chest was gone, nothing but an ugly hole. The other guys were already dead. Somehow, I crawled out of the vehicle. I tried to get up and walk, but—" He chuckles grimly. "It took me a minute to realize what I was seeing when I looked down at what was left of my leg. I was still crawling through the blood and twisted metal and body parts when another unit rolled up and pulled me out of there."

"Gabriel." All I can manage is a whisper. I don't want to break down in front of him, but the pain I feel for him is staggering. When I know any words I have to say will prove inadequate, even harmful, I reach out and wrap him in my arms.

"I wanted to die too," he says, his breath warm in my hair. "I know what it's like to survive and wake up some days wishing you hadn't. But you get through. Whatever it takes, you get through."

I don't know if he's giving me a command, or if he needs the reassurance as well. Either way, I hug him closer. His arms cocoon me against his strong body, and I think I could stay here like this forever.

But all we get are a few moments.

His phone rings, and I reluctantly let him go as he reaches down to retrieve it from atop his folded pants on the edge of the tub.

"Don't tell me that's my brother or Nick calling you at this hour."

"No," he says, frowning. "It's my brother, Jake. I have to take this."

He answers, and while he listens, I catch only snippets of the deep voice on the other end, speaking in an urgent tone. Gabe's face goes slack. A curse punches out of him.

"Okay. Yeah, I'm on my way now."

My heart was already heavy, but now it's filled with cold dread when I see the bleak look on his face. "What's wrong?"

"My father's had a stroke. The ambulance just picked him and my mother up. I have to get to the hospital right now."

20

~ Gabriel ~

The intensive care unit's doors swing open in the short hall outside the general waiting room. A grieving family exits together, their muffled sobs growing louder as the group moves listlessly toward the ICU floor's elevator.

It's been a constant stream of people in and out of the ward all day, some in tears, others walking in shell-shocked silence, a few so distraught they've melted down in sobbing puddles right outside the unit. I'd almost forgotten what a critical care area of a hospital sounded like, but in the sixteen hours since I arrived, it's all come crashing back to vivid life again.

Idly, I check my phone for the hundredth time. I won't find the number I really want to see. I left Evelyn's place without asking how to reach her, and it's not as if I can call her brother for the information. Instead, I kill a few minutes rereading texts from O'Connor and other members of my security team. There's one from Dominic Baine, too, reiterating what he'd told me on the phone early this morning, that work would wait and I should take all the time I need to be with my family.

My family are some of the lucky ones today. According to Dad's doctors, the clot that caused his stroke has been mitigated and if he continues to improve as they expect, he should make a full recovery in time. The good news hasn't kept my mother from worrying, though. She's been in his room most of the day. As the unit's doors whisk open again, I hear her voice in the hallway. It's strained and weary, even as she insists to my brothers who accompany her that she wants to be back first thing tomorrow.

I rise from the uncomfortable waiting room chair as she enters with Jake and our next oldest brother, Ethan.

"Oh, honey. You're still here?" She reaches for my hand, her slender fingers feeling cold and small in my grasp. "I thought you left a couple of hours ago with Shane."

I shake my head. "I wanted to stay."

She squeezes my hand, and I can almost feel her leaning on me for balance. My mother is petite and delicate looking, her sable hair shot through with silver strands, yet I know better than to think she's anything but formidable.

Tonight, however, I am reminded that she is mortal. Just like my old man.

"How's he doing?"

Ethan answers. "He's been sleeping for the past few hours. They've got him on blood thinners and they're running a bunch of tests, but it's looking good. The doctors think he could be back home in about a week."

I exhale a sigh, genuinely relieved. "That's great news."

Ethan nods in agreement. He slides a glance at Mom and runs a hand over the short waves of his chestnut-brown hair. "Dad's almost out of the woods. Now, we need to keep this one in line."

She scoffs lightly. "My heart is in that hospital room in there. I can count on one hand how many times your father and I have slept apart in our forty-three years together. I just hate leaving him here."

Jake rests his hand on her back. "He'll be home before you know it."

"Jake's right," Ethan tells her, his deep voice grim. "And we all have you to thank for saving him, Mom. If you hadn't called 911 right away, things would've turned out very different."

She closes her eyes for a moment, nodding her head. "He didn't want me to call. He was embarrassed. Stubborn man kept insisting he was fine."

"What happened?" I ask. Until now, I haven't wanted to press her for details.

"He woke up early this morning to go to the bathroom. I noticed he was a little off balance and he told me his leg had fallen asleep. Well, no sooner had he reached the toilet than I heard him fall. I ran in and found he'd collapsed on the floor. He was confused, and he was having trouble talking."

"Classic warning signs," Ethan interjects.

As a police officer also trained in basic emergency medical response, he should know. I'm personally aware of three instances where Ethan's skills have saved lives.

And as a widower and father of an eight-year-old

son, he, of all of us, truly understands the fragility of life.

"I've never seen your dad so upset," Mom continues. "He could hardly form a coherent sentence, but he made it crystal clear that he did not want me calling an ambulance to come and find him naked in front of the toilet."

Jake gives her a reassuring smile. "Nothing the EMTs haven't seen before, I'm sure. Better the old man gets a little embarrassed than the alternative."

"I know that," she admits quietly. "I only hope he'll agree."

"If he doesn't," Jake says, "he'll have to contend with all four of his sons."

I meet my brother's glance and nod. I may not be on the best terms with the old man, but I'm damn glad he's going to be okay. Mom would be lost without him, and I don't doubt that my brothers would be too.

Ethan releases a heavy sigh. "I'm going to take Mom home to my house tonight. Liam's over at a neighbor's while I've been here. He'll be asleep by now, but I want him to wake up in his own bed. Besides, I'm sure he'll be thrilled to have breakfast with Grandma."

Mom smiles. "I'd like that too, sweetheart."

She turns to Jake and tells him goodbye, hugging him close and kissing his cheek. Then she does the same with me. She holds on to me for an extra moment. "You've been here in the waiting room all day. You should go in and see your father before you go."

I shrug. "Dad needs rest. I'll look in on him next time I'm here."

"Promise?"

"Yeah, Mom. I promise."

She pats my cheek the way she used to when I was

her grandson's age. "I'm sorry for all of this stress today. Especially for you, Gabriel. The last place you probably want to be is in a hospital. And I know how busy you must be with your new promotion."

I shake my head. "It's all right. Don't ever hesitate to call me if something's wrong with you or Dad."

We say goodbye and Ethan escorts Mom to the elevator.

As they go, for what isn't the first time, my thoughts return to where I was when Jake called this morning. Evelyn's been on my mind more than I want to admit. The memory of her softness as she moved beneath me in her bed. Her exquisite, addictive sensuality. Her soothing, tender care after I'd withdrawn in self-directed anger for having let myself lose control with her.

I'm no better than my old man in a lot of ways. Yet she'd handled me with patience, with affection. With a trust I haven't earned and don't deserve.

I can't deny the stark dread that shot through me when she joked about telling anyone that we'd been together. I'd acted like a dick, pushing her away and then losing my shit while I was donning my prosthesis.

If not for my job and her brother, everything would be different.

Everything but me. I'll still be the same fucked up asshole I've always been, and she deserves something more.

That doesn't mean I crave her any less.

If I had her phone number, I would have called her already. Not because I want to get between her legs again, although I do want that. Desperately. More than anything, I just really want to hear her voice.

As much as that ought to scare the ever-living shit

out of me, it doesn't.

With Mom and Ethan gone, Jake stares at me for a moment. "Awfully nice of Kelsey to stop by earlier tonight."

"O'Connor? Yeah." I nod. She'd come by the hospital for a few minutes on her way home from work, bringing a bag of fast food burgers and fries, which my brothers and I devoured on the spot. "I told her when she texted me this morning that she didn't have to go to the trouble, but you see how far that got me with her."

Jake smiles, still studying me. "She cares about you, man."

"She's a good friend."

He clears his throat. "That all?"

I glance at him, frowning. "That's all."

"So, you and her . . . you two have never—"

"Slept together? Fuck no." My scowl deepens. "And don't you think about it, either. Like I said, she's my friend. I'd hate to have to kill you if you touch her, brother."

He backs off, holding up his hands. "Okay, okay. Point taken. It's called a bro code for a reason."

Bro code. Shit. What kind of hypocrite am I to hold Jake to any kind of sacred code when I'm breaching the one I have with Beck?

At this point, I don't think any level of threat would be enough to keep me away from Evelyn. And while guarding her body is part of my current job description, I'm pretty sure doing it while naked is grounds enough to cost me both my job and another limb. Or three.

"You know what? Fuck me," I tell Jake. "Fuck everything I just said. She digs you, in case you aren't aware."

He perks up again. "Yeah? You think so?"

I nod begrudgingly. "Yeah, she does."

Although Jake's a dedicated bachelor and makes no excuses for that fact, I know that deep down, where it matters, he's a good man. Better than me, that's for damn sure. And as much as I want to protect my friend O'Connor from heartache, she's a grown woman capable of making her own decisions.

I scowl at my brother's lopsided grin. "Get one thing clear, though. You hurt her, and you answer to me."

"Done." Jake cuffs my shoulder. "What do you say we get out of here? You up for a beer?"

I shake my head, even before my brain kicks in. "Long day. I'm just going to head back to the city."

I hardly ever turn down a chance to hang with my brother, but right now it's not alcohol I'm craving. It's not hard, anonymous sex at one of Jared Rush's private-invitation clubs, either, which astonishes me to realize. Normally, after a stressful day like this one, I turn to either one of those outlets—often both.

Right now, I can think of only one thing I need.

Jake and I walk down to our cars, and he drives off toward Bayside. I head for the Queensboro Bridge and the fastest route back to Manhattan. Back to the Upper East Side apartment building I have no business being at, yet cannot seem to drive past.

Using Evelyn's garage code from last night, I park next to her Volvo and take the elevator up to the tenth floor. My palms are damp, my heart pounding like a drum in my chest. I stand outside her door for a long minute before I raise my hand and knock.

Shuffling footsteps sound from inside, then a pause. I flick my gaze to the peephole.

"Gabe?" Her voice is muted by the panel that separates us, but the locks are already snicking free and then she pulls the door open and stares at me. She's wearing a wine-colored camisole and loose black pajama pants. No makeup, her dark hair swept up in a messy bun.

And Christ, she's never looked more beautiful.

I can see the questions in her eyes. I can see the worry. It's the soft affection that humbles me the most.

I have things I want to say to her—apologies for this morning, and for the way I've showed up on her doorstep late tonight without permission or explanation.

There are a hundred different things I want to tell her, all of them jammed in my throat. And they all boil down to just one truth, anyway.

"There's nowhere else I want to be right now."

She opens her arms, and I walk into them.

21

~ Evelyn ~

After nearly a week of incredible nights spent in Gabe's arms, my Friday morning at L'Opale could not be off to a worse start.

Katrina storms into my office carrying one of our signature bespoke boxes and drops it on my desk with a hard thump. "I've had it, Eve. I have fucking had it with that man!"

Shocked at her outburst, I turn away from my design table where I'm working on one of Avery's pieces. Kat's temper is on a full boil, which is difficult enough to deal with in private sometimes, but especially when I know we have a sales floor and dressing rooms busy with shopping customers today at the other end of the corridor from our offices.

Frowning, I motion for her to shut my door, which she does with an equal lack of discretion. It bangs closed and I stand up, confused and displeased. "What's going on, Kat?"

She reaches into the open tulle-stuffed box. "Too much lace," she says sharply, holding up a lovely custom-designed bra. She chucks the piece into my trash bin and grabs a pale mint negligee from the box. "Wrong shade of green."

That, too, is thrown into the bin. She pulls out a third, a beautiful black silk and Leavers lace bustier, some of Kat's most stunning work, which I personally modeled and sized for Jane's final stitching earlier this week.

"Too slutty," Kat announces, sneering.

When she starts to toss that piece into the trash, I reach out and take it from her hands. "Enough."

"Hennings has rejected them all, Eve. Every. Fucking. Piece. He's just left the shop after refusing this entire order."

It's no secret that Katrina's gotten off to a rocky start with Mr. Hennings. She hadn't been excited when I asked her to take over his account for me after I landed Avery Ross's project, and it seems their working relationship has only deteriorated. It's been a lot of strain and miscommunication on both sides, from forgotten appointments with Hennings—which Kat not only denies but refuses to apologize for—to constant back-and-forth over designs. All unusual problems for Kat, whose work ethic with other clients has always been impeccable. But she and Walter Hennings have clashed from day one.

And now this.

I walk around to retrieve the other two pieces from my trash bin and release a heavy sigh. "Would you like me to talk to him?"

"No," she snaps. "I'd like you to take back his account. It's obvious that's what he really wants. And I can't keep working like this, Eve. I won't."

"What are you saying?"

Her jaw tightens. "Either you take me off his account, or I'm done."

Her ultimatum hits me like a slap. "Done?"

She fists her hands at her sides as though girding for battle. "I have other design clients here at L'Opale and I've never had issues working with them. This man has been sabotaging me at every turn—"

"Sabotaging you?" I shake my head, taken aback by her drama. "Kat, do you hear yourself? You sound paranoid and that's not like you."

"I'm not paranoid, I'm pissed off. I take meticulous notes on all of his design changes, only to have him contradict everything the next time we meet. He signs off on paper, then finds fault with the finished piece." She scoffs. "Honestly, I don't know how you've been able to deal with him all this time, but I can't. And for the record, I never scheduled that appointment with him on the day I requested off last week."

"It was on your calendar," I remind her. Gently, because I can see how upset she truly is. "Megan showed me the boutique client schedule. The appointment was on the computer, and Mr. Hennings certainly thought he was supposed to be here to meet with you."

She shakes her head, a vigorous denial. "I never scheduled it."

I pinch the bridge of my nose, feeling a headache coming on. "It doesn't matter. I'm sure we can figure everything out. Maybe if you and I both talk to Mr.

Hennings together—"

"No, Eve. Take me off his account, or I'm removing myself right now."

She's serious. But she's also pushing me into a corner like a pouting child or a spurned lover, and I don't like the feeling. "Dammit, I understand you're frustrated. But you're talking about a loyal client who's spent more with us in the past few months than many accounts bring in over several years. We can't afford to lose him. I don't have enough hours in the day to personally devote to both him and Avery Ross. Especially now that she's awarded L'Opale the design contract for her wedding and honeymoon collection."

Kat stares at me, her cool blue eyes sharp, even glacial. "I guess I have my answer."

She pivots around, reaching for the door. But as she steps out of my office she pauses, sending a brittle glance over her shoulder. "You know, I almost said no after I interviewed here and you offered me this job. I could have started over with my own boutique. I could have created designs under my own name. Instead, I poured everything into L'Opale because I believed in this shop, and in you. Because I thought maybe, for once, I had found someplace I could truly belong. I thought I was going to be part of something truly special. Whatever, though. My mistake."

Her uncharacteristic display of emotion stuns me. She's furious over Hennings, that's clear. But right now, it's obvious that she's equally upset with me. She stalks out of my office before I can tell her that she does belong—that as a design team we have created something special together at L'Opale.

With her purse and keys in hand, she nearly crashes

into Gabe and the middle-aged man accompanying him as she races out the back door of the boutique in a furious huff.

"Everything all right?" Gabe asks, resting his hand protectively on my shoulder for a moment before he catches himself and lets his touch fall away.

I slant him a weary look. "No, everything's a mess. Kat just quit."

He frowns. "I'm sorry to hear that. If this isn't a good time, we can come back."

It's only then that I recall he mentioned he'd be stopping by with an electrician today to prep the utility room for the security system upgrade. I shake my head, offering a smile to the man with the tool belt around his waist and the coil of wires and cables looped over his shoulder.

"No, it's fine. Now is as good a time as any."

Gabe nods to him. "Go ahead and get started, Don. I've got some things I need to discuss with Ms. Beckham and then I'll come back and check in with you."

The electrician lopes off and Gabe follows me into my office. He closes the door behind us and quietly turns the lock. My blinds are already closed, so there's no one to see when he gathers me into his arms and gives me a slow, sweet, toe-curling kiss that I wish could go on forever.

"I missed you last night," he murmurs against my parted lips.

"I know. I missed you too." He was at the hospital with his family, then stayed overnight at his parents' house in Bayside to help install a hospital bed and other temporary accessibility modifications in preparation for his father's imminent return home. "How's your dad doing?"

"He was discharged this morning. The doctors say he's doing great."

"That's good news." And because I can see the reticence in his handsome face, I have to ask the real question. "Have you spent any time with him yet?"

He shrugs. "I will . . . eventually. He's trying to get settled back at home now. Mom says my brothers are keeping a close eye on him, so I'm sure he doesn't need me. Which is just as well."

"Oh, Gabe." I sigh, wishing there was a way to mend the wound that exists between him and his father. Death may have taken one of my parents, but Gabe's loss is worse, I believe. Because he's been living with the inexplicable, prolonged absence of his father's love all these years.

And whether he wants to admit it to himself or not, I see the pain it's caused him. I've felt the grief in him this past week that his father's been ill.

He draws back, frowning. "I didn't come in here to talk about my old man. Tell me what just happened with you and Katrina. You both looked awfully upset."

"She inherited a client from me recently and let's just say it was a bad fit for both of them. Today he rejected a box full of Kat's custom designs and she decided she'd had enough."

Gabe cocks his head, gaze narrowed. "He?"

"Walter Hennings. He's a widower with a large bank account and a young girlfriend from overseas whom he likes to spoil with expensive, bespoke lingerie." I roll my eyes at his dubious look. "I know. But he's one of our best clients and Kat demanded I either let her drop him or she was going to walk."

"Not the smartest thing to say to your boss."

I rub my temples and slowly shake my head. "I've been working with Katrina for a long time. We haven't always agreed on everything, but I respect her. She's an amazing designer with a great work ethic. Today I saw a different side of her."

Gabe's brow furrows slightly. "How so?"

"She was mad, Gabe. Worse than that, I think I really hurt her. It wasn't my intention, but she wasn't allowing me much room to find a compromise. I must've really wounded her, if she was mad enough to quit like she did."

"Do you think she might be a problem?" His question is so guarded, so grimly protective, it takes me aback.

"What do you mean? A problem, as in dangerous?" I sound incredulous because I am. And Gabe looks too serious to be joking. "She's angry and upset, that's all. Granted, I've never seen her like this, but no, I'm not worried about anything like that. Why? Do you think I should be?"

"Just needed to ask." An odd emotion flickers in his gaze, but it's shuttered by the fall of his thick lashes almost as quickly as it appeared. His expression relaxes as he draws me against him once more. "I'm in the security business, remember?"

I smile up into his intense, hazel eyes. "And you're never off duty, right?"

He grunts, his mouth a flat line. "Right."

I move my thigh between his, rubbing my hip against his erection. Wetting my lips, I can't resist sliding my hand down to caress the hard ridge of his cock over the fabric of his dark suit pants. "Definitely armed and ready for duty right here."

His nostrils flare and he closes his eyes on a low groan. "You're playing with fire. I've gone without you for an entire night now. Don't think that was easy."

"It wasn't easy on me, either." I tilt my mouth to his and kiss him, pushing my tongue past his lips as I tug down his zipper and slip my hand into his boxer briefs. He fills my hand, his skin hot and velvety, his thick shaft pulsing in my grasp.

"Ah, Christ," he hisses against my cheek. His hips jerk as I stroke him, his breath sawing out of his lungs. His hands are on the hem of my skirt, inching it higher up my thighs. His fingers sweep aside the crotch of my panties and cleave into the wetness of my pussy. He moans. "I don't have any protection on me."

"I don't care." I kiss him some more, using both hands to unbuckle his belt so I can free him completely. "Right now, I just need you inside me. Right here."

He rears his head back, a desperate look in his heated stare. "I always use protection. I promise you, I'm clean."

"Me too. And I'm on the pill."

"Fuck."

I grin up at him and nod. "Now you're getting the idea."

His hands move around to grip my ass. He squeezes tightly, possessively. Then he spins me around and bends me over the top of my desk, moving aside the lingerie box and potted rosebush with a sweep of his arm. One hand moves under me to knead my breast while his other hand strokes my back for a moment, before sliding onto my backside, which is fully exposed to him. On a jagged curse, he yanks my panties down and spreads me open with a harsh grasp.

"You're so fucking beautiful like this," he whispers, his voice rough and raw as he urges my legs apart then slips his hand between them. "One of these times, I want to tie you up with some of these pretty things you make."

Oh, God. My sex throbs at the very idea.

"Yes," I gasp.

And then it's all I can do to bite back my pleasured scream as he takes hold of my hip in one hand, his cock in the other, then plunges into me in a powerful thrust that makes me see stars.

There is no need to take things slowly, or to ease into what we both crave the most right now. My sex is drenched and aching for him, and his cock delivers everything I need and more.

He pounds into me fast and hard, brutal strokes that excite me for their ferocity as much as I am aroused by the realization that I am the one driving him to this wildness. I feel it inside me too. As much as I want to prolong the spiraling tempest of the wave that's cresting beneath me, I can't hold on. My orgasm breaks and splinters, carrying me away on a flood of bliss and pounding, delicious release.

Gabe bends over me, our clothing rasping, his hips rocking against me in a fevered tempo. His breath is rapid and shallow as he pumps deeper and stronger inside me, and then he slams home on a low snarl as he comes, his big body shuddering with the force of his climax.

He holds me for a moment, his lips brushing the side of my cheek as we both recover from the aftershocks of our pleasure and the Earth slowly tilts back onto its axis.

Pressed atop me over the desk, he kisses the corner

of my slack mouth. "Are you okay?"

I hum a little moan. "Better now."

"Me too. Except now I don't want to stop."

Outside my office, muffled voices carry from the rest of the shop. I'm not afraid anyone heard us or could be aware of what just occurred, but at this moment I wouldn't care either way. Having Gabe on top of me—still moving in a slow rhythm inside me—makes everything else reduce to total insignificance.

But then he groans and I feel him carefully withdraw even though he's still hard. He nips my shoulder before leaving my body completely.

I'm smiling as he helps me up and turns me around to face him. "That was amazing."

"You're amazing," he says, as I adjust my skirt as he stuffs his firm cock back into his tailored suit pants. "Let's do this again soon, Ms. Beckham."

"I'd like that very much, Mr. Noble," I say, playing along. "What are you doing for lunch?"

"Hopefully you." His grin is pure sin. He reaches over to my desk and picks up the black silk corset I spared from Kat's fury. "What are the chances of my convincing you to wear this for me later?"

I arch a brow. "With or without panties?"

"Definitely without," he growls, closing the distance between us and taking me in a bone-melting kiss. Then he smacks my ass. "I need to get out of here before you give me any other wicked ideas."

We straighten ourselves and arrange our clothing, then Gabe walks to the door and silently unlocks it. He sends one last heated glance at me before he exits. No sooner does he step outside than the electrician calls to him from the back room of the boutique.

"Hey, Gabe? There's something here I think you should take a look at."

"Sure thing, Don."

I walk out of my office a second after him, just to get another glimpse of Gabe striding down the hallway looking all business once more and sexy as hell.

It's virtually impossible for me to curb my satisfied smile—or to tamp down my desire for the man who's not only seduced my body, but my heart as well. With my purse in hand and my body still buzzing with residual pleasure, I head for the staff washroom to freshen up and wait impatiently for that lunch date he promised me.

22

~ Gabriel ~

Dominic Baine and Andrew Beckham are seated together at the executive suite conference table reviewing a large collection of blueprints when Nick's assistant, Lily, shows me into the office.

"Sorry to interrupt," I tell both men. "I didn't want to discuss this over the phone, but I didn't think it should wait."

In fact, I left L'Opale as soon as I saw what the electrician had discovered in the utility room a short time ago. Making excuses to Evelyn about postponing our lunch date, I headed directly back to Baine headquarters. I hated lying to her about my abrupt need to leave. Realizing that she trusts me so implicitly she had accepted those excuses without question doesn't make me feel any better, either.

I owe her the truth. Not only about my role as her

protector and my suspicions that her safety could be compromised, but about everything. Including how much she means to me.

But as I step inside Nick's office, the only thing stronger than my guilt over all of the secrets I've been asked to keep from Evelyn is the grave concern that's sitting like a cold rock in my stomach.

Nick glances up in question. "What's going on, Gabe?"

Once Lily has left and closed the door behind her, I reach into my jacket pocket and remove the small square of black plastic and the singed wires attached to it. The men stand up to look at the device I've placed on the conference table.

"What the hell is it?" Beck asks, his dark brows furrowed.

"Some kind of digital intercept device. The electrician found it in the boutique's utility room."

Nick frowns. "Someone bugged the shop?"

"From the looks of it, yes."

"Jesus Christ," Beck hisses. "Bugged it for what reason?"

"Specifically? I haven't determined that yet. But this kind of device coupled with specialized software can enable someone to hack into just about anything. Computers, mobile connections, cell phones, cameras. It can even tap into security systems, if the operator knows what they're doing."

"Shit." Beck swallows, and I see some of the same cold fear in his face that I've been feeling ever since I was alerted to the problem. "Are you saying someone had to be physically inside the shop in order to install this fucking thing?"

I nod. "I'm going to be looking into L'Opale employees, current and former, as well as chasing down a list of service and maintenance workers. Anyone who may have had access to the shop in recent weeks or months."

Beck swears under his breath. "You think it's been there that long?"

"I don't know. But it's possible." I clamp my jaw, if only to maintain some level of calm when I consider that someone has had digital access to Evelyn and her workplace for an indeterminate time. "According to the electrician, equipment like this can suck down a lot of energy when it's in use. This one caused an overload on the shop's electrical system, which is why the power went out last week. The only good news is the surge also fried the components of the device."

"Evie was working late that night by herself. She said she thought she heard someone trying to get in the back door."

"Yes. All the more reason to expedite the new security system and camera installations. I made a few calls on my way here. I have a crew available to work the weekend to get it completed as soon as possible."

"Okay, I agree." Beck lets out a weary breath. "I appreciate all you're doing, Gabe."

Nick nods in confirmation. "Whatever you need, consider it yours."

"Thank you."

Beck's serious gaze moves from Nick to me. "Does Evie know about any of this?"

"No. Not yet. I wanted to bring it to you first."

"Good. Let's keep it that way for now."

"Yeah, about that." I clear my throat, working up to

what I've been wanting to suggest for several days. "This actually might be a good time to bring her up to speed on everything. I don't think we need to keep her in the dark. In fact, I prefer we don't. As the one tasked with keeping her safe, it's my opinion that it will be easier to do that if she's informed."

"You'd rather scare her before we have answers?"

"From what I've seen, she's a level-headed, strong woman. She can handle this."

Beck's misgiving is written all over his face. "You've known my sister for, what, barely a couple of weeks? You've been watching her from a distance, Gabe. I've known Evie all her life. I'm fairly certain I know what she can handle, or not. I've seen up close what stress and anxiety will do to her."

I sympathize with him, all the more now that Evelyn has shared some of her past struggles with me. I also know that it was her brother who protected her. He's still trying to fill that role now, still seeing her as the fragile young woman she had been when her life had spun so dangerously out of control.

The last thing I want to see is a repeat of those troubles for her. The woman I know is stronger than that. I've seen it myself. I trust that she can handle anything life throws at her now, but at the end of the day, that's not my call to make. I'm the hired help, even if my feelings have crossed that line a long time ago.

"Someone slashed her tires the other day," I remind both men. "And now we've got hard evidence that the boutique has been compromised. Not to mention her personal belongings. I don't think her purse went missing by accident last week."

"You think one of the employees took it?" Beck

asks.

I shrug. "I think someone did. And I think if we find out who it was, we'll find out who's responsible for everything else that's going on."

"Then go dig up those answers, Gabe. When you get to the bottom of this, then I'll explain everything to my sister. But don't expect me to put her through any unnecessary pain in the meantime. I love her too much to see her hurt for any reason."

I can't argue that. No more than I'm prepared to admit just how intimate my knowledge of Evelyn has become. And I can't tell him how every moment I withhold the truth from her—about the potential threats I'm aware of, and about my covert responsibility to protect her—is the worst kind of torture I've ever endured.

Beck seems to take my silence as agreement.

"Do you think she's in danger right now?" he asks me, his low voice filled only with concern.

"Not if I have anything to say about it, no."

"That's what I'm counting on," he says. "I'm counting on you, Gabe. I know you're not going to let me down. I also know I don't need to tell you how grateful I am for everything you're doing for us. I can't thank you enough for dropping everything to watch over her."

I nod, trying to ignore the pang of guilt that claws at me. My friend wouldn't be thanking me if he knew how I'd greeted his sister this morning. Or all the other mornings—and nights—I've spent in Evelyn's bed this week.

I avert my gaze, looking at Nick as he inspects the cooked spying device. "What are you thinking this is about, Gabe? Corporate espionage, or something more personal?"

"I don't think we can rule out anything." I glance at Beck. "How much do you know about her coworker Kat?"

He shrugs. "Only the basics, and things my sister's told me. I do know Katrina Davis came to L'Opale from another lingerie house. She's been Evie's design partner all this time, so that's five years now. Why do you ask?"

"She walked off the job today."

"You got to be kidding."

I give a sober shake of my head. "When the electrician and I arrived, Kat was storming out of the shop after what sounded like a heated argument with Evelyn over a difficult client."

"Shit." Beck scrubs a hand over his jaw. "That doesn't sound like Kat. To hear my sister tell it, she's always been a consummate professional."

I nod. "That's my understanding too. Even so, I'd like permission to check her background. Just to see if there are any red flags we should be aware of."

"Are you saying you think she might have something to do with all of this?"

"Like I said, we shouldn't rule out anything." I glance at both men. "I want to run background checks on all L'Opale employees and everyone with access to the boutique."

"Fine with me," Beck says.

Nick gives an affirmative dip of his head too. "Based on this development today, I'd personally feel a lot better knowing Evelyn has eyes on her around the clock."

"Gabe, do you have the resources on hand for that?"

I practically choke at the idea of putting other

security personnel on Evelyn's watch. Especially when the person she's spending the most time with lately is me.

"I'll make sure she's covered," I answer, mentally signing myself up for the job.

It's not as though I would entrust her safety to anyone else, no matter how much confidence I have in my other team members.

Evelyn's well-being, and her exquisite body, are mine to protect.

And as I agree to extend my secret duty to watch over her, I can only hope that this decision to covertly keep her safe isn't going to cost me her heart one day.

23

~ Evelyn ~

Gabe's rain check for our missed lunch date yesterday was an early dinner of Chinese takeout and a sleepover at my place.

Not that either one of us got much sleep.

I'm pretty sure my satisfied smile hasn't faded even a little since I arrived at the boutique this Saturday morning. Of course, it doesn't help that he's spent nearly the whole day in the shop with me, he and a small crew of technicians showing up first thing to install the new security cameras and wireless alarm system that I thought weren't due to arrive until next week.

Megan and I closed the boutique early to give the guys space to work, and I sent her and the weekend sales team home to enjoy some time away from the shop for once.

I have to admit, it doesn't seem the same without

Kat here. I still regret the way things ended yesterday. I've tried calling her a few times since she walked out, but she won't pick up. Meanwhile, I'm scrambling to decide between gearing up to hire someone new or finding a way to juggle all of L'Opale's clients on my own.

It's after five o'clock and I've still got several projects open in front of me on my design table when Gabe appears in my open doorway. His white shirt is unbuttoned at the collar, the sleeves rolled up over his sexy forearms. He wore jeans in to the shop today, and I'm not sure which Gabe I find hotter—laid-back in denim or take-no-prisoners in his usual dark suit and tie.

Fortunately, I don't have to choose. I have them both. And I must have done something right in this life, because by some gift of fate, I also have naked and glorious Gabe, which is the version I'm craving now.

"The guys are wrapping things up and taking off," he says, his tone low enough not to be heard over the sounds of chatter and jangling equipment carrying in from the back of the shop. "How long do you need before you're ready to call it a day?"

I glance at my desk full of work. "About three months. But how does five minutes sound?"

"Like four minutes too long," he says, giving me a hungry look that almost melts me in my seat. "I want to take you out tonight, Ms. Beckham. Not here, but in my neck of the woods. I want to show you where I live."

I raise my brows, surprised and delighted by the invitation. "I'd like that very much, Mr. Noble. What do you intend to do with me?"

"Everything." He studies me for a moment, his hazel eyes serious and contemplative, promising more than just a date. "Five minutes, Ms. Beckham. Then you're at my mercy for the entire weekend."

I lick my lips, my pulse skittering with excitement. "I can hardly wait."

When we get to my apartment, Gabe instructs me to change into casual clothes and pack an overnight bag. Wearing a T-shirt, jeans, and sneakers, I have no idea where we're going, or what to expect when we get there.

I'm even more confused twenty minutes later, when he parks outside a gymnasium near Harlem. There are only a couple dozen vehicles in the lot, mostly pickups of various types and a few beefy SUVs. Although the lights are on in the building, for a Saturday evening in New York, the place is far from busy.

Gabe turns off the Lexus's engine and smiles at me. "You like watching basketball?"

I frown, confused. "Sure."

"I was hoping you'd say that. Come on."

We get out of the car and he grabs a black nylon duffel bag from the trunk. With the bag in one hand and my fingers caught in his other, he takes me into the large square building. Inside the lobby are bulletin boards filled with schedule sheets and activity calendars, as well as brochures and flyers offering various services and counseling centers geared toward veterans.

We walk past, Gabe leading me down a wide corridor toward the open doors of the gymnasium. The rhythmic thud of basketballs bouncing on hardwood and the inviting sounds of men and women laughing and conversing echo out to the hallway.

As we near the entrance, a blond man in a wheelchair

rolls out to the corridor. He's thirty-something and good-looking, and although he's got all of his limbs, his legs are thin and immobile beneath the knee-length hems of his red basketball shorts.

He stops when he sees Gabe, and his face breaks into a wide smile. "Hey, Noble. Good to see you, man."

Gabe lets go of my hand to clasp his friend's. "How's it going, Webber?"

"Oh, you know. Same shit, different day." He says it with an affable grin, his gaze cutting to me every few seconds. "Hello."

I smile. "Hi."

Gabe clears his throat. "Sorry. Webber, this is Evelyn. Evelyn, this is Chris Webber."

"Nice to meet you." He stares for a longer moment, his head tilted, eyes narrowing in contemplation. "Anyone ever tell you that you kind of look like that famous model from a few years ago?"

"I have heard that comment once or twice before, yes." My smile broadens with my wry reply. "Probably because I am her. Or used to be, that is."

His brows shoot up, and I swear I don't know who looks more surprised by my casual admission—Gabe, or his friend. I have to admit, I've surprised myself too.

If I'd encountered this question even a few weeks ago, I would have been tempted to shut it down with a polite deflection—maybe even a sharp denial. But now, standing next to Gabe, I don't feel trapped by who I used to be. I don't feel exposed, or fearful.

Instead, with Gabe's warm gaze on me, and his hand slipping easily around mine, I feel strangely liberated. I feel comfortable, free.

I feel safe in a way that I haven't felt for a very long

time.

Gabe smiles at me, a private glance that is both a comfort and an enticing promise.

"Well, damn." Webber chuckles, reaching up to punch Gabe in the arm. "No wonder we haven't seen you around here lately. O'Connor's been trying to cover for you, said you were putting in a lot of hours at that swank security job you're working."

Gabe grunts, seeming a bit uncomfortable with the subject of his job. "Is O'Connor here?"

"Yeah, she's inside with everyone else. Now we're only waiting on Nicholson and then we can start the game." Webber gives me a nod. "Good to meet you. 'Scuse me for a minute. I gotta go call Nicholson and light a fire under his ass to get down here."

Webber rolls away and Gabe leads me into the gymnasium. Inside is a regulation-size basketball court where a group of seven men and women are gathered on the sidelines, some in wheelchairs like Webber, others standing on prosthetic limbs.

Near the group is a collection of ten specially designed chairs with low backs, tilted wheels, and a metal frame fitted around the bottom of the chair with a small caster at each corner.

"Gabe!" His friend O'Connor raises her left hand in greeting as soon as she spots us.

She breaks from the group to walk toward us and I realize that not only does she have a prosthetic right arm and hand, but she also wears a prosthesis on her right leg. The gleaming metal and plastic limb extends from her sneakered foot to above her knee in the cutoff sweats she's wearing.

"I'm glad you made it tonight," she says as she nears

us, smiling at him for a moment before turning her warm greeting on me. "Hi, Evelyn. We haven't formally met yet. I'm Kelsey. Although most people I know call me O'Connor, so take your pick. Anyway, it's really nice to meet you."

I nod. "Thanks. I'm happy to meet you too."

She swivels another look at Gabe, giving him an impatient up-and-down wave of her hand. "Are you just going to stand there, or are you going to suit up and strap into a chair so my team and I can kick your team's butt all over this court?"

"You can try, anyway," Gabe quips.

"Wait a second." I can't mask my surprise. "You play wheelchair basketball?"

"Most every Saturday night for the past year or so," he says with a shrug. "O'Connor talked me into joining the group. Come on. I'll introduce you to everyone."

We walk over with Kelsey to where the other players are gathered and I meet the four men—Rob Sanchez, Denny Adams, John Tuttle, and Bruce Goldberg—and the two women—Tameka Jenkins and Lori Murphy. Everyone is friendly and inviting, so when Gabe excuses himself to the locker room to change out of his office clothes, I fall into the relaxed conversations as if I might actually belong here.

When he returns a few minutes later I have to add another version of Gabe's hotness to my list, because he is rocking the hell out of a basic black basketball jersey and shorts. The jersey showcases his powerful arms and broad shoulders, and the waistband of the loose-fitting shorts cling to his trim hips below the muscled taper of his waist and abs.

He strolls up with an easy, confident stride and a

dimpled smile that makes my mouth water and my core bloom with instant heat as I mentally undress him with my eyes.

He leans in close, his mouth hovering beside my ear. "If I knew you'd look at me like that, I would've brought to you one of these games a lot sooner than now."

It's all I can do not to wrap my arms around him. Not only to give in to the arousal that's stirring to life inside me, but out of simple joy and affection.

Dear God, I'm falling fast and hard for this man.

But it's more than that.

If I'm being honest with myself, I already have fallen.

The admission sits on the tip of my tongue as he draws back from me, his hazel eyes lit with amusement and something more elusive. Something solemn and intense. I hold my breath because for a moment, I wonder if he's feeling the same way toward me.

"Eve . . ." My name is a rough whisper as he rests his palm tenderly on the side of my face.

I don't know what he might have wanted to say, because in the next heartbeat Webber rolls back into the gymnasium to announce that Nicholson won't be coming tonight, after all.

Groans go up from several of the players.

"Shit." Sanchez, a triple amputee, lets his curse fly along with the ball he's been holding in his lap. The basketball swishes into the center of the net, a three-point field goal wasted.

Another player, one of the two women, Tameka Jenkins, holds up her hand. "I'll sit out. We can manage playing with teams of four tonight."

Webber shakes his head at the tall, dark-skinned beauty whose left arm is nothing but a short stump at her shoulder. "No way, Jenkins. You're our best center, and I want you on my team."

"You know, guys," O'Connor says, "we do have a tenth person on the court tonight."

All heads swivel in my direction. My panicked gaze moves from Gabe to each of his friends, who are staring at me in expectant silence.

"W-what? Me?" I stammer in response, shaking my head. "Ah . . . I don't—"

"I think it's a great idea." Gabe's deep voice is calm, leaving me little room to argue. His hand drifts down to mine, idly stroking my fingers, quelling the little bubble of alarm rising up in me. "Do you know how to play?"

"Yes. But I'm not—"

"Missing a limb?" Jenkins asks, a note of challenge in her voice.

"I was going to say I'm not dressed to play," I clarify, glancing down at my jeans and T-shirt. "But I've never used a wheelchair before, either."

"Good," Jenkins replies. "Then you'll be easier to beat."

She grins, and I immediately relax, realizing she was only giving me a hard time.

Before I know it, we've split up into two teams of five, all of us strapped into the specialized wheelchairs. After explaining the difference in game rules for this adaptive sport versus the one I used to play growing up, Gabe gives me a quick lesson in how to maneuver the chair, demonstrating the pivot action of the wheels and the anti-tip qualities of the frame and casters.

"I'll be lucky if I manage to move and dribble the ball at the same time," I tell him. "If I don't crash in the process, it'll be a miracle."

"I'll be right beside you," he says. "I'll catch you if you fall, I promise. But you won't need me to, because you can do anything you set your mind to, Evelyn."

He really means that; I can see it in his eyes. He can't know how much that simple statement means to me, how much it bolsters me to know I have him in my corner. Tonight, on the basketball court, we'll be on the same team. But for me it's much more than that.

In the short time we've come to know each other, I trust him as a friend, a confidant.

As a lover.

I trust him as the partner I never dreamed I'd find.

"Ready to roll, beautiful?" he asks me.

"Yeah." I nod. "I think I'm ready for anything with you, Gabe."

He stares at me for so long, I almost can't take the intensity of his gaze. Then he catches my face in both his hands and draws me toward him, slanting his mouth over mine in a brief, but achingly deep, kiss that arcs through every cell in my body like an electrical current.

"Let's go get 'em," he says, and together we move into the center of the court.

24

~ Gabriel ~

We lost to a lucky free throw by Webber in the final seconds of the game.

Not that I actually care about the score or who won. The best part of the game was watching Evelyn play it. Seeing her not only step up to a challenge, but fearlessly conquer it. Hearing her laughing with my friends. Working together with her as part of a team, as partners.

That's something I haven't had in a very long time. And never like this.

It's not anything I've been looking for, but I know at least enough to recognize something special when it's right in front of me. And Evelyn Beckham is special. She's all that and more, and I can't pretend there is anything casual about the way I feel about her.

What I feel is powerful. It is complicated.

And it is real.

As real as it can be, so long as her well-being remains a part of my job description.

Bringing her into my world this weekend had been an idea borne of practicality—and genuine concern. Beck and Nick want security on her 24/7 now that it's clear that someone has not only tampered with her vehicle, but with the boutique as well.

I couldn't agree more. Evelyn's round-the-clock protection is a plan I fully support and intend to carry out personally. I can't think of anywhere she'll be safer this weekend than in Inwood with me.

It's the rest of the days ahead that bother me the most. Because while I'm confident that I can shield her from harm while we're together, this arrangement will eventually have to come to an end. I don't know how long I can continue to uphold my duty to her brother and Nick when it means denying Evelyn the truth. Not just about the potential threat to her safety, but about my current, covert role in her life.

And until that potential threat to her is resolved and eliminated, I'm not about to surrender my job to anyone else.

Even at the risk of her hating me for it one day.

Those thoughts weigh heavily on me as Evelyn eagerly agrees to dinner with my friends following the game. We've all hit the locker rooms for showers and a change of clothes, then the ten of us head out for one of the pubs on Broadway in Harlem, not far from the veterans center gymnasium.

Her easy camaraderie with everyone, especially the three women of the group, carries on over a round of burgers and beers. While Evelyn answers questions from

O'Connor, Jenkins, and Murphy about the fashion world and her work at L'Opale, I notice Webber and the other guys can hardly take their eyes off her.

Then again, neither can I.

Seated beside me at the long table, she rests her hand on my left thigh. Her warmth permeates the silicone and cushioned sleeve that covers my leg, that soft touch both a comfort and a temptation that has rendered me hard as stone. Each time she turns her head to glance at me, it's all I can do not to pounce on her gorgeous mouth and kiss her senseless.

I hadn't intended to share her with my friends for this long, but I can hardly regret the time when she's clearly enjoying herself. That doesn't keep me from signaling for the check as soon as we've all finished eating. I pass my card to the server and, over the protests of everyone at the table, tell the woman to charge the whole tab to me.

I'm not doing it to show off or to wave my fancy job in everyone's face. But my motives are far from altruistic, either. I'm impatient to have Evelyn all to myself, and I'd rather not wait on my buddies to dissect the bill and pony up for their portions.

As the rest of the table grumbles and groans about the check, Evelyn bumps her shoulder against my arm, her pale green eyes glimmering in the low light of the bar. "So, is this our first official date?"

I stare at her. Since the rest of our time alone together has mainly consisted of long, sleepless hours spent naked in her bed, or hot, breathless minutes with her pinned beneath me on other flat surfaces, I realize that, shit, she's right. This is the first time I've taken her out somewhere. Not that I could risk doing this on the

Upper East Side or anywhere that we might run into her brother or someone else from Baine International.

I frown, wishing I'd done better for her tonight. "I'm sure this isn't the kind of date you're used to. I'm sorry about that."

Her fine dark brows arch. "What kind of dates do you think I'm used to?"

I try to picture her with other men—men with intact bodies and bank accounts that could afford multimillion-dollar apartments and the elegant designer clothes that line her massive closet. I don't want to see her with any other man, real or imagined, past or present. And trying to picture her with someone else only makes me feel even less deserving of her.

She's out of my league by a long mile, something I've known from day one. But it's easy to forget that when she's looking at me like I'm the only man in the room.

Glancing away from her studying gaze, I pick up my mug and drain the flat mouthful of beer that's gone warm at the bottom of it.

"I wish I'd taken you somewhere special tonight instead, that's all."

She makes a small noise in the back of her throat, barely audible over the combined din of bar clamor, music, and conversations taking place all around us. But I can hear the note of doubt in that faint exhalation.

"Am I the only woman you've felt you had to apologize to after bringing her to one of your basketball games?"

"Yeah. You are." She gives me a wounded look that cuts through me. I reach out and smooth the pad of my thumb over the soft velvet of her cheek. "You're the only woman I've ever brought to a game. I told you before, I don't do this . . . relationships. I don't do dates, either. Not very well, obviously."

She smiles, turning her face into my open palm to press a brief kiss there. "I've got news for you, Gabriel Noble. As far as dates go, this one has been pretty perfect so far."

"Yeah?" My voice rasps, arousal competing with the jolt of relief her reply has just given me. She nods, her long-lashed gaze flicking from my eyes to my mouth. She licks her lips and my heart rate speeds, desire coiling into a fist inside me. I lean in close and whisper beside her ear. "Sweetheart, this date is just getting started."

With the check taken care of and a crowd of people waiting for us to leave our table, we all head out of the pub to say our goodbyes on the wide sidewalk outside. As I exchange handshakes and chuckle over smack talk with the guys, Evelyn is drawn into warm embraces by the women. As we all part company, I overhear the women making plans to meet up for lunch and a visit to L'Opale in a couple weeks.

I take Evelyn's hand as we make the short walk around the block to where my car is parked. As soon as we're locked in the vehicle and I start the engine, I can't contain my need to touch her, to feel her lips on mine. I pivot toward her and draw her into a long, slow kiss.

"I've been dying to do that all night."

Just one kiss, and the arousal that had me in its talons at the pub increases to a fevered need. I take her again, stroking my tongue past her parted lips and into the hot sweetness of her mouth.

I am hard as steel against the zipper of my jeans, every cell in my body on fire for her.

She breaks away from my kiss on a ragged gasp.

"How far is your apartment from here?"

My lust-drenched brain takes a second to calculate the distance. "About ten minutes."

Her lips are glistening from my kiss as they curve into a sexy smile. "That's nine minutes too long."

She moves closer and reaches into my lap to unfasten the button at my waistband. The zipper rasps as she tugs it down over the thick bulge of my erection. Then she slips her fingers into my boxer briefs to free my stiffened cock.

"Ah, Christ." I groan as she begins to stroke me. Then I let out a choked curse as she covers the head of my shaft with her hot, wet mouth and sucks me deep. *"Fuck."*

I lean my head back, one hand in her long hair, the other gripping the wheel like a lifeline as her tongue slides along the underside of my cock and her throat opens to take me farther in. Her fingers stroke me at the same time, one hand cupping my balls while the other pumps me from root to tip, moving in tempo with the incredible friction of her mouth.

I look down at her as she bobs in my lap, the wet sounds and hungry moans that vibrate through me taking me swiftly to the edge. "That feels so good, baby. I'm not going to last if you keep that up."

Paused with her lips teasing the head of my cock, she glances up at me. Her smile is pure sin. "Then you'd better drive fast, Boy Scout."

"Yes, ma'am," I croak.

I put the vehicle into gear and punch the gas.

I'm fairly certain I set a new land speed record, which is no small feat considering it also takes a miracle of self-control and focus to withstand the sensual onslaught of

Eve's perfect mouth and ruthless tongue. But my iron will can only last so long.

As soon as I'm parked in my space in the small lot behind the old brick apartment building, I kill the engine, pack up my hard-on, and grab our bags. I practically drag Evelyn up the short flight of stairs to my unit on the second floor. Holding my free hand, she giggles in amusement as I drop the duffels and fumble for my keys in the hallway outside my door.

I can't help the shaking of my fingers. I've disabled bomb detonation devices and I've reloaded weapons without breaking a sweat while taking on heavy gunfire, yet knowing I'm only moments away from having Evelyn naked beneath me and I doubt right now I'd even be able to tie a damn shoelace if my life depended on it.

Finally, I push the apartment door open on a curse and toss the bags in. Then I pull her inside with me. We crash together in a clumsy, urgent need, kissing and tugging at each other's clothing as I guide us through the combination living room and dining room, toward the hallway that passes the bathroom and terminates at the single bedroom at the end.

Beneath her dark T-shirt and faded jeans, Evelyn is wearing a scarlet silk bra and matching panties. I am careful with the pretty underthings this time, unfastening the clasp on her bra and drawing it off her beautiful breasts. I tuck the bra into the pocket of my jeans because I have plans for the pretty length of silk and lace.

With Evelyn stripped down to just her panties and me shirtless in my jeans, I take her hand and walk briskly down the rest of the hallway.

She nips my shoulder as I walk her into my bedroom. "Aren't you going to give me a tour?"

I chuckle, but it's a dark, hungry sound. "I just did. I think you'll agree this is the best room in the place."

I guide her onto the king-size bed and sit her down on the edge of it. Her hands caress me, running up and down my bare torso and around to my back. Her touch inflames me, but I refuse to let it own me. Not this time.

Right now, she's on my turf. On my terms. And I need her to recognize that.

Hell, I need to prove it to myself too.

Because this woman is becoming an addiction I'm not sure I can break. What's worse is I can't imagine I'll want to—not even if it means losing everything I've worked to achieve.

She is mine.

Even though I know I don't have the right to stake that claim, it's alive inside me.

"Lie back," I command her, my voice low and harsh.

When she obeys, I lean over her, taking possession of her mouth in a deep, unhurried kiss. She shudders as my lips move onto her throat, my tongue stroking along the line of her shoulders, then down onto the pretty swells of her breasts.

"Gabriel," she whispers as I suck one dark nipple between my teeth. "Oh, God."

She writhes and pants beneath my roving mouth, the scent of her desire punching into my senses and lighting fire to my veins. I skim my hands along her sides, then onto the curves of her hips. With my thumbs hooked into the sides of her panties, I remove the small scrap of silk and set it aside on the floor beside her bare feet.

Her ankle is delicate in my grasp, her calf firm and soft against my lips as I kiss my way back up the long length of her leg. Her breath is shallow and rapid, her thighs quivering as I take them in my hands and open her to my hungry gaze.

"So beautiful." I stroke the dark, glistening folds of her sex, first with my fingers, then with my tongue. She sighs, a small tremor rippling through her and into me as I circle her clit and suck it into my mouth.

I draw back on a groan, wishing I had all night to savor her. I've hardly begun and already I can tell she's teetering at the brink of release.

"Don't come," I order her. "Don't come until I say so, baby. Can you do that?"

Her answer is a moan and a nod, her lip caught under her straight white teeth.

I smile up at her. "That's my girl. Not afraid of any challenge. Now, move up to the center of the bed for me."

She does what I ask, and I stand up, facing her while I unfasten my jeans. Her heavy-lidded eyes watch every move of my hands as I slide the zipper down and push the denim and black boxer briefs over my hips and off the bulge of my erection.

The throaty noise she makes as my cock springs free is so carnal it nearly kills me. With her gaze riveted on me, I grasp my shaft and stroke it a few times. "Look how hard you've got me. I can't wait to get inside you, baby. But first I'm going to feel you come against my mouth."

She licks her lips and I feel it all the way to my balls.

"Touch yourself," I tell her, my voice sounding strangled. I ease up on my cock and pivot to take a seat on the edge of the mattress to finish removing my pants. "Show me how you want me to touch you, sweetheart. Let me see your pleasure—but not too far. Your orgasm belongs to me."

I watch as she caresses her breasts, her dusky green eyes closing on a thready sigh. "I want your hands on me," she complains quietly. "Gabe, please . . . I need you."

I smile, taking too much satisfaction in that unabashed admission. My arousal edges on the verge of agony, my shaft jutting hard and hot against my abdomen as I watch her touch roam farther down her body. "You're so fucking sexy, baby. I can still taste your sweetness on my tongue. Maybe I'll feast on you all night."

She lets out a cry, and her fingers wade into the bare slit of her pussy. She circles her clit, then pushes two digits inside her sex, and it's a wonder my molars don't crack for how tightly I have to clench my jaw to keep from pouncing on her.

I shove my jeans down past the socket of my prosthesis and push the suction valve to free my leg. She opens her eyes, watching me as she continues to stroke herself, her thighs squeezing around her hand as her body undulates on the bed. Her fine muscles are straining, her light brown skin flushing a deeper, rosy hue. I've never seen anything so hot, so irresistibly sensual.

"Fuck," I utter hoarsely, reverently. "Don't you come yet, Eve."

She tosses her head in denial, but I can see she's struggling to hold on. I roll the sleeve off my stump and cast it aside, along with my prosthesis. Chucking the sneaker from my right foot, I remove my pants the rest of the way, pausing only long enough to pull the red bra out of the pocket.

I move onto the bed with her, positioning myself between her spread legs. Gently, I still her hand and bring her fingertips to my mouth. Her juices are sweet and hot, more intoxicating than the strongest liquor.

When I tie one end of the bra around her wrist, her eyes fly open. Her movements still, but her breath keeps soughing out of her, her pulse ticking furiously in the hollow below her throat.

"Earlier tonight, you said you were ready to go anywhere I wanted to take you." With the knot tied firmly, but comfortably, around her wrist, I kiss the center of her open palm. "Is this all right?"

She swallows, her eyes rooted on mine. Then she nods.

I growl, swamped by everything I feel for her right now. "Give me your other hand, sweetheart."

She obeys, and I finish binding her wrists with the length of scarlet silk and lace. I guide both of her arms up over her head, resting them on the pillow. "Keep them there, or I won't let you come. Do you understand?"

"Yes." Her answer is little more than a gasp.

I reward her with a slow, deep kiss before moving over her body. She pants and shivers under my mouth as I kiss a path from her mouth to her neck. I move lower, tasting every inch of her from the tight buds of her nipples, to the sweet hollow of her navel.

As I savor the tender skin at her hip, I slide my fingers into her wet, silky cleft. I want to take it slow, wrestle back some of my fleeting control, but my need for her is too wild.

I press my hands to her thighs and spread her open to my fevered gaze. Then I lower my head and claim her with my mouth. She moans, bucking against the sensual onslaught of my tongue and lips. "Please," she gasps. "Oh, God . . . Gabe, please."

"Please what?" I murmur against her tender flesh.

"I want . . . I want you inside me now." She shudders as I continue to lick and suck at her sex. Her shoulders come off the pillows and for an instant I think she's going to break her promise to keep her hands where I've placed them, but she falls back down on a groan. "Oh, God. I need to come so bad, Gabe."

Her desperation is swiftly becoming my own. I tongue her swollen clit, arousal ruling both of us now. My face is wet from her juices, my senses swamped with desire for her. Every nerve ending in my body is lit up and sizzling, every tendon and sinew ratcheted to the breaking point. And my cock has never been harder, ready to explode.

"Come for me now, baby."

That's all it takes. With my name a strangled cry, she breaks on my tongue in wave after powerful wave. I want to savor every hard tremor and nuanced vibration, but my need is too urgent now.

I flip her over to her stomach, drawing her hips back until she's on her knees before me, her head down on the pillows in a nest of her loose dark hair, her bound wrists stretched above her.

"Christ, you're gorgeous like this. Tell me you enjoy this. Tell me this is what you want."

"Yes," she gasps, her body still thrumming under my fingers. "I want this. I want you, Gabe . . . now."

I stroke my hand down the length of her spine, from the top of her nape to the seam of her sweet, rounded ass and the drenched, molten haven below it. I move in behind her and guide my cock to the mouth of her sex. I drive home in one long, hard thrust, too far gone to even think I have the ability or the will to take things any slower now.

A possessive growl unfurls deep inside me as I pump within the tight, hot walls of her body. "Fuck, Eve." My voice is guttural and ragged, my release building like a tidal wave. "You're mine. *Mine.*"

"Yes. Oh, God, Gabriel . . . yes."

"You belong to me. No matter what," I snarl. "Say it."

"I am yours." The pledge gusts out of her on a sharp sigh. "No matter what, Gabe. I belong only to you."

Her reply is enough to snap the leash on my control, but it is the feel of her sex convulsing around me in climax that sends me hurtling over the edge. She cries out with her release, and I slam into her feverishly, savagely, my body tensing with every rapid pound of my hips against her backside. My orgasm erupts in a scalding rush.

I've barely finished coming as I reposition her on her back and strip the bindings off her wrists. I sink between her legs again, picking up a tempo that's even more relentless, more fevered. She wraps her arms around me, her thighs hooked around my hips.

"Don't stop," she whispers. "Please, Gabe . . . don't stop."

I couldn't if I tried. The white-hot explosion of pleasure is still rippling through every cell in my body, but I want more. Need more.

With this woman, I know I won't be content with anything less than all of her.

25

~ Evelyn ~

The next morning, after showering and brushing my teeth in the apartment's sole bathroom, I pad barefoot in a fresh camisole and yoga pants toward the small kitchen, where the aromas of brewing coffee and sizzling bacon make my stomach growl with interest.

That's not the only thing that stokes my hunger.

Gabe must have been up for a while. Long enough that he's already clean and has breakfast more than half under way. He pivots from the stove as I approach, alerted to me even though my steps are silent on the beige thick-pile carpet of the hall.

Holding a black spatula in his hand, he is naked except for the low-slung, gray sweatpants he wears, all of those delicious planes and roped muscles of his body bared for my appreciation. As for the bulge of his cock, the baggy fabric hardly conceals its thick, heavy outline. And the loose waistband of his pants only accentuates the obvious, sagging enticingly on the lean cut of his hips.

I can't imagine ever tiring of seeing him like this. The fact that he's cooking breakfast for me and has a pot of coffee waiting only makes me adore him even more.

His mouth curves in a slow, sexy smile. "Good morning."

"Mm, morning." I can't look at him today without feeling the soft abrasion of the bonds he'd placed on my wrists last night. The faint ache lingers there, along with a deep thrum of yearning that still clings to me now, even after I eventually fell asleep boneless and exhausted from pleasure last night.

He rests the spatula next to a griddle and a bowl of pancake batter he's about to pour into it. He strolls up to me and lifts my chin on the edge of his fingers, lowering his mouth to mine for a kiss. It's too tender, too brief by half. I moan, biting my lip as he withdraws.

"Insatiable," he murmurs, his grin waking those twin dimples that never fail to weaken my knees and my resistance. "Coffee?"

"Love some. Just black, please."

"Coming right up. Have a seat." He indicates one of the two stools that sit on the other side of the short L-shaped counter. And he was right about his kitchen window. It does, indeed, look into a unit in the brick building next door.

I smile to myself as I take my phone out of the pocket of my stretchy black pants and set it next to me on the granite. I notice his glance as I place it there, and the flicker of question in his expression.

"I talked to Andrew this morning," I volunteer as Gabe pours a mug of coffee for me and brings it over. "He called before I got in the shower. He said he just wanted to say hi, but I think he was afraid to admit he was checking up on me. We haven't spoken since our blowup in the boutique."

"What did you tell him?" Gabe's voice is as measured as his stare.

"That I was spending the weekend with a friend." I smooth my finger idly over the rim of the phone's case. "It's not a lie, but it feels like one."

"I know." He frowns, making a low noise in the back of his throat. "I'm sorry."

"I don't like keeping secrets, Gabe."

He nods, his brow creasing into a deeper furrow. "I need to fix this. I *will* fix it. Right now, I just need you to trust me."

"I do." I swallow, resting my palm against his cheek. "I trust you completely. Last night should've been evidence enough of that."

"Last night was amazing," he growls, his consternation replaced by a look of dark, male desire. His hands frame my face, lifting me toward him for another kiss, this one long and unrushed, hot and possessive. "If you're not careful, you might find yourself bound to my bed for the rest of the weekend. Maybe longer."

I smile against his sinful mouth. "That doesn't sound so bad to me."

He chuckles. "Maybe the better plan would be to hold you captive in your apartment instead. I think I warned you my place didn't have much to recommend it."

"It has you. And besides, I think it's a nice place." I draw out of his loose hold, glancing at my surroundings. The rooms are organized and orderly, neat as a pin. "Sure, it's compact, but this is New York, after all. And I have to say, I'm particularly impressed with the lack of clutter. Even your furniture is arranged with exacting precision."

He smirks. "Interior decorating skills courtesy of Uncle Sam."

"Is that also where you got your baking skills?" I gesture to a basket of obviously homemade blueberry muffins that sit on the counter next to the toaster.

"Those? They're a gift from my neighbor down the hall in Apartment 5."

"You have a neighbor who bakes for you?"

"Every week." He shrugs, all charm and dimples. "I try to warn Mrs. Bernstein that she's spoiling me, but I think that's the point. She makes me a fresh batch on Saturday mornings and drops them off at my door."

"I'm sure she does," I remark, giving him a flat look. "And does this tart down the hall expect something in exchange for giving you her fresh muffins every week?"

He grins at my double entendre. "Considering she's in her eighties, the only muffins I'm getting from her are the ones over there on the counter."

"Good." I laugh, happy to replace the image of a married cougar on the prowl with one of a gray-haired little old lady who probably views Gabe as a grandson more than a juicy hunk of man-meat.

He fetches the basket and offers it to me. And, dammit, the muffins do look and smell amazing. I select one and start peeling off the paper wrapper. Breaking the crumbly muffin in half, I hand him one piece. I take a bite and can't hold back my sigh.

"Oh, my God," I moan around a mouthful of blueberry goodness. "This is incredible."

He nods, watching me chew in my state of culinary rapture. "Maybe I really should sleep with her, right?"

I almost choke on my laughter. "Maybe we both should."

"No," he says, his dark tone close to a demand. "I don't intend to share you with anyone, Ms. Beckham."

I bite my lip. "Not even eighty-year-old ladies bearing muffin baskets?"

The corner of his mouth quirks, but the rest of him is vibrating with sexual energy. "No one."

The air between us shifts, as it has so often since we met. It doesn't take more than a breath for his mood to change from playful and charming to sexual and commanding. It takes even less for everything female in me to respond to the storm gathering in him.

He reaches for my hand. Bringing my fingers to his mouth, he licks off the crumbs before sucking my index finger into his mouth. Slowly, he lets it go, his eyes full of carnal promise. "Do you remember what you told me last night?"

My mind buzzes with all of the desperate promises and breathless whispers he coaxed from me under the barrage of pleasure he delivered. I meant every one. Especially the one that sits perched on the tip of my tongue even now.

"I am yours."

He inclines his head in a tight nod, his gaze scorching everywhere it touches me. Leaning over the countertop, he captures my mouth in a searing kiss, dragging me up off the stool and halfway onto the granite surface. I crawl up the rest of the way, impatient to put my hands on him. I kiss him in a frenzy, my fingers in his hair, on his back, clawing at him in raw lust and a need to be taken hard by him.

"I'm only yours, Gabriel."

His eyes never leave me. They consume me as completely as a blaze.

With a sweep of his arm, he pushes aside my phone and the mug of coffee and the rest of the smattering of things on the countertop. Then he takes hold of me by my hips, dragging me across the granite to the opposite edge where he stands. My yoga pants and panties are yanked down with impatient hands, cool air rushing against the drenched seam of my sex as he parts my thighs.

The sound he makes as he looks at me, spread open and ready for him, is fevered, possessive.

His hand moves to the front of his pants, and I watch in rapt fascination as he pulls out his cock and guides it between my legs. He is fully erect, sliding along my wetness like heated steel, unyielding, demanding. He finds my center and I whimper with the need for him to fill me, to claim me.

Desire rules my voice and every fiber of my being. I toss my head back on a desperate cry. "Please . . ."

He captures my mouth in a brutal kiss and thrusts inside me. Hard and thick and unrelenting, almost more than I can bear. He lifts his head to watch me as he pounds into me, his strokes furious and deep and wild. His handsome face seems so tortured in that moment, awash with a hundred things he cannot, or will not, say.

So, I say the words for him.

"You're mine, Gabriel." With one hand braced

behind me, I wrap my other around the back of his strong neck, our eyes locked on each other. "No matter what . . . you belong to me."

My demand pushes him over the edge of his control.

Hauling me closer, he powers into me now. He doesn't let up, not until I am crazed with sensation, tears leaking from my release breaking over me in an explosion of pleasure and emotion. He comes with me, my name boiling out of his throat like a curse and a prayer.

26

~ Gabriel ~

As appealing as I found the idea of keeping Evelyn bound to my bed for the entire weekend, eventually our stomachs overruled my plans.

Having spent most of my free time last week on the Upper East Side at her place, food options in my kitchen were limited to random breakfast items, a few frozen dinners, and the basket of blueberry muffins. Instead, Evelyn persuaded me into a trip to the farmers market and lunch at a neighborhood café.

We are seated at a table in the small green space out back, enjoying deli sandwiches and iced teas. A woven tote stuffed with fresh produce, including a carton of tiny wild blueberries, sits on the gray patio bricks at my feet.

"You realize this is setting a bad precedent with Mrs. Bernstein," I tell Eve, my arm draped over the back of her hard wooden chair next to me. Garbed in a breezy summer dress and flats, she turns a radiant smile on me, her pale green eyes sparkling in the sunshine. "I've made the occasional pharmacy run for her and carried up her parcels from time to time, but you're really forcing me to up my game now."

She laughs, leaning over to kiss me. "I couldn't pass up the blueberries, and I'm sure she'll appreciate having a few days' worth of fresh vegetables."

I make a skeptical sound, but I like that Evelyn thought of it. Christ, I like everything about being out with her today, doing things I see normal couples do every weekend. It's a foreign concept to me, sharing my day and my neighborhood with someone. While I would have expected it to feel strange or awkward, with Evelyn it is neither of those things.

If anything, it is the sense of contentment I feel that alarms me the most.

It's too easy to weave her into the fabric of my world when I look at her right now. Too easy to let down my guard and forget that someone has been watching her— someone who still has the benefit of hiding in the shadows, lurking just out of my reach.

Until I'm certain she's safe and that every threat is eliminated, I have to be first and foremost the man committed to her protection. Not the man distracted by his desire for her . . . and the deepening affection that I can no longer deny, least of all to myself.

For what isn't the first time today, she reaches into her purse and takes out a small spiral notepad and adds a few details to a lingerie sketch she's working on. Sheepishly, she glances at me and finds me watching her draw.

"Sorry," she says, snapping the notebook closed. "I get a little obsessive sometimes when it comes to new designs."

"Don't be sorry. Can I look?"

She hesitates for a moment, seeming a bit uncertain before opening the little sketch pad and handing it to me. It's a detail drawing of a lovely bra with delicate, pearl-studded straps and lacy cups. Below the sketch showing it from the front is one displaying the unusual side-closure of the piece.

"There are no hooks or clasps," she explains, leaning closer and pointing to the sketch. "It stays on using a touch fastener instead, see? It can be done with one hand. All the wearer needs to do is press the two ends of the bra together and it's set. It comes off just as easily. And it can be custom-made to close on either side, based on customer preference or need."

I lift my gaze to her bright, excited expression. "This is an adaptive design. For someone missing a limb."

She nods. "I started thinking about it back in the locker room at the gym last night with Kelsey and Tameka and Lori. I have some ideas for panties and bustiers, too." She shrugs, taking the notepad out of my loose grasp. "Anyway, they're just ideas. I won't be the first designer to offer adaptive lingerie, but I want L'Opale's pieces to be as beautiful and unique as anything else we create."

I'm staring, but damn if I can help it. I'm more than impressed. I'm proud of her. And I'm touched to think that she would take this kind of interest in my friends. My chest is heavy with all of the emotions she inspires within me.

She slips the pad back into her purse. When she

pivots back around toward me, I slide my hands into her loose hair and slant my lips over hers.

"What's that for?" she asks, smiling up at me after I kiss her, her forehead resting against mine.

"You, Evelyn. Just for being who you are."

Her gaze softens, but I see the sultry edge of desire that's still simmering below the surface. I see the question in her eyes, and I would be only too happy to oblige. "Shall we go?"

"Yes."

I put cash on the bill that's lying next to my elbow on the table. I'm reaching for the bag from the market when my phone chimes with an incoming call. I know the custom ringtone, even though I don't hear it very often.

"I need to take this." At Evelyn's nod, I unlock the screen and accept the call. "Hi, Mom. Everything okay?"

"Oh, honey." My mother's voice sounds breathless and strained. "I'm sorry to bother you, but your brothers are all at work or I would've called them first."

I glance at Evelyn, who's staring at me in quiet concern. "What's going on, Mom?"

"It's your father. He fell in the bedroom just now." She exhales, and it comes out as a sob. "I tried to help him up, but I'm not strong enough. And you know how he feels about calling the paramedics—"

"It's okay. I'll be there." Evelyn is on her feet alongside me while I talk. We collect our things and start heading out of the restaurant at an urgent pace. "I'm leaving right now, Mom. I'll get there as fast as I can."

The thirty-minute drive to Bayside takes less than

LARA ADRIAN

twenty.

Maybe I should have insisted that Evelyn stay behind at my apartment, but I feel better with her beside me. Not only because her well-being is still my primary focus and concern, but for the simple fact that I want her with me. I need her.

We get out of my car and approach the front door of my parents' mid-century brick Cape Cod house where my mother waits behind the screen door, watching for me to arrive. She's petite, but she looks even more so today. The stress of my father's stroke is wearing on her. I'm sure his explosive temper hasn't helped the situation.

"Are you all right?" I ask my mother, after hastily introducing the two women who matter the most in my life. This isn't the way I would have preferred for them to meet for the first time, but since when has my father ever made a damn thing easy for me? "Where is he?"

"In the master bedroom," she says, her doe-brown eyes red-rimmed and weighted with puffy shadows beneath them. "I think he's okay, but he can't get up. Stubborn man. He just won't listen to me when I tell him he has to take things easy."

I squeeze her shoulder. "It'll be fine, Mom. I'll handle him."

Evelyn gives me a reassuring nod. Leaving her to look after my mom, I pivot and stalk down the central hallway to look for my father.

I find him lying in a heap only a few paces away from his side of the old queen-size bed in the master bedroom. He's always been a big man, solid muscles on a tall, substantial frame. Now all of his bulk is dead weight on the floor. No wonder Mom stood no chance of lifting him.

The old man knows I'm in the room, but he doesn't even attempt to look up as I step inside. "What the fuck are you doing here?"

"I came to help."

As I near him, I smell the ammonia punch of urine. The front of his faded blue cotton pajama bottoms are soaked with it.

His thinning, copper-and-gray hair is matted and damp. His silver beard has grown in even more since he was admitted to the hospital, but it is unkempt and patchy. His jowly cheeks sag, in particular the left one.

My chest tightens at the sight of him like this. I grew up seeing a man with an immutable pride. That he's been reduced to this, even temporarily, blunts some of the anger I feel toward him for his disregard of me all these years.

I hunker down beside him and put my hand on the rounded hump of his shoulder. He shakes off my touch as if I'm diseased.

"Do I look like I want your help?" His voice is hoarse, some of his words slurred.

"No, Pop. I don't imagine you want my help. But it looks like you need it."

"Linda!" He bellows for my mother as if I'm not in the room. "Goddamn it, did you call him?"

She comes to the open doorway, panic in her face. "Is everything all right?"

I nod, telling myself to treat this situation like I would if he were an injured comrade. No emotion, taking nothing that is said or done personally. "We're fine," I reassure my mom. "I've got this, I promise."

Once she's retreated back to the living room with Evelyn, I turn a flat look on my dad. "You're scaring

Mom. You need to take things slow for a while. Do it for her, at least."

"Don't tell me what I need to do."

"Someone has to. You obviously don't want to listen to your doctors or Mom."

He glowers up at me, those narrowed, light hazel eyes shooting pure venom. "I want you to leave."

"I will," I tell him tonelessly. "First, I need to get you cleaned up and back in bed."

He grumbles but starts to move. I take him under the arm and try to support him, but it's clear that my once formidable father can't even stand up right now.

He sags back down to the floor on a grunted exhalation. From the other end of the hallway, I can hear Evelyn's soft voice talking to my mother.

My father hears her too. "Who's out there?"

"Her name is Evelyn. She's with me."

I'm not sure how to introduce her to my parents. To call her my girlfriend after only a couple of weeks feels abrupt, and yet the affection I hold for her in my heart makes the term seem inadequate.

No label I'd give her right now is significant enough to describe what she means to me.

Not that it matters to my father right now. He curses tightly. "Christ, you brought an audience with you? You think I'm some goddamn sideshow?"

I ignore his rancor. God knows, I'm experienced enough at dealing with it that it no longer intimidates me. It hasn't since I was a boy.

"Come on, old man. Stow your pride for a minute and let's get this done."

I heft him up to his feet and quickly place my shoulder under his arm. I walk him into the bathroom and sit him down on the closed toilet seat. There is a metal bar running waist-high along the wall now, an update installed sometime after he had the stroke.

"Hold on to the rail," I order him, shocked to see him comply. He slumps there, looking haggard and beaten down. "Where do you keep your clean underwear and pajamas?"

He jerks his hand in the direction of the bedroom bureau. I go there and retrieve what I need. As I walk back into the bathroom, he is struggling with the buttons of his pajama top.

"I'll get that."

He drops his arms and I unfasten the shirt and push it off his rounded shoulders and the spongy muscles of his once powerful biceps. He watches me work on him, rage simmering in his eyes even though I can see that he's losing steam.

"I'll bet you like seeing me like this," he remarks weakly. His breath wheezes out of him on a bitter chuckle. "I'll bet you couldn't wait to see me lying in there unable to do a damn thing for myself. Like some pitiful, lame—"

He stops himself from saying the rest, but I hear it anyway. "Like me, Pop?"

He glances away quickly, his lips pressed flat, his jaw quivering behind the tight line of his mouth. "It's not what I meant."

"Sure it is." I was wrong when I told myself his disdain didn't hurt. I can see the shame in his face, and it sears me to think my injury has given him the excuse to think even less of me than he did before. "You want to know the truth? My life got infinitely better after I lost my leg."

His head slowly swings back to me, disbelief in his glassy eyes. I give him a cold smile.

"It got better because I got away from Bayside, away from this house. Away from your contempt for me. I made a better life for myself."

He swallows, his scowl deepening, a mottled redness filling his sallow cheeks. For one perverse moment, I wish he had better control of his motor skills, if only so he would strike me. God knows, I've wanted to bruise him too.

And now that I've torn the dressing off this wound, I have to let it bleed out.

"You know, it shouldn't have surprised me that you never came to see me—not even once—while I was at Walter Reed. Sometimes, I actually think it helped. Your absence during those months of my recovery. Your total disregard for me, even before my injury. I got better just to spite you, because I knew you didn't give a shit if I lived or died."

He stares at me. "At least you give me credit for something. All this time, I assumed you only blamed me for fucking up your life."

I take a step back from him, blowing out a sharp breath. I push my hand through my hair and curse, low and bitter, through my clenched teeth. "You don't know a fucking thing about me. You never even tried. Why the hell should I care if you're lying in a puddle of your own piss on the floor? Why should I lift a goddamn finger to help you? I shouldn't give a damn what happens to you, old man."

He's trembling now, whether in humiliation or futile rage, I have no idea. "You think I want pity from you? Of all people, you think I want you feeling sorry for me?"

He tries to stand up, but only stumbles back down. His ass drops onto the toilet seat, the stench of urine and sweat invading my nostrils as I reach for his pajama bottoms and ruthlessly strip them off. I throw all of it into the tub beside us.

I wet a washcloth with warm water and soap and hand it to him to clean off. He really needs a shower or a bath, but Mom told me when we arrived that a visiting nurse was coming in the morning to look after him. He'll survive a few hours until then.

And the way my blood is seething in my veins, I can't get out of his house fast enough.

When I see that he's finished with the washcloth, I take it from him and rinse it out, then make quick work of dressing him in fresh underwear and pajamas. I know he's spitting mad. I can feel his depleted body vibrating with useless anger. But he's too weak to fight back.

I hoist him to his feet and shuffle him back into the bedroom, easing him down onto the mattress. Tears leak from the corners of his eyes as he lay there, glaring up at me.

"Go back to the city," he orders me in a low, raspy voice. "Do us both a favor. Don't come back."

I nod as if it's a reasonable request. As if it's exactly what I want to hear, I start walking away. But I'm angry too. I'm hurting, which only worsens my rage.

I pause at the threshold and lower my head on a curse. Then I glance back at him, my calm belying the furious storm that's lashing me from the inside.

"I know I must be a terrible disappointment to you. You sure as fuck never hid that opinion of me. But I want you know that my life on the other side of that bridge out there is damn good. In spite of your low expectations of me, I'm doing fucking great. Better than you can even fathom."

When he shows no reaction, I feel a jab of spite pricking me. I have the need to wound him the way he's wounded me, but I know the only soft target on my father is his Noble pride. As a provider, as the head of our family, and as a man.

"You want to know why I never wanted to be a cop like my brothers and you? Because I wanted to be something more. I didn't want to live in your shadow or that of the rest of the Nobles."

"And how'd that work out for you, son?" His flat reply hits me like a fist.

I feel the blow, but damn it, it's not enough. I wish he and I had let this fight happen years ago. Would have saved us both a lot of time and grief.

"You tell me, old man. With the promotion I got a couple weeks ago, it won't be long before I'm pulling down more in a year than you made in twenty busting your hump behind a badge."

My father looks at me for a moment, seeming intent on denying me the satisfaction of his anger now. He simply nods. "Congratulations. I guess I had you pegged right all along, Gabriel. You always were too good for this family."

I scoff sharply. "Everyone but you, right, Pop?"

I don't wait for him to reply, not that he would.

As soon as I step into the hallway, I am met with the shocked and saddened stares of both my mother and Evelyn.

Fuck. It's one thing for me to show such a humiliating lack of control in front of my old man. For my mother to see it—to have heard probably every demeaning word that he and I exchanged—shames me even more than anything my father could ever say or do.

"I'm sorry," I tell her, my voice low and clipped. "I'm leaving now."

I hate that I've hurt her tonight when I only came to help. I want to reach out for her, but I don't have any gentleness in me right now.

I've hurt Evelyn too. But her pain is for me.

And that only makes my self-directed contempt burn even more intensely.

I want to punch something.

More than anything, I need to release the pressure of the rage that's swirling inside me.

I know where I would go if Evelyn weren't with me. But I haven't stepped foot in one of Jared Rush's anonymous sex clubs since I met her.

I can't do it now, even though it would be the easiest, safest outlet for the volatility churning inside me. All I do know is that Evelyn won't be safe with me tonight.

Maybe not ever, if I am being honest with myself . . . and with her.

I grab her hand. "I need to get you out of here."

27

~ Evelyn ~

I have never seen Gabe this way.

The terrifying silence that filled the drive back to the city has deepened into a black and expanding void as we exit his car and walk up to his apartment. I can feel the rage that has cloaked him since his confrontation with his father.

I can feel the pain in him too.

I've been too uncertain to try to reach him while we were in the car, too afraid he would reject my compassion. Now, as we enter his apartment, all I want is to bridge the chasm I fear is opening up between us tonight.

He walks ahead of me into the darkness, pausing just inside to turn on the light switch. I close the door behind me and move toward him, placing my palm gently on his shoulder. His muscles are tense beneath his dark T-shirt.

The firm sinews flinch at my contact, his spine going rigid.

"Are you all right?" I whisper, pressing a kiss to his back. He lets his breath go, a restrained exhalation that only confirms the fact that, no, he is not all right at all. Not even close. I wrap my arms around him from behind. "I'm sorry about what happened with your father tonight."

I feel him take air into his lungs, but he doesn't respond. His strong hands cover my forearms where they are banded loosely around his waist. Instead of holding on to me, he opens the circle of my embrace and steps out of it.

"You need to stay away from me right now," he says, without turning around to look at me. His deep voice sounds wooden, edged with a strange tension I don't understand. "I don't need consoling. All I need is space."

Since he won't tolerate my hands on him, I wrap my arms around myself. The warmth helps, because staring at his back, I am suddenly feeling very cold.

He doesn't seem to want to talk to me any more than he wants me touching him, but I can't let him bear his anger and pain without letting him know that I am here for him. God, he has to know that. I want him to know I always will be.

"I think being alone is the last thing you really need right now, Gabe."

His answering scoff is barely audible. He says nothing, just walks away from me, heading toward the bedroom at the back of the hallway. Each step he takes feels like a mile to me. I feel empty, confused . . . rejected.

But I go after him anyway.

I enter the bedroom and see he's got my duffel bag

in his hand. He starts gathering my things and placing them inside. The pair of sneakers I wore to the basketball game. The camisole I left folded on the nightstand after our lovemaking moved from the kitchen countertop to the bed this morning.

"What are you doing?"

"You can't be here tonight. I'm taking you home where you belong." He walks past me to the hallway bathroom to continue removing all evidence of me from the apartment. My hair dryer and makeup bag. The case that holds my toothbrush.

"I thought you invited me to stay here for the weekend. It's not over until tomorrow."

He slants me a regretful look. "This weekend was a nice little fantasy. But that's all it was. That's all it can be."

"What are you talking about?" I am standing in the open doorway of the bathroom, effectively blocking him inside. I know he would never hurt me, but I can't shake the feeling that I'm facing off against a caged tiger. Something wild and dangerous. "Gabe, there is nowhere else I want to be. I just want you to talk to me. Please."

"Don't you get it?" His nostrils flare, his handsome face twisted into an enraged scowl. "It's not talking I need right now. Not when I'm like this."

Even though I jump at his sharp tone, I take a step inside, shrinking the distance between us because I'm that desperate to reach him. "Then tell me what you need. Show me."

I can see the desire in his flashing, furious eyes. I can see the jagged need. Not even his anger can hide the fact that he wants me in spite of what he's saying.

I glance down and see that he is erect behind the

zipper of his dark jeans. On the sides of his neck, veins stand out like cables, pulsing so intensely I can almost hear the drum of his heartbeat in the thickened, electrified air between us.

Right now, he is coiled, dark energy in need of an outlet.

Maybe I should be afraid of everything I see in him tonight, but I'm not.

He pulls my silk kimono off the hook near the towel bar. He's about to stuff it into the duffel bag, but I halt his hand. I take the garment from him.

"Dammit, Gabriel. Don't shut me out."

His gaze bores into mine, the hazel turned stormy gray beneath the harsh slashes of his brows. "I can't give you what you want, Eve. And you can't give me what I need."

"Bullshit." I shake my head. "That's bullshit, and you know it."

"You want me to use you?" His scowl deepens. His voice is rife with torment, but also arousal. I know him enough to recognize the rawness of his lust. "You deserve more than this. Christ, you deserve a hell of a lot more than me."

I take another step closer. "Why don't you let me decide that for myself?"

He swears under his breath, then brushes past me, stalking out toward the living area with my duffel bag gripped in his hand.

I should go. If that's really what he wants, if he's just going to keep pushing me away, I should leave him to his solitude and save myself the heartache of loving someone who cannot—or will not—love me in return.

Because that's what this is, this burgeoning sense of

yearning I feel for him. Love.

Oh, God. I am so in love with Gabriel Noble, it hurts.

I drift out to the hallway, the kimono grasped numbly in my fingers. I find Gabe standing near the door, waiting for me to concede to his demand that I go. No matter what either one of us truly wants.

He needs this control.

That's how he copes with pain, be it emotional or physical. He reaches for control.

He needs it more than solitude. Maybe even more than he needs me.

I don't know why it's taken me this long to see it, but now it seems so clear. I think back to the bondage we played at last night, how it excited him to be in control of my body, in control of my pleasure as well as his own.

It excited me too.

As I walk slowly toward him, I pull the silk belt off the kimono and let the garment fall to the floor. Gabe looks at me as I approach, his gaze flicking to my fingers as I tie one end of the belt around my left wrist.

His face is a mask of fury and desire. "What the fuck are you doing?"

I don't answer until I am standing in front of him with only a foot of space to separate us. "Don't you remember what I told you? I am yours, Gabriel. So, now the rest is up to you. Are you mine?" I hold the loose end of the belt out to him. "If you are, then take me. Take me the way you need to, whatever that has to mean to you tonight. Let me be what you need."

"You are." The words gust out of him, thick and raw.

He grabs the silk ribbon from my fingers and yanks me forward. I crash against the front of his big body, my tethered hand pinned between us. And then his mouth is on mine. His kiss is brutal. A hard claiming that steals my breath and sends a current of fire licking through every fiber of my being.

I melt into him, his name a jagged sob as our tongues clash and our bodies press and grind together. Relief floods me as his mouth consumes me. I haven't lost him tonight. Far from it.

I think, for the first time since we've met, we are truly only just discovering each other now.

He breaks away from our kiss, his eyes wild with hunger. My summery dress has buttons down the front from bodice to hem. Gabe manages only the first few before he rips it open on a dark curse. He dips his head, his mouth latching on to the curve of my bared shoulder.

"I'll buy you another," he snarls against my skin. "I'll buy you a hundred new dresses."

"I don't care." I moan, the ruined dress already forgotten as he unfastens my bra and lifts one of my breasts to his lowered mouth. He tongues my nipple before catching it between his teeth. I cry out at the pleasurable pain, which arcs through my body like lightning.

Dominating my mouth again with his kiss, he caresses and strokes me, smoothly ridding me of my panties before sliding his hand between my legs. His thumb teases my clit, his fingers delving into the molten heat of my sex.

"Please," I beg, writhing into his touch.

And I need to feel him too. I find the hem of his T-shirt and start to slip my hand under the material. I feel a tug on my wrist and realize he still holds the silk belt. He tightens the slack, at the same time stepping back to take hold of my other hand now too.

He binds my wrists together, tying the belt too tight for me to escape. Not that the thought of it even occurs to me. I have no fear, only wild excitement . . . and complete trust.

I stand before him naked and bound, and trembling with anticipation.

Gabe's fevered gaze drinks me in, a slow perusal that only makes the bulge of his erection appear on the verge of bursting out of his jeans.

He raises my tied arms up over my head, a silent command to keep them there.

His touch sears me, both hands moving over every inch of my body. Then he abruptly turns me around and presses me forward against the wall until my cheek rests against the cool drywall. His denim-clad thigh nudges my legs farther apart—wider, then wider still.

I jolt when his kiss lands on the center of my spine. I squirm when his tongue drifts lower, licking a trail of fire all the way down to the cleft of my ass. A finger invades my sex, then another, pushing deep, spreading my juices and stroking my inner walls until I am panting with arousal and quivering on unsteady legs.

"I can't be gentle," he warns me. "Not this time."

I shake my head. "I don't want you to be."

I hear the rasp of his zipper behind me, then the rough tug of his clothing in the instant before I feel the thick head of his cock at the drenched seam of my body. He doesn't undress. It seems he has no patience for that.

He rams into me, fucking me with savage thrusts. His strokes are hard and unhinged, one hand clutching my hip while the other is fisted in my hair. Our coupling is primal, a relentless, animal act.

And I have never been more aroused in my life.

The words he utters are filthy, worshipful. His voice low and coarse, like gravel and velvet. I am lost to the overwhelming power of him now. Pleasure streaks into my nerve endings, bright white, lightning hot.

If control was what he needed tonight, I am only too glad to surrender all of mine. Anything if it means he'll keep driving his cock into me as if he can't get close enough, can't go deep enough. He needs this, and I revel in the fact that it is me who's giving him this.

"Fuck," he growls beside my ear. "I'm gonna come." He powers into me without losing his pace, his thrusts rough and urgent, verging on violent. "I need to come."

He's not asking for permission. Tonight, he has only need. Need for this domination, this fevered release.

And, yes, need for me.

I need it too—this connection to him that is both primitive and sublime. I want him to go on like this forever, but his release is already slamming into him. Behind me, his heavy frame goes rigid. He drives deep, so deep it wrenches a small scream from my throat. His strangled roar erupts out of him and he pulls me tight against his body as a shudder rakes him and the scorching blast of his release fills me.

He keeps pumping, his arm locked around my waist as the aftershocks convulse over him. His shaft is still hard, each slick thrust inflaming my unspent desire. He curses, his hot breath skating across the back of my neck.

"I didn't wait for you."

I can't see his face, but I can hear the self-recrimination in his raspy voice. I hear the apology in his words. I shake my head. "It's all right. Never hold back with me. I love that I can give you this. I love . . ."

My confession drifts off when I feel him reaching up to untie the bonds at my wrists. He gently pulls out of me, and I can't help moaning at the loss. But then he turns me around, his strong arms still caging me against the wall. His face is intense with emotion, with so much tender care and deep affection it makes my throat catch.

He lowers his head and kisses me. It is slow and restrained, but I can taste the wildness still thrumming inside him.

"This wasn't supposed to happen, Eve. *You* weren't supposed to happen." He strokes my cheek with trembling fingers. "I need you. Christ . . . I've just used you like a fucking animal, and I still need you."

"Then have me, Gabriel."

With the silk ribbon still dangling from one wrist, I reach down to caress his erection, which is still thick and jutting from his open jeans, still slick and hot from his release. He holds my stare, his handsome face caught between pleasure and torment as I run my hand over him.

He closes his eyes for a moment, his head dropped back on a low moan. Taking me in his arms, he lifts me off my feet and wraps my legs around him.

Then he walks me into the bedroom, where we have all night to express the endless and erotic depths of our mutual need for each other.

28

~ Gabriel ~

Evelyn yawns as I gather her close in the shower after we've washed each other. "I don't want to Monday today."

I kiss the top of her head, smiling as she burrows deep into my chest. "Unfortunately, I have some business at headquarters, so we need to get out of here in about an hour."

She groans. "You're no fun."

I grunt, tweaking her nipple. "That's not what you said last night."

I don't think either of us got more than a couple hours of sleep once we hit my bed. This morning came too damn early, but I can hardly complain when Evelyn woke me with soft, demanding kisses and questing hands.

We made love slowly as dawn illuminated the

bedroom. After a night of seemingly unquenchable need, today my desire for her has calmed into a slow-burning, deep ache that I feel as intensely in my chest as I do in my blood.

Maybe even more.

She lifts her head, frowning up at me. "I thought you were coming to L'Opale with me this morning for a walk-through of the new security system with the staff?"

The smile I intend to be reassuring instead feels forced. "I'll drop you there, and then I'll come back later, once my business is finished with your brother and Nick."

I'm not exactly comfortable with the idea of leaving her at the boutique without eyes on her, so as soon I have a minute alone, I'll have to call O'Connor or another of my team to park a vehicle nearby and watch the shop until I return.

A playful light shines in Evelyn's eyes as she kisses my chin. "A little timeout today is probably a good idea. I'm not sure I can be around you this morning without either smiling like a cat in the cream or wanting to tear your clothes off."

"Believe me, the feeling is mutual, Ms. Beckham."

Last night her complete surrender to me is a gift I'll always cherish. She was the balm I needed after my confrontation with my father. Her acceptance of me—even at my weakest, even when I was trying to push her away—is the glue that's keeping me together now, when I know I could be just a few hours away from losing everything.

Because I can't go another day without telling her the truth.

No matter what that costs me with Andrew

Beckham and Dominic Baine, today I need to explain to them that I'm involved with her.

And then I need to alert Evelyn about the danger I believe she's in, and the fact that I have been assigned to watch over her.

There is so much more I need to tell her. Words I almost said last night.

Words I long to say now, as I hold her under the warm spray of the shower and feel her heartbeat drumming against my chest.

That I can't imagine being with another woman now that I've found her.

That I want to build a future with her.

Most of all, that I love her.

I keep all of those words inside for now. It wouldn't be fair to say them before she knows all the rest. Instead I lift her lips to mine and kiss her, wishing we didn't have to start this day I'm already beginning to dread.

"Gabe," she murmurs. "I don't want to go."

I swallow, smoothing my thumb over her cheek. "I know, baby."

Does she feel the same sense of foreboding that I do? The worry that this weekend really was the unsustainable fantasy I tried to claim it was last night? She had refused to accept it then. Now, it seems like we're both afraid to be the first to let go.

With the water still raining down on my back, I kiss her deeply, moving my mouth over hers in an unrushed joining of our lips and tongues and shallow breaths.

She skims her hands over my chest and shoulders, a fluid caress that wrings a low moan from me. Her touch soothes every bit as much as it inflames. Her fingers skate lower, and even the briefest attention she gives my cock makes it stir to life all over again.

I touch her, too, stroking the pretty softness of her neck, curving my palm under the perfect curves of her breasts. I lower my head and suckle each tight nipple, taking things slowly this time, savoring every taste of her, every gasp and sigh.

Her sex is silky and hot against my fingertips. She melts into my palm, her mouth locked onto mine as I gentle her into a shivery, breathless climax.

It's enough for me, but before I realize what she's doing, she sinks down in front of me. Her palms trail down the length of my thighs. She doesn't shy away from the blunted end of my left leg. Her caress encompasses all of me, her gaze following her touch with a reverence that staggers me.

Feeling unworthy of the depth of her care right now, I suck in a breath, then push it out on a dark chuckle. "You know, I never considered my stump to be an erogenous zone, but you're changing my mind."

I mean it to lighten the mood, but it seems to have the exact opposite effect. Her mouth curves with devilish amusement. Then her hands move languidly up to my hardened cock once more. "What about this erogenous zone?"

Kneeling on the shower floor in front of me, she closes her lips over my erection and takes me deep into her mouth. *Ah, Christ.* My hips buck in response to the wet grip of her lips and tongue moving up and down my shaft.

"Eve." I reach down to tangle my fingers through the wet strands of her dark hair.

She is my anchor, grounding me in more ways than simply keeping me upright.

I stare down at her as she draws me into the haven of her mouth. The pleasure is too intense. So is my love for this woman. The combination rockets through me like wildfire.

I clench my molars together and bellow as the pressure coils to the breaking point. I should be depleted after last night and this morning. The simple fact is, I'll never reach my limit when it comes to her.

"Baby." It's a warning she doesn't heed. Nor does she yield to the tightening of my hand in her hair. Her mouth takes me deeper, her cheeks holding me firmer as my release boils at the base of my shaft. It is an invitation I'm too far gone to resist.

I come on a roar. She answers with a soft moan as I erupt against the back of her throat.

"Fuck." A deep shudder racks me. When my leg starts to shake beneath me, Evelyn gives my shaft one last lick, then rises up, lending her body for support as I hobble over to the teak bench at the back of the stall. I drop onto it and sag back against the cold tiles, breathing heavily.

She looks far too satisfied as she kneels between my parted thighs, then takes my face in her hands and gives me a firm kiss. "You okay?"

I manage a smirk. "Never better. Now, get out of this shower before you kill me, woman."

She laughs. "I'll go get dressed and make some coffee. You need anything?"

"I'm good." Hell, I'm better than good, I think as I watch step out of the shower and wrap herself in a towel.

After a few minutes, I rally enough energy to stand up and soap off again, then I cut the water and towel off while I hear her in the kitchen, filling the coffee maker.

She pops her head into the bathroom a moment later, looking fresh and beautiful in one of the summer dresses she brought for the weekend and her damp, dark hair swept into a loose twist on top of her head. "Coffee's on. I'm going to drop that market bag at Mrs. Bernstein's door, then warm up a couple of her blueberry muffins for us for breakfast."

"All right."

I almost tell her not to bother with the produce, but she's already gone back to the kitchen to get it. I tie a towel around my hips and hop back to the bedroom to get dressed and don my prosthesis.

"Be right back," she calls from the kitchen.

I hear the twist of the deadbolts on my apartment as she opens the door to leave.

For an instant—one awful, time-frozen instant—everything goes perfectly silent.

Then Evelyn screams.

29

~ Gabriel ~

I bolt from the bedroom, stumbling more than running.

I've never hated my prosthesis more than in the seconds it takes me to reach the corridor outside my apartment. My suit pants are half-zipped, my white dress shirt flapping behind me like a sail.

My heart is lodged like a boulder in my throat. "Evelyn!"

I race to where she has fallen on her bent knees just past the open door. The bag of produce is spilled where she dropped it, leafy green vegetables and tiny blueberries scattered in all directions on the floor of the corridor.

Her horrified scream has turned into a low, wounded-animal howl as she rocks herself, staring aghast at the disturbing images and obscene scrawl that someone has plastered on the wall across from my apartment.

Pictures of Evelyn.

Fashion show photographs, candids, and selfies. A random and varied collection of images, all of them featuring the emaciated, virtually skeletal, very ill young woman she had been years ago. There are dozens of them, each one documenting her drastic decline.

And one image that's not nearly as old as the others.

That one is just days old. Not a photo at all, but a closeup, intimate screenshot captured of the two of us on Friday at L'Opale when I impulsively made love to Evelyn on top of her desk.

"Jesus Christ."

As if the images weren't enough to convey the deranged state of the perpetrator's mind, they are accompanied by two furious messages scribbled in some kind of red ink.

BITCH.

WHORE.

On a broken cry, Evelyn scrambles to her feet and flies at the wall, tearing at the printed photos in a frenzy and trying to scrub away the hideous words with her hands.

Some of my neighbors come out to see what the disturbance is. I bark at them to get back inside, that this is a private issue and I've got it under control.

But this situation is neither of those things.

Whoever did this just took it public, and the fact that it occurred not ten feet from my home tells me just how close I've come to failing Evelyn.

I don't have a fucking thing under control right now. Least of all, my fury.

Or my bone-deep fear for her safety.

I stalk to the wall and rip down the rest of the images, starting with the one taken via the camera that's obviously been obscured inside her office. In something on her desk, from the looks of it. Evelyn's so overwhelmed right now, I'm not sure she's processed the full scope of what she's seeing.

I stuff some of the images in my pockets—including the infuriatingly invasive one from the other day. The rest I crush in my fist. As for the red words now smeared over the painted drywall, I glance down and see an open tube of designer lipstick lying discarded against the baseboard. I pick it up carefully, using the edges of a photo to avoid compromising any fingerprints that may be on it.

A wave of black rage pours over me to think that someone was out here delivering this cowardly, malicious attack no more than a few hours ago. While I was on the other side of the door losing myself in the pleasure of Evelyn's body and rationalizing that so long as she was with me she was safe.

"It's okay," I tell her, struggling to keep the violence out of my voice. "Sweetheart, I'll take care of this. I'm going to make it go away."

She can't hear me. She's hyperventilating, a thready, endless moan leaking out of her as she scrubs at the words with a crumpled wad of photos.

"My phone," she murmurs. "Someone took these off my phone. Oh, my God. How did they get them?" Her voice climbs in confusion. In rising hysteria. "Who would do this to me? Why?"

I don't have those answers for her, but damn it, I'm not going to rest until I know.

When I find out who's responsible, I will be merciless.

I will fucking end them.

"Come on, baby." I wrap my arm around her shaking shoulders and physically pull her away from the wall. "I need to get you out of here."

I have to take her to the only place where I know for certain she'll be safe now.

She doesn't resist. The fight is seeping out of her by the second. She's withdrawing, falling into a vacant-eyed silence that guts me even more than her screams and tears.

As soon as we're inside my apartment, I take the pictures out of her hands and dump them in the trash. Then I fetch the rest of my clothes and my service weapon, shrugging into it all as I grab my keys and hustle her out of the unit.

She doesn't ask where we're going.

She doesn't utter a single word for the entire drive down to the Baine Building. Just sits in the passenger seat beside me staring out the windshield with shell-shocked eyes and tears drying in chalky streaks on her face and chin. In her lap, her hands are stained red from the lipstick, fingers trembling.

Damn it. I glance at her, knowing I am to blame for this as much as anyone—including the sadistic asshole who put up those photos.

When we reach the building, I don't bother with the garage. It will take too long and right now the most important thing is getting Evelyn inside and somewhere comfortable. Leaving my Lexus parked at the curb, I hold Eve under my arm and walk her into the lobby.

It's early, but O'Connor has already reported to

work. She's at the desk with another member of the security team, but rushes toward me as soon as she sees me come in with Evelyn.

"What happened?"

"Long story, and I don't have time to explain now. I need to see Beck right away. Will you find someplace quiet for Evelyn?"

"There's no one in fitness room lounge. I was just up there working out before my shift started a few minutes ago."

I nod. "Take her there and stay with her."

Evelyn blinks slowly. "I'm all right," she murmurs, not actually sounding like it, but at least she's starting to come back around. She glances down at herself and winces. "God, look at me. I'm a mess."

I stroke her cheek. "You're going to be fine. Kelsey's going to help you clean up."

"Of course, I will," O'Connor says. She puts her arm around Evelyn, slanting a concerned look at me. "What about you, Gabe? Are you okay?"

I don't know how to answer that yet, so I don't. "I need to let Beck know she's here."

Her brow knits, but she nods. "He's in his office, last I knew."

I take the elevator up to the executive floor and head straight past Beck's assistant. His door is open. I must look like hell because when he glances up from his laptop, some of the color drains from his face. "Something's happened."

I struggle to collect myself enough to explain the situation. "First, you need to know that Evelyn is all right. She's here in the building with O'Connor."

Frowning, he vaults up, long strides carrying him

around to the front his big desk. "What's going on?"

"Whoever's been watching her just got too fucking close."

"What are you talking about?"

I take out the crumpled photos that are in my pants pocket and slam them down on the desk—all but the explicit one, which I've sequestered in my jacket when I arrived at the Baine Building. "Someone stole these pictures off her phone and plastered them where they knew she would find them this morning."

He stares at the images of his sister looking almost unrecognizably frail and unhealthy. His frown furrows deeper. There is confusion in his eyes. Along with horror . . . and anguish.

When he speaks, his tone is smoldering with the same kind of thinly held outrage that's also burning in me. "Who did this?"

"I don't know. But we need to tell her everything we do know so far." I force myself to look away from the pictures. "We've kept her in the dark to avoid scaring her, Beck, but the sick fuck who got his hands on these photos just took that choice away from us. She's terrified. I can only imagine how violated she must feel right now."

"Jesus." Beck's hands shake a little as he picks up one of the torn and wrinkled photographs.

It's an image of Evelyn in a flesh-baring couture outfit that shows the worst ravages of her eating disorder. Her long legs are little more than bones, her ribs and shoulders so pronounced she could pass for a prisoner of war.

But it's her face that's even more tragic to see in that image. Beneath the stage makeup, her cheeks are sunken and sallow. Her gorgeous green eyes seem huge in her gaunt face, ringed with thick black lashes that don't quite hide the dull resignation in her stare. Despite her sultry smile, she looks only moments from collapse in the photo. Yet she is beautiful. Stunning, even though someone would have to be blind not to recognize her disease.

"I remember this photo," Beck murmurs. "It was taken when she was doing a show in Paris. Her last show, as it turned out. She went into heart failure that night. The doctors only narrowly saved her."

I nod in acknowledgment of what Eve told me about that time in her life. "You flew there and brought her home."

"I thought I was going to lose her. It was nothing short of hell seeing my sister go through all of that." He swallows hard and seems to regroup a bit before he drops the photo and looks at me. "Where did you say you found these? At the boutique?"

"No." I feel a tendon jump in my jaw. "Someone stuck them to a wall outside my apartment."

I don't miss the flicker of confusion that passes over his face. He tilts his head, and his dark brows lower over suspicious eyes. "You said Eve's seen them."

"Yes, she has. She was with me this morning."

"With you." There is a dangerous undercurrent to his response. It takes him a moment before he puts my remark into context. "You don't mean guarding her."

"No, Beck. She spent the weekend with me at my place." His gaze hardens as I speak. I don't know if the truth will make things better or worse between us, but either way he has to know. "We've become . . . involved. I'm in love with her."

He scoffs, incredulous. "What the hell do you mean, you're in love with her?"

"I want her to be part of my life. I think she wants that too."

"You're telling me you fucked my sister?"

He leans hard on the accusation. I can't argue that he's got a right to be disgusted with me. Hell, I'm disgusted with myself for breaking my friend's trust. But I can't apologize for how I feel about Evelyn.

"I realize this isn't what you want to hear, especially right now. But I'm not asking for your permission, Beck. I love her—"

I'm not expecting his punch. It comes up on my left and cracks me hard under the jaw. I stagger back on my prosthesis, tasting blood in my mouth.

"You son of a bitch," Beck hisses. "She's not one of Jared Rush's shiny, brainless playthings from one of his clubs. She's my sister."

"You think I don't know that?"

He glowers at me, fury rolling off him. "Your job was to protect her, not fuck her and put her in danger. You were supposed to watch over her. Keep her safe, whatever that took. That was your promise to me, Gabe. Goddamn it, that's what you're being paid to do."

I feel a shift in the charged air that surrounds us. Then I hear the sudden, hitched inhalation from somewhere behind me.

I swivel my head and see Evelyn standing in the open doorway.

My heart sinks when I see her stricken expression.

"Gabe . . . is that true?"

30

~ Evelyn ~

I don't know what hurts my heart more—seeing Gabe's cut lip and guilty expression, or hearing Andrew state that Gabe's being paid to care about what happens to me.

"Is it true?"

"Evelyn." Gabe takes a step toward me and I take one back.

As much as I want to feel his arms around me, as much as I need his comfort after everything that happened this morning, first, I have to know.

"Am I part of your job description?"

His hazel eyes flick down, and it's as if the floor beneath me has gone soft. "I wanted to tell you. I should have."

I draw air into my lungs, but it doesn't feel like enough to keep me standing. I am already wrung out and shaken after seeing the hideous photos and ugly words wielded against me like weapons in the hands of an invisible enemy.

Now, I feel as if I am looking a different enemy in the face.

Both of them.

Andrew's voice is solemn with concern. "Evie, the important thing here is you're okay."

Mutely, I shake my head. I'm not looking at my brother. I'm staring at Gabriel Noble. The man whose silence is breaking my heart.

Andrew exhales a sigh and starts walking toward me. "Come on. You look as if you're wilting. No wonder, considering what you've been through this morning. I'm sorry for how upsetting this must be, Evie."

"I'm not wilting." I glance at him. "Yes, I'm upset. I'm confused and angry, but I'm not wilting."

Even I can hear the steel in my voice. Andrew stares at me for a moment, as if weighing my resolve. "Evelyn, I think—"

"Go, Andrew. Please. I want to talk to Gabe."

"All right." His hand falls slowly to his side, then he crosses the large office, pausing by me at the door. "I'll be in the conference room just down the hall if you need me."

I don't reply. I can't turn off my affection for my brother, no more than I can be surprised to learn that he would go so far as to hire a personal security guard to look after me without my knowledge.

I'm angry with him for that, but Gabe's participation is the deeper pain.

We're alone in the big room, but neither one of us makes any move to lessen the space between us. It only seems to grow as I study him in his stoic silence.

"How long, Gabe?"

His jaw looks tight, his gaze sober as he holds mine. "That day at the zoo. After I discovered your tire had been slashed."

"Slashed?" My head tilts back, the word cutting through me. "I thought it was just a flat."

"I know," he says. "Because we made the decision not to tell you."

"*We*," I repeat. "You and my brother, working together. Making decisions about my life without bothering to include me."

"Andrew didn't think you could handle what I suspected was going on."

"Which was?"

"That you were singled out deliberately. That someone had their eye on you, not only while you were at the event that day, but for a while. I couldn't prove it. All I had to go on were my instincts." Now, he takes a step toward me. Just one. His tongue sweeps his split lower lip, erasing the blood that's gathering near the rising bruise of what I assume came at the end of my brother's fist. "I didn't know Beck and Nick were going to tap me to watch over you. I should have refused, but—"

I scoff, starting to understand. "But by then, I'd already thrown myself at you—that first night you came to the shop after the power went out, and again, after you drove me home from the zoo. Especially then."

He scowls at me, shaking his head. "That's exactly why I should've told your brother no. But the fact is, I couldn't imagine putting your safety in anyone else's hands."

"It wasn't only my safety you wanted in your hands, was it, Boy Scout?"

I don't want to be this bitter. I can't believe I have it in me when roughly an hour ago all I felt was numb and in shock as I sat in that hallway outside Gabe's apartment.

"I can't say you didn't warn me, though, right? You told me you were always on duty. I just didn't realize how literally you meant it."

He curses under his breath. "The concern for your well-being all this time was justified. Those photos this morning are damn clear evidence of that."

"Do you know who put them there?"

"No. But I'm going to find out." He clears his throat. "Evelyn, there's something else you should know. Someone has been watching you at the shop. There was a monitoring device installed in the utility room. A device intended for digital spying. I'm talking about access to the shop's computers and data, your phone, possibly even the original security system. We believe it was an energy overload in the device that caused the power to go out in the boutique that one night. The good news is, that surge killed the device at the same time."

"A spying device." I swallow, trying to dislodge the knot of alarm that's suddenly settled in my throat. "You mean, that's how someone got access to the photos on my phone?"

"It's possible, yes. Or someone took them before, possibly while your purse was out of your hands the day you came here for your meeting with Avery Ross."

A detail leaps into my consciousness, something I saw in the hallway outside Gabe's apartment. "My red Dior lipstick. It was in my purse that day. I thought I lost it, but now I remember it was in my purse that morning. It wasn't there after the purse was found. Whoever took those pictures off my phone also had my lipstick. That's what they used to write those words on the wall." I feel sick over the next thought that invades my mind, but considering the way Katrina had been acting lately . . . "Do you think someone from L'Opale is behind all of this?"

"I'm looking into the possibility," he admits grimly. "I've got background checks in process for all of the boutique employees, past and present. If anything turns up, my brother Jake will let me know. There is . . . something more, Eve."

He pulls a crumpled photo out of his jacket pocket and holds it out to me where he stands across the room. I don't have to move any closer to see what it shows. Gabe and me, locked in a graphic pose on top of my desk.

"This was on the wall with the others," I murmur, just now realizing I've glimpsed the image earlier today. In my shock, it blurred into the overall horror of the entire display.

I'm repulsed to see it now. Not by anything Gabe and I did together, but at the idea that our privacy had been compromised. Violated.

The image had to have been taken on Friday. Just a few days ago.

I glance at him, confused. "You said the device stopped working the night of the power outage."

"This is something different. A hidden camera, obviously concealed in something in your office."

"Oh, my God." My stomach lurches. Nausea washes over me, cold and dizzying.

Slashed tires.

Background checks.

Spying devices and hidden cameras.

The shock of hearing all of this presses down on me. But even worse is the fact that neither my brother nor Gabe felt it necessary to discuss it with me.

Especially Gabe.

"How long would you have kept all of this from me? If this morning hadn't happened, how long would you and my brother have been willing to lie to me, to betray me? You let me make a fool of myself with you."

"No. Damn it." His mouth compresses. "It wasn't like that, Eve."

I scoff. "I told you things I never told anyone else in my life, not even Andrew. Not my friends. No one. And the whole time, you weren't being honest with me."

"I was," he insists. "About everything but this, I was. I wanted to tell you. I told your brother it wasn't right to keep you in the dark—"

"But you did. You had a choice, and you made it."

"Beck's my friend, Evelyn. He and Nick both."

"And let's not forget that Baine International is also your employer," I reply brittly. "That wonderful promotion and big raise you just received. More money in a year than your father's made in twenty, right? You couldn't jeopardize that."

Something hardens in his eyes. "Is that what you think?"

"I don't know what to think."

"Will it make a difference if I tell you that I love you? Because I do, Evelyn. I love you."

God, how I want to believe him. I want to run into his arms and never let go.

But my feet stay rooted to the floor. My heart continues to pound heavily, coldly, in my breast. Because today my trust in him was shattered.

I'm not sure how I'll get it back, no matter how desperately I wish I could.

And while he may have feelings for me, they weren't enough for him to trust me, either.

If he had, he wouldn't be standing here breaking my heart.

Emotion jams in my throat, a conflicting storm of regret and pain. It tastes like acid on my tongue, filling my mouth as he stares at me, his expression stoic in my lengthening silence.

When he speaks, his low voice is quiet, toneless. "Aren't you going to say anything?"

"Yes, Gabe. I think I need to say goodbye."

A stillness washes over him.

I want him to fight for me. As unfair and selfish as it is, dammit, I am waiting for him to fight. But he only stares at me for a long moment, a look of resignation in his eyes.

He walks forward, his steps controlled and measured, his carriage military precise. He pauses for a moment, just out of my reach.

"I'm sorry, Evelyn. I'm sorry for everything."

I stand there, my breath trapped in my lungs as he walks past me and out the door.

When I'm certain he's gone, when the muffled ding of the elevator signals its arrival to carry him away, I let the air go. It escapes my lips on a ragged sob.

31

~ Gabriel ~

O'Connor walks into my office a few minutes after I get there. "Evelyn went to look for you a few minutes ago. I know you told me to keep her in the fitness room lounge, but she insisted she didn't need a babysitter and I . . . Oh, shit."

She stops short, glancing at my holster and service weapon, which I've just removed and placed on my desk. The Baine International pin clatters as I set it down beside the other accoutrements of my job.

Former job.

I must look as pathetic as I feel, because her expression mutates into a soft sympathy that sets my teeth on edge. "What are you doing, Gabe?"

"What I should've done as soon as I realized how I felt about Evelyn."

"You're quitting?"

I give her a curt nod. "My resignation email should've already hit Dominic Baine's in-box."

"God, you're serious." She gapes at me. "What the hell just happened up there?"

"I fucked up." I shrug as if it's no big deal. As if my heart doesn't feel like it's just gone through a shredder.

I should have refused to let Evelyn push me away. I should have fought with every weapon at my command to convince her how I feel. That after having her in my life these past weeks, I can't imagine a day—or a night—without her. Nor do I want to imagine it.

Damn it, I should have told her it was her brother who insisted I shield her from the facts, even when I pressed him to tell her everything. To let me tell her the truth—all of it, including the fact that I was tasked with her personal security. That she was, in fact, part of my job description.

But she was never only that. Fuck, not even close.

I know I could have put the bulk of the blame on Beck. The secrets were his idea, his insistence. I know he wouldn't refute that. But blaming him would've only worsened the conflict between Evelyn and her brother. I know what it feels like to be estranged from family, to be so at odds you can't even be in the same room together. I would never wish that for Evelyn and Beck. I'm not about to use that kind of damaging leverage to bolster my own wants and desires.

Even if I were willing to destroy their bond to try to strengthen mine with Evelyn, it wouldn't change the fact that I chose duty over telling her the truth. She was right. I had a choice and I made it.

I was afraid to put my job on the line, or to jeopardize my friendship with Beck and Nick. I felt I owed them both for taking a chance on me, for taking a leap of faith when no one else in my life had.

Now, I've blown everything to pieces.

The worst loss of all, the only one that means anything now, is the loss of Evelyn's faith in me. The loss of her friendship and trust.

The loss of her love.

I rake a hand through my hair and heave a sigh. "I crossed a line with Evelyn and I don't think there's any coming back from it."

O'Connor studies me. "You're in love with her."

"Desperately."

"You're in love with her, but you're leaving."

"It's what she wants."

"Shit, Gabe. I'm sorry."

"Yeah. Me too." Impatient to be gone before I no longer have the strength to adhere to Evelyn's wishes, I grab my jacket off the back of my chair, then swipe my keys from the edge of the desk. "I gotta go."

"Where to?"

I shrug. "I don't know. I just know I can't stay here."

That much is true. But despite the fact that I'm no longer part of the Baine security team, I will for damn sure be paying a visit to the boutique to turn Evelyn's office upside down to locate and destroy the camera someone's hidden there. In the meantime, I'll have one of my brothers test the lipstick tube at my apartment for fingerprints and sic a computer forensics investigator on all of the other evidence uncovered at the shop.

Simply put, I'm not going to rest until I've taken care of Evelyn's stalker. After this morning, it's clear that the situation is only going to escalate unless someone puts a stop to it.

I intend for that person to be me, whether or not I've got the authority or the right to see this through to the end.

"I'll catch you later, O'Connor. Right now, I need to talk to my brother. Jake's running some background checks on L'Opale employees. I want to make sure he's got those in hand before the end of the day."

She stares at me. "Jake's at the hospital, Gabe."

"How do you know that?"

"Umm." Color blooms in her cheeks. "Because he told me when we spoke on the phone this morning."

My brows rise at her admission, but I don't have time to deal with that newsflash, or the implications of it. Right now, I'm more concerned with getting a hold of my brother. "What's he doing at the hospital?"

"He's there with your parents. Your dad was admitted again overnight."

"Jesus. Another stroke?"

She shakes her head. "Angina. He's okay. I'm sorry I didn't say anything to you sooner. I thought you knew . . ."

"No. I didn't know."

And why would anyone tell me after the way I behaved at my parents' house the other night? Evidently, I've ensured that every corner of my life is scorched Earth now.

I walk past my friend, trying not to see her pitying expression. "Thanks for letting me know, Kelsey. I need to go see Jake."

My brother is seated in my father's hospital recovery room when I arrive twenty minutes later.

It appears he's been here a while. His face is shadowed with dark whiskers and he's out of uniform, dressed in jeans and a black T-shirt, slouched in one of the three guest chairs lined up along the wall at the foot of Dad's bed. Straightening in his seat when he sees me outside, he motions for me to come in.

My father's eyes are closed, his chest rising and falling in a sedate rhythm as he sleeps. Beside him, machines hiss and beep softly at the ends of the monitoring lines and IVs attached to his chest and arms.

"You just missed everyone," Jake tells me. "Shane and Ethan just took Mom down for some breakfast in the cafeteria. You want to go join them?"

"No. I need to talk to you."

I indicate the hallway, but Jake gives a faint shake of his head. He nods in Dad's direction. "We won't disturb him. He's okay, been asleep for a couple of hours. Besides, I think he rests better hearing a little conversation going on around him instead of all these machines and hospital noises. What's going on, brother?"

Since I don't plan on staying long, I just lean my shoulder against the wall and jump right in. "Were you able to run those background checks I asked you about?"

He nods. "I was going to call you this morning once I got in the office, but then I ended up here. Anyway, yeah. They all came back clean, every one of them."

"Even Katrina Davis?"

"Yep. Unless you count a couple of parking tickets."

"Shit." I cross my arms, my disappointment obvious. "And nothing on any of the former employees, either? No red flags that could turn into bigger problems down the road?"

Now he frowns. "No, Gabe. Like I said, there's nothing to report. You want to tell me what this is about now? Obviously, these weren't just routine checks like you wanted me to believe when you asked for this favor."

"No. This is about Evelyn Beckham."

Jake tilts his head. "The woman you brought to the house on Saturday? Mom said it looked like you were serious about her." He scoffs quietly. "Not that you've mentioned any of this to me."

Great. Now, I've dug myself into a hole with my closest brother too. "It's complicated between Evelyn and me. *Was* complicated. I screwed it all up and now she doesn't want anything to do with me."

"Evelyn Beckham, you said?" He stares at me, latching on to her last name. "As in, related to Dominic Baine's right arm, his attorney, Andrew Beckham? I thought you were tight with that guy?"

"Until about fifteen minutes ago, I was. Eve's his sister."

Jake arches a brow, then pushes out a sigh. "You fucking idiot, bro. You and his sister? I guess that explains the busted condition of your lip."

"Never mind about any of that right now. She's in danger." I give him a rundown of everything that's happened so far, including the discovery of the photos outside my apartment and my resignation from Baine International a short time ago. "Evelyn's landed on some sick fuck's radar, and I need to find out who it is."

"You want me to put a tail on her? I can make a call now and I can have eyes on her in five minutes. Plainclothes or uniform, I'll arrange for either one."

As tempting as the offer is, I shake my head. "She would have to agree to it first. And after today, I don't expect she'll agree to anything I have to say. She made it clear she just wants me to stay out of her life."

"So, where does that leave you?"

"If those employee background checks are a wash, I'm back at zero. Less than zero, because if anything happens to her, I'll never forgive myself. If she gets hurt, or worse—"

I push out a breath, and there's no masking the choked quality of my voice. If that makes me some kind of pussy in front of my hardass older brother, I don't give a shit.

"She means everything to me," I utter thickly. "I love her, Jake. *Fuck*. I love her. She's the best goddamn thing that's ever happened to me and I've lost her."

"*Gabe.*"

My father's rusty voice draws my attention to the bed. His eyes are open now, unblinking and trained solely on me. I hate the idea that he may have heard some of my conversation, or all of it. If he can see that I'm in pain, especially this self-inflicted wound I've sustained today, I don't know what I'll do if he shows me even a hint of satisfaction in my suffering.

I don't answer him. Silent, I exchange a glance with Jake before turning to head for the door.

"Gabriel." He says again. Then, "Son, please . . . wait."

I pause, even though it's the last thing I want to do.

Jake steps past me. "I'll go see what's keeping Mom and the guys."

And just like that, I am left alone in the room with my old man. The air feels heavy, like the coming of a storm. Or maybe it's the aftermath of one, considering how he and I left things last night at his house.

It seems like it's been a week. Longer, when I consider how my life went from as close to perfect as it had ever been, to completely shot to shit in the space of one weekend.

"Help me with this bed, will you?"

My father's words are sluggish, but there's no mistaking that his mind is sharp and clear. So is his gaze. Those shrewd, often demeaning, hazel eyes stay locked on me as I walk over and take the multi-buttoned remote for the bed out of his weak grasp.

"How do you want it?"

"Sit me up," he says. "I need to talk to you."

The plastic-covered mattress groans as I hold down the button to tilt the bed under my father's head. He nods when he's where he wants to be. I set down the remote but ignore the empty chair that sits close the bed.

I unclench my jaw as I stand there looking down at him. "What do you want?"

He seems to consider the question for a long moment. Still looking at me, he exhales a long and heavy sigh.

"You weren't supposed to happen," he states bluntly and without preamble. "A year before you were born, your mother and I had separated. I thought we were heading for divorce. I think we would've ended up there eventually, even though we were trying to make things work. Then we learned you were on the way."

I scoff under my breath. "Yeah, Pop. I already know this story."

"No, you don't," he says tersely. "Not all of it." A wheeze shakes his chest for a moment, then he continues. "I wasn't a good husband. Probably not a good father, even at that time. I had other women. I drank too much. I loved your mother—I adored her—but I couldn't seem to stop doing the selfish things that hurt her. Finally, she left me. She took your brothers to her parents' house, and she wasn't going to come back."

He's right. I haven't heard this part. It's not a conversation I want to have right now, when all I want to be doing is turning over every rock in the city until I uncover Evelyn's stalker. But the old man keeps talking, as if he needs to get it off his chest.

"She forgave me, thank God. Her forgiveness has been the biggest miracle of my life. And I never strayed again. Sometimes, though, I think she shouldn't have come back. She deserved someone who had never hurt her, who would never let her down. Your brothers would've been upset if I'd gone, but they would've survived. But you, Gabe? You deserved to have a better father than me."

"What are you talking about?"

"I was a weak man. A failure as a husband. A poor example of a father. And every time I looked at you, I saw a mirror that reflected all of those shortcomings back at me. You were supposed to be a new beginning for your mom and me. Our angel baby, she used to call you. But all I could see was a daily reminder of that lowest point in my life. When I looked at you, I didn't see a new beginning. I saw another possibility that I would ruin something good."

I frown, shaking my head. Trying to understand. "That's why you've hated me all my life?"

"Hated you?" His mottled brow furrows. "I never hated you, Gabriel."

"That's not what it sounded like the other night." I say the words carefully, refusing to let him see how deeply he'd wounded me. Maybe we both wounded each other. "You mocked me. You said you had me pegged right along, that I always thought I was better than you."

"You were better, Gabe. You *are* better, in all the ways it matters, even then." He looks at his hands, a tendon ticking in his sagging cheek. "I didn't know how to be a father to you. You were always bright and curious, independent. Hell, you were a defiant little shit from the moment we brought you home."

He chuckles—actually chuckles, the first time I can recall seeing him express any joy when talking about me. My chest constricts, but my guard is still up. He's taught me well, after all.

He looks up at me again, sobering. "The only kinds of kids I knew how to raise were obedient little soldiers. That's how my father did it, and his father before him. But their methods didn't work on you. Instead of falling in line, you pushed back. You challenged me at every turn, always ready to lock horns. Unlike your brothers, you never needed my approval."

"That's not true." I shake my head, incredulous that he could think as much. "I did need it. But you never gave it."

A sound seems to strangle in his throat as he stares at me. He glances away and doesn't look back, not for a very long time. When he finally does, his eyes are glassy and wet. "Do you blame me, Son?" He swallows hard and tries again. "Do you blame me for what happened to you in the war?"

His guilt clings to the humid air in the room. His remorse stuns me. I've never heard the emotion in his voice before.

"An IED took my leg, not you. It was an unlucky stretch of road on an unlucky day. So, no. I don't blame you, Pop."

He doesn't seem satisfied with my answer. His gaze stays rooted on mine, his mouth trembling. "I didn't want you to join the army. I told you that." He smiles ruefully. "I demanded you didn't join, as I recall. I thought you enlisted just to spite me."

I shrug, unable to hold back my smirk. "I did."

His barrel chest shakes with his laugh, but there are tears leaking from the corners of his eyes. When he's quieted, he reaches for my hand, which I realize only now is gripped on the rail of the bed like a vise. "I should've come to see you in the hospital. I wanted to, but I didn't know how to handle it. I didn't know how to face you, realizing what my failure as a father had cost you."

I exhale, and it's as if every last particle of air leaves my lungs. "That's why you never showed up there?"

"I'm sorry, Gabe." His fingers curl around mine on the bed rail. "I'm so very sorry. After you came home, I felt ashamed for staying away. I didn't want to hear you say you hated me, even though I knew you must. How could you not?"

"I didn't." My voice is choked. "Ah, fuck, Dad. I never hated you. Not even the other night. I'm sorry too."

He pats my hand and rolls his head away again, staring at the wall. I can hear his quiet sobs, the thickness of his throat working.

When I feel I have control enough of my own voice, I ask, "Why are you telling me all of this now?"

"Because I heard you talking with Jacob." He looks at me, his gaze studying me, probably seeing all of my misery. God knows I'm too split open to hide it, even from him. "I heard you talking about the woman you care for. Evelyn. And because your mother told me the other night that it was obvious the two of you are in love."

I shake my head. "I screwed up with her. I broke her trust. She feels betrayed, and I wasn't able to convince her that it won't happen again."

"Will it?"

"No. Never. I don't know if she'll ever believe that. Right now, I'm not even sure she can forgive me."

"But what if she can, Son? If she loves you, then you haven't lost her yet."

I stare at him, measuring his advice, another gift he's never given me until this very moment. But I hold on to it now. If my father never gives me another word of encouragement, it will be worth it for the hope he's instilling in me now.

"Go after her, Gabriel. Maybe you're due for a miracle too."

32

~ Evelyn ~

My brother is waiting for me in the hallway when I come out of the executive floor ladies' room. He is a solemn figure in his bespoke midnight-blue suit and crisp white shirt. His tie is askew, the top button of his collar unfastened below his throat. His dark head is bent, his broad back leaning against the mahogany wood paneled wall, hands stuffed in his pants pockets.

He looks as though he's been through hell and back. I'm sure I do too.

I've spent the last forty-five minutes in the bathroom, trying to wash the blood-red lipstick stains from my dress and fingers. Really, what I've been doing is hiding in the solitude of the luxurious restroom, giving myself a chance to grieve the loss of Gabriel Noble.

Because that's what this feels like. Death. Mourning.

A soul-deep emptiness.

He's gone from my life, and while I am still hurting from the reason we're not together, being without him is only making the pain worse.

"I came back to my office and you were gone," Andrew says, his deep voice cautious, compassionate. His light green eyes watch me with regret as I approach him. "Lily told me where to find you."

"How long have you been out here?"

He shrugs faintly. "A while. Are you okay?"

"No."

His gaze drops from mine and he utters a quiet curse. "Evie, I'm sorry. I'm sorry about all of this. I never wanted you to get hurt. That's what this whole thing was about."

I shake my head. "No, Andrew. That's not what this was about. It was about you treating me like a child. You didn't respect me enough to give me the truth."

He frowns. "I do respect you. More than you know."

"How can you say that when instead of being honest with me, you went behind my back and hired someone to guard me like I'm a piece of property? You still want to handle me as if I'm that sick, broken girl you brought home from Paris."

His face is filled with consternation. "I can't get that image out of my mind. When I got the call that you were in the hospital three-thousand miles away, my world just about stopped. And then, when I got there and saw how sick you'd become . . . Christ, Evelyn. I should've known. I'm your brother. I should've done something more to get you out of that situation before it nearly killed you."

"You did get me out of there," I remind him, gently,

because I can hear the anguish that's still fresh in his deep voice. Anguish he's held all this time, because of me. "You tried to help me, numerous times. In the end, you were the only one who did help, Andrew."

A heavy sigh gusts out of him as his gaze meets mine. "Every day after I brought you home, all those months you were in therapy, I dreaded I'd get a call telling me you were gone. I watched you fight your way back. You were so brave, Evie, so fucking strong. Stronger than I would've been. Hell, you're stronger than I am now. I don't know why it's taken me this long to see it."

I want to hold on to my anger for my brother, but it's hard to feel anything but remorse now.

I understood how deeply he cared for me during all the years of my ordeal, but now I can see that although I got better, he is still living with the scars of watching me suffer.

He shakes his head. "I'm sorry I kept the truth from you. I should've told you. Hell, I should have taken the whole thing to the police right away. Instead, I dragged Gabe into this, too. Now, you've both got every right to despise me."

I reach out to him, briefly placing my hand against his cheek. "I don't despise you, Andrew. I never could. As for Gabe, I'm sure he'll get over it. After all, he was only doing his job."

"No, that's not all, Evelyn. He cares about you. That was obvious to me today. I've known him for more than a year and I've never seen him like this. Not about anything, or anyone. He told me he's in love with you."

I close my eyes against the words I so desperately want to believe. Words I was afraid to trust when Gabe said them to me, because my heart had been cracked open from the hurt of his betrayal. It may never heal from that.

"He lied to me. He let me think I meant something to him, when the whole time he was being paid to care about me."

Andrew slowly shakes his head. "He wanted to tell you everything. It was me who insisted against it."

"You insisted."

He gives me a rueful look. "I demanded Gabe's silence, as his friend and colleague. I thought you would be better off without knowing about any of it—about the fact that someone was targeting you, about Gabe's covert role in protecting you—at least until we had the situation contained. He disagreed with me on that, more than once. But I told him I knew best. I really believed I did. Now, I realize I was wrong. Gabe knew I was, but he kept those secrets from you only because I made him promise that he would. He's a good man, Evie. He's been a good friend, too. I'm sorry to see what that friendship has cost him with you."

A piece of my outrage calves away from the larger ache still filling my chest. Gabe never said it was Andrew who insisted on the secrets, so I just assumed he participated without qualms.

How would I have reacted if he'd laid the blame at my brother's feet today? I'm not sure, and as much as it kindles a small hope in me to hear that betraying me hadn't come easily to him, it doesn't change the end result.

"No. He chose," I remind my brother as well as myself. "You gave him a job to do, and he did it. He chose that job over everything else, over me. That's how much he loves me."

Andrew's brows lower. "Evelyn, Gabe resigned."

Shock takes me aback for a moment. I gape at my brother. "He did? When?"

"After you and he spoke. He tendered his resignation, and from what I'm told, he left the building."

A flood of emotion pours over me. I can't believe he would quit the job that means so much to him. The job I accused him of trying to preserve at the cost of our relationship. Instead, it was his bond as Andrew's friend that kept Gabe's silence as much as anything else. Perhaps more so.

And then today, after the hurtful things I said to him, Gabe threw it all away.

"Where did he go?"

Andrew shakes his head. "I have no idea. Kelsey O'Connor turned his service pistol in to Nick, so I believe she was the last person to talk with Gabe before he left."

My feet are in motion even before my brother finishes his sentence. I race for the elevator and punch the down button.

"Evie, wait." Andrew jogs up behind me as I enter the waiting lift.

He stops outside of it, but he doesn't challenge me, not this time. We've moved past that now, even though I can see he's struggling to allow me the space enough to make my own decisions, to risk my own mistakes.

He's not going to stop me from going after the man I love, even though his expression is filled with reservation.

"I need to find him, Andrew. I just . . . need him."

I see his nod in the instant before the doors slide

closed between us.

Down in the lobby, Luis at the desk tells me where to find Kelsey. I race to the meeting room where she is speaking with several of the security team. I know I should knock, but I have no restraint right now. I catch the tail end of her announcement that Gabe has resigned, but then everyone goes silent as I open the door.

"Where is he, Kelsey?"

Her eyes widen, as if she's not quite sure how to respond. Stepping out of the room, she closes the door to speak privately with me in the hallway.

"Please," I implore her. "I need to see Gabe. I need to tell him that I love him."

A smile breaks over her face. "New York Hospital on Bell Boulevard in Queens. His father was admitted for chest pains this morning, but he's fine. Gabe was heading there to see his brother Jake."

Shit. The hospital is across the bridge and I have no car to get there. I also realize in a flood of misery that my purse, wallet, and phone are all back in Gabe's apartment. We left in such a hurry, and I was so distraught, I didn't stop to grab it.

"I don't have my purse." I give her a sheepish smile. "Do you, ah, do you have any money I could borrow for a taxi?"

"I have a MetroCard for the subway, if that will help?"

Oh, God. The subway. A sudden wave of anxiety seeps through me at the thought.

Kelsey notices my hesitation. "Or you could use my phone to call him?"

No, I can't do that, no matter how much I would

prefer to avoid going anywhere near the subway. But what I need to say to Gabe can't be done over the phone.

I need to see his face. I need to be able to touch him, to kiss him.

I need to be able to look into his soul-stirring hazel eyes and tell him that I love him. I'll get on my knees and beg him to forgive me for pushing him away, if that's what it will take to win him back.

Even if I have to face the subway in order to reach him.

I'm no longer the scared and self-destructive young woman who stood at the edge of those subterranean tracks on the lowest day of her life. I'm not afraid to live anymore. I want it more than ever, but especially if I can share some part of it with Gabe.

And not even a lake a fire could keep me from going to him now.

"Your MetroCard would be great, Kelsey. Thanks."

She runs to fetch it, then returns with the card and places it in my hand.

"Wish me luck with him?" I ask her, my smile shaky on my lips.

She hugs me tight. "Oh, girl. You aren't going to need it."

33

~ Gabriel ~

I race back into the city, the Lexus roaring through the morning traffic while my father's encouragement pounds like a battle drum in my head.

He says maybe I'm due a miracle today. The truth is, I've already been granted one. It happened the day I met Evelyn Beckham in the Baine Building garage.

I have to see her now.

Even if she refuses to believe me, I have to tell her what she means to me. That she is the only woman I want. The only woman I will ever need.

That I will spend nothing less than the rest of my life loving her.

All I need now is the chance to show her that. I have to try to regain her trust, if it takes me weeks or months or years to prove myself to her again.

I know I don't deserve her. And even if she rejects me in the end, right now, I just have to convince her to at least let me try to get her back.

Because in a word, what she means to me is . . . *everything.*

It is that thought that spurs me as I round the corner onto West 57th Street. I see the gleaming, dark glass tower of the Baine Building up ahead. I punch the gas, maneuvering around a slow-moving sedan.

I left less than two hours ago, and I only hope she's still there. I'm not sure I would have called, even if her phone wasn't left in her purse back at my apartment. I don't want to give her the opportunity to shut me down again before I've even started to plead my case.

I just need to see her.

I need to hold her in my arms and pray I haven't squandered all her affection for me.

Downshifting as I speed to make a light, I nearly rear-end the truck in front of me when I pass Evelyn walking swiftly up the sidewalk several hundred yards in the opposite direction of Baine headquarters.

Holy shit.

Where's she going?

I glance in the mirror, trying to keep an eye on her while I navigate the river of traffic all around me. She's soon engulfed in a crowd of pedestrians, all of them heading somewhere en masse.

The subway station.

What the fuck?

It's the last place I would expect to see her heading. Confused, I veer toward the curb and dial O'Connor's number on my vehicle's speaker while I drive.

"Hey, Gabe." She sounds chipper and a little coy,

which confuses the hell out of me.

"Do you know where Evelyn's going?"

"She just left to find you."

"Find me? How does she know where I am?"

"Uh, because I told her. I just saw her here a couple of minutes ago. She borrowed my MetroCard and she's on her way to the hospital in Queens right now."

"Fuck."

"What's wrong?"

"I'm in the city," I bark in a clipped voice. "I'm rolling up to the building right now. Shit, I need to catch her."

"Then go," O'Connor tells me. "I see you outside at the curb right now. Leave your car. I'll take care of it. Just go get her, soldier."

I chuckle in spite of the torrent of emotions swamping me. "I owe you one, O'Connor."

I end the call and jump out of the car.

Then I start running, ignoring the protests of my stump as my feet chew up the distance between me and the miracle I hope is waiting for me at the other end.

34

~ Evelyn ~

I'm nervous.

Not because of the dankness of the subway station or the crushing press of the other commuters who surround me on the platform.

Not even because of the steep edge on the other side of the concrete floor, with its dark tracks and yawning tunnels on either end.

I'm nervous because now that I'm here, I'm afraid of what awaits me at the end of this journey.

What if Gabe is too angry to listen to me?

What if I've pushed him too hard and he wants nothing to do with me?

I've cost him his job. He left it voluntarily, yes. But his resignation has everything to do with me.

After my talk with Andrew, I am hopeful that Gabe still has a place at Baine International . . . if he wants it.

I know my brother still considers him a friend as well.

Maybe all of us will find a way to repair the damage we've done to one another.

I hug myself, needing some sense of reassurance as I stand with the crowd filling the station to await the next train. A little old lady seated on one of the thick-hewn wooden benches in the center of the platform stares at me in open curiosity.

I glance down at myself, suddenly reminded of the ruined state of my dress. The red lipstick stains are faded to pink, but still obvious. An ugly reminder of the morning that now seems like it happened days ago.

"Eve."

I turn around at the sound of the familiar voice. I'm not expecting to hear my name here, and especially not spoken so intimately by the man who just said it.

He is standing a few people back from me. His round face is unsmiling, his balding head shining with perspiration under the milky wash of the fluorescent lights.

"Mr. Hennings."

He steps forward, melting out of the surrounding crowd. His gaze is oddly disapproving, unblinking as he approaches.

My instincts recognize the threat in him, even before I glance down and see the blunt barrel of a gun partially concealed by the fall of his suit jacket and held low in his hand.

Oh, God. "It was you."

He stands in front of me now, and despite that we are hemmed in by hundreds of other commuters, my focus narrows to just him and me.

And the pistol that he's aiming squarely at the center

of my body.

I take a small step back, a reflexive, fractional retreat. His raised brow is as effective as a shouted command to halt.

"Do not be a fool, Eve. I've tried to be patient with you. I'd hoped you would come around to my way of thinking. Now, I see you require more direct methods."

"What are you talking about?"

"You and me, of course." His tone is conversational, if measured.

He steps closer, until we're standing scant inches apart, the same as any two people would while having a friendly exchange. Except this is nothing close to friendly.

The screech of the incoming train vibrates all the way into my marrow. I am chilled and trembling, panic beginning to collect behind my sternum. I glance on either side of me, hoping someone will notice I'm in peril.

Hennings bares his teeth in a menacing smile, his lips barely moving as he speaks in a soft murmur. "Sound any alarm, and I will start shooting into the crowd. Do you understand, Eve? Nod if you do, please."

I bob my head shakily. Within moments, the train is in the station and the people begin to crowd onto it. The little old lady on the sturdy bench shuffles past me without so much as a glance, as if I am invisible.

In the city, that's nothing unusual. But right now, I feel as insubstantial as a ghost.

I feel as if I am trapped in a nightmare.

Hennings flicks his gaze to my stained dress. "I see you got my message this morning."

My stomach lurches at the thought of him standing

outside Gabe's apartment, scrawling hateful words, exposing photos of me at the lowest points in my life— my personal photos. I am mortified that Gabe has seen them.

I'm sure that was the point.

"You stole my purse that day in the boutique."

He chuckles. "I was clumsy about it. I nearly got caught by that bitch, Katrina. It was all I could do to ditch the damn thing in the nearest hiding place after I transferred your photos to my phone and took the other things I needed."

"The photos you put up outside Gabe's apartment. The lipstick you used to write that filth today. You stole it from my purse too."

He shrugs mildly. "A personal indulgence, because I enjoy having things you've touched. Things you've used on your body, or on those provocative lips of yours. I've amassed quite an impressive collection of memorabilia on you over the years, Eve. I'm not ashamed to say that I've been your biggest fan from the first time I saw you parading half-naked down a runway. I told myself that one day we would be together. And here we are, at last."

I shudder inwardly, feeling a cold dread swamp me. He's sick, deranged.

And all this time, he's been obsessed with me.

"There is no girlfriend waiting for you overseas, is there? All that lingerie you've bought from the boutique, you weren't buying it for anyone."

"That's not true. I was buying it for you." He sneers, pursing his thin lips. "I thought you were enjoying the time we spent together in the boutique. Then you pushed me off without a care. Did you really think I would stand for working with anyone else? Steps had to be taken, Eve."

So, Kat was right. Hennings was sabotaging her. I don't doubt that he even found a way to manipulate the shop's calendar program to make her look negligent, when all along he was to blame.

And I didn't want to believe her.

"You set her up to fail. You made me doubt her. She quit because of you."

God, I feel like an idiot to have not seen all of this until now.

"You hacked into my computer and my phone. You've been spying on me. You put a monitoring device in the boutique. You have a camera hidden in my office." Nausea swells inside me when I think of what he's seen, everything he's done. "You were at the back door that night the power went out, weren't you? I heard the lock rattling. It was you, trying to get in."

He stares at me without a speck of remorse. "The device I installed had been working fine for months. I don't know why it started shorting out. Technology can be so unreliable sometimes," he says, as if he's discussing the weather. "I needed to repair it or replace it before anyone might start poking around in there, so I swiped your purse for a few minutes while I was visiting the shop that week and I made an impression of the key, so I could come back the next night and work without interruptions."

He pauses, waiting for the last of the people in the station to step into the waiting train. The doors thump closed, and suddenly it is just him and me alone on the platform.

"As I was saying, I intended to return the next night to investigate the device malfunction, but you were working late. I watched you for a while using the camera on your desk—"

"The rosebush." I practically gag on the word. "That's why you brought me that so-called gift."

"I decided to follow through with my plan anyway," he says, not so much as a pause to acknowledge the sickness of his acts. "I decided I would go the shop, and if you were still there, I would bring you home with me that night."

I can't hide my revulsion. "You mean abduct me."

Something dark flickers in his expression. He glances down at the gun still aimed at me, moved farther out in the open now. "If I had come prepared that night like I am today, we would already be together, Eve. But the key was a bad copy. It stuck in the lock, made too much noise. I knew you'd hear. I worried that you would call the police."

That's exactly what I should have done. Instead, I dismissed the noise, too afraid to rouse my brother's overbearingly protective instincts, should he learn I'd panicked and called for help. I was stubborn and defensive of his concern—and now I'm paying the steepest price.

Hennings steps closer to me, forcing me to either step back or let him come nearer. I know the edge of the platform is somewhere behind me. I can only hope my choices don't boil down to facing off against a bullet or the third rail of the subway tracks.

Absurdly, I pray if I die here today, that Gabe won't hear about this and blame himself.

I balked at his protection too. Now, I would give anything to be safe in his arms.

"My luck took a turn a few minutes later," Hennings

says. "I considered it fate when the device in your utility room shorted out completely and the power cut off. I waited outside the back door for a while, hoping the darkness would drive you out to me. But then a vehicle approached, and I had no choice but to run back to my car a few streets away."

Thank God, Gabe had come that night. He is all that saved me from Hennings' sick plans.

I swallow a cold knot of horror to hear him breezily recount everything. And he hadn't stopped with just those acts, either. "You followed me to the zoo. You slashed my tires."

"Yes, I did," he says, ice moving into his eyes. "You disappointed me, Eve. I never took you for a slut, not until you started spending time with that other man. That cripple."

I flinch at the awful word, and the venom with which he speaks it. What's also disturbing is that he talks about Gabe as if he is rival for my affection.

He straightens, eyeing me with a new resolve under the glare of the station lights. "I'm glad to see the message I delivered today served its purpose. I wanted the interloper to see the real you, Eve. Not the mask you've been wearing for him. I knew if he saw who you truly are, he wouldn't stay. And, yes, I wanted to punish you, too."

As he speaks, a pair of rushing footsteps sound on the stairs leading down to the platform. I recognize the gait. I swivel my head at the same time Gabe comes into view.

"Gabe, stop!"

He hesitates, his face the grimmest I've ever seen it. "Evelyn. Ah, Christ."

In that same instant, Hennings snags me with his free hand, yanking me against him. The nose of the pistol jams coldly into my temple.

35

~ Gabriel ~

It is as if my entire body freezes in the space of a moment.

Like the instant between the first firecracker pop of a triggered IED and the explosion that will send twisted metal and body parts flying in all directions, I stand in a brief state of stunned incredulity as my mind tries to process the sight of Evelyn caught at the end of a madman's gun.

My heart halts, giving my brain a chance to formulate a plan.

Without a weapon of my own, I don't have a lot of choice.

"Let her go."

I take a step down the stairs, moving by degrees while looking for ways to disarm her assailant. The man is shorter than her and sturdy. He is not young, in his sixties by my guess. Dressed well, he's obviously a man of some means in his tailored suit and polished shoes.

But he is crazy. I can see the wildness of insanity in his eyes.

"Put the gun down. You don't want to do this."

He sneers at me. "She's mine. Tell him, Eve."

A strangled cry leaks from her. Her eyes are rounded, her breath panting shallowly through her trembling lips. "Mr. Hennings . . . Walter, please don't do this."

I flick a glance at Evelyn, a silent acknowledgment of her courage in giving me the bastard's name. Not that I'm going to need it. By the time I get her out of here, Walter Hennings will be dead—or wishing like hell he was.

"Stay back," he growls at me. "I'm going to take Eve out of here now."

There is a stairwell on both ends of the station; the one I'm standing at the bottom of, and another one about a hundred feet in the opposite direction. I hear other people's voices and footsteps approaching. Any second now, the station is going to begin filling with commuters.

Hennings starts inching my way, sidling past the row of squatty wooden benches in the middle of the platform.

"It's okay, man. You're the boss." I raise my hands in a surrendering gesture meant to relax him, while I consider my options. The way I see it, I have only two. Draw his fire away from Evelyn, or charge the bastard.

I take an easy step toward him.

He catches on and his round face burns red with rage. "Fucker, I said stay back!"

The gun swings forward, his finger curling tight

around the trigger. As soon as the weapon leaves Evelyn's temple, she brings her arm up under his, throwing off his aim.

The shot he fires hits one of the fluorescent tubes overhead. The light explodes, and the sound of gunfire scatters the few people who've trickled onto the platform at the other end of the station.

At the same time, Hennings bellows, slamming the butt of the pistol into the side of Evelyn's head. She goes down, landing on her side at his feet.

I charge him, shoving him away from Evelyn as I grab his gun arm and push it up at a ninety-degree angle. He claws at me, his strength a surprise. No doubt he's running on adrenaline now, in addition to psychopathic rage.

He manages to punch me in the side of the head with his left hand. I shake it off and head-butt him. The bastard retaliates with a hard kick to my left knee.

My prosthesis wrenches and we go down together in a heap on the concrete. The back of his head hits hard and he loses his grip on the pistol. With the impact of our inelegant fall, the weapon skitters under one of the benches.

With Hennings dazed and unmoving, I scramble for the gun, my stump screaming in its skewed socket. The pain is inconsequential, but the lameness of my limb shaves off precious instants as I dive and shimmy beneath the low bench to grab the weapon.

I hear Evelyn's scream in the same second that I'm lifting my shoulders up off the ground, the pistol gripped in both hands and trained on Hennings.

He's standing near the edge of the platform, holding Evelyn in front of him like a shield. I can't shoot through her, and one wrong move by her assailant and she could fall to her death on the tracks below.

Hennings peers around her. He is breathing hard, spittle collecting at the corners of his mouth. "You've ruined everything," he says to me, seething with fury. "You've ruined her, fouling her with your body. Now this."

He shakes his head, glancing at the ceiling of the station, where the pound of booted footfalls sounds from above. The gunfire and screams will have brought law enforcement from all directions. The station is probably already on lockdown, police only seconds away. Hennings knows it as well as I do.

"There's only one way out now," he says, rubbing his cheek in Evelyn's long, unbound hair. "They won't let me leave with her. So, I'm going to have to take her with me another way."

Ah, Christ.

The tracks.

Evelyn's terror is a palpable thing as she stares at me, her lovely face stricken with fear. I hold her gaze across the space that separates us, making a silent promise that I will fix this. All I need is the sliver of a chance.

Her breathing slows as our eyes lock and hold. I watch as a calmness settles over her, a resolve that awes me, especially when every fiber in my body is stretched to the breaking point with stark, cold dread.

"Walter," she says quietly. Although he can't see her face, I can. I can see the fortitude it takes for her to lift her hand and gently caress the arm that's banded around her. "Walter, you're right, darling. We can't be together in this world. But, please . . . before we go on to the next one, I want to feel your lips on mine. Just once, my darling."

I stand as still as statue, watching as the madness in Walter Hennings responds to the siren sweetness of Evelyn's voice. He relaxes his iron hold on her, just enough for her to slowly pivot in his terrible embrace.

"Oh, my love," he murmurs, taking his eyes off me to gaze into hers.

He moves his mouth toward her. But instead of kissing him, Evelyn brings her hand up and rakes her fingernails down his face, hard enough to draw blood.

The assault startles him, staggers him back on his heels with a roar.

And in the split second of his inattention, with Evelyn now ducked out of the way, I adjust my aim and pull the trigger.

The head shot topples him.

I set down the gun as his dead weight tumbles over the edge of the platform and onto the rails below.

"Gabe!" Evelyn launches to her feet and runs to me where I'm still on my ass on the floor.

She dives into my arms, and I wrap her in my embrace.

Her sobs gust against my neck. "Oh, God. I was so scared."

"I know, baby. Me too." I hug her tighter, emotion thickening my throat. "I've got you now."

She lifts her head, searching my eyes. "I love you, Gabriel. I should've told you. I shouldn't have let you leave—"

"I'm here," I say, kissing her trembling lips. "I'm here, and I'm holding you, and I love you. I love you so much, Evelyn. I'm never letting you go."

"Promise?"

I nod. "It's more than a promise. It's a vow."

She kisses me, and I draw away from her lips reluctantly when I hear police officers clambering down the stairs with weapons at the ready. I recognize one of them as a cousin and give him a nod and crooked smirk in greeting.

They will have questions, of course. There will be statements for us to give, and evidence to collect from the boutique and my apartment.

But all of that can wait.

The rest of the world will have to wait, because right now, I've got Evelyn safe and warm in my arms, and I'm not about to let her go.

Not for anything.

Epilogue

~ Evelyn ~

One month later . . .

"Kat, what do you think about the lace on this demi-bra? I went with Leavers, but now I think the Chantilly might be a better complement to the piece."

She walks around to my side of our shared design table and glances down at the swatches I've laid out. "Chantilly, no question. And I agree with you about the silk piping over the rosettes. It's a beautiful design, Eve."

I meet her approving gaze and smile. "Thank you."

It feels good to be working with Katrina again. I wasn't sure she would come back after the way I'd hurt her with my doubt.

As it turned out, Walter Hennings' derangement had gone much deeper than stalking and cyber sabotage. At his home, the police discovered reams of image files and documents going back to the beginning of my modeling career. He'd kept a journal of my appearances, and copies of every article ever written about me.

If that wasn't disturbing enough, he also had a life-size silicone doll molded in my likeness. The officers found the thing dressed in lingerie I had designed, its mouth painted in the red lipstick Hennings stole from my purse. And, yes, he had collected other, random personal belongings of mine over the years too, just as he'd bragged to me in the subway station. He had handcuffs and shackles as well, and a cabinet full of ropes and weapons.

I still shudder to think what he would have done with me if he had managed to abduct me like he'd planned. But Walter Hennings is no more. It's rare that I think of him weeks after Gabe saved me from him. Being busy with work helps.

Once the news media got a hold of Walter Hennings' death and the details of his sick obsession with me, Katrina called to see how I was doing. Thankfully, she accepted my apology for not believing her when I should have trusted her. She forgave me.

Since she's come back to L'Opale, our working relationship has never been stronger. Our friendship has strengthened, too. I couldn't ask for a better creative partner on the boutique's newest launch.

With Avery Ross's wedding and honeymoon ensemble making headlines, the shop has been inundated with new clients. We've hired more designers and seamstresses, but Kat and I are working alone on the concepts for the lingerie project that means the most to me now.

Kelsey O'Connor steps out of the dressing room wearing our newest prototype. "Well, how do I look?"

I smile, taking in the gorgeous sight of my friend. She's wearing a sheer black lace, boned bustier with balconette cups and a touch fastener along the right side with matching panties. She looks fierce and sexy. Most of all, she looks beautiful.

"Stunning," Kat says, beaming at her.

I nod in agreement. "Do you like it?"

"I love it." She smooths her hands along the front of the piece, the hand that's flesh and bone, and the one she's wearing today that's fashioned of sleek titanium and carbon, the fingers gleaming like polished silver. She glances up at me, grinning. "I think Jake's going to love it too."

"Oh, I'm sure of that."

"Speaking of," she says, "they're going to be here to pick us up any minute now."

As if she's conjured the Noble brothers by mentioning them, I hear the electronic beep of the boutique front entrance chime. I tap my phone and the security camera image appears, one of the new features of the state-of-the-art system Gabe and his team at Baine International installed.

"Better get dressed, unless you want to spoil the surprise and let him see you in that before it's finished," I tell Kelsey.

She darts back into the room on an excited squeal while I walk out to meet Gabe and his brother.

He's chatting with Megan, but as soon as he glances up and sees me, he smiles and starts heading my way. I hardly have a chance to say hello before he sweeps me into a warm embrace and a kiss that makes my toes curl.

"Ready to go?" he murmurs against my lips.

"Almost. Kelsey's getting changed." I lightly smack my hand against his chest. "You still haven't told me where we're going today."

He smiles, something cryptic, almost uncertain, in his loving gaze. "You'll see soon enough."

Kelsey walks out to join us, slipping her hand easily into Jake's. He grins at Gabe, revealing the same pair of dimples that have charmed me more often than I care to admit with his brother. "Let's go."

I ride beside Gabe in the passenger seat of his Lexus, curious as we cross the bridge to Queens, then proceed toward Bayside, his old hometown. He pulls into the parking lot behind a small pub called McGilly's. The place is crowded, and as we stroll inside, I see a lot of familiar faces. Some I haven't seen in months.

"Daddy?" I gasp to see my father stroll up to us alongside my brother. My father enfolds me in a big bear hug, pressing a kiss to my cheek. "When did you get in the city?"

"I came down last night and stayed with Andrew. It's so good to see you, Evie."

I nod, overcome with happiness—and not a little confusion. I glance at my brother. "Why didn't you tell me?"

"Gabe wanted it to be a surprise."

The two men exchange a private smile before my brother gives Gabe a friendly cuff to his shoulder. They are back to being friends and colleagues, which is one of the best things about the past month. Now, seeing the three men who matter most in my life together in one room is practically overwhelming.

In the next few moments, Gabe and I are greeted by

other friends and family, too. His parents. His older brothers, Ethan and Shane. Avery and Nick are here as well. All of our combined family and closest friends are gathered in the pub.

"Come on," Gabe says, after we've been welcomed by everyone. Taking my hand, he leads me to the small, empty dance floor. "Dance with me."

"Dance?" I arch a brow as he takes me tenderly in his arms and we begin to sway together to the ballad that's competing with the chatter of a ball game on the TVs overhead. "You must be feeling romantic, Mr. Noble."

"In fact, I am. I'm feeling everything because of you, Ms. Beckham." He gazes solemnly into my eyes. "I never realized how numb I was before I met you. I used to seek out that feeling, I made it part of my life. Pain killers. Control. Meaningless time spent with forgettable women. Willful estrangement from the people I cared about. I thought the war had taken more than my leg. Hell, I had allowed it to take more than that. Then you showed up." He lifts his hand between us, gently caressing my cheek. "You shook my world in an instant. You challenged me to feel again, Evelyn. Not only with my body and senses . . . but with my heart."

"Gabe," I whisper, trying to hold back the sudden swell of elation his words are causing inside me. Trying, and failing. A small cry spills from my lips. "That's how you make me feel too. Your love saved me—not only that awful day we almost lost each other, but from the beginning. I love you."

He kisses me, right there in front of everyone. "Dance with me, Eve."

I smile against the warmth of his lips. "In case you

haven't noticed, Boy Scout, I am."

"I mean forever." He draws back from me, his hazel eyes filled with raw emotion. Then he slowly, carefully sinks down onto his left knee. "Marry me, Evelyn. I don't know why you chose me over all the other, far better men you deserve, but I'm not going to wait around and let you think better of it. I love you, Evelyn Beckham. Please, marry me."

I can't curb the smile that breaks over my face as he takes my hand in his and reaches into his pocket for a glittering diamond ring.

Joy fills me, so immense I can't hold it inside. And I don't need to. I don't need to hold anything inside with this man. Least of all, my love for him.

"Yes, Gabriel Noble." I nod my head, tears streaming down my cheeks as he slips the beautiful solitaire onto my finger.

The pub room erupts in cheers and applause as I drop down with him on the floor, throwing my arms around his neck. We kiss, surrounded by love, and wrapped in the promise of a future we cannot wait to begin. Together.

~ * ~

You met brilliant artist Jared Rush in the 100
Series. Unravel his darkest secrets and desires in
this emotional standalone novel!

Play My Game

Available Now

eBook * Paperback * Unabridged audiobook

"Adrian simply does billionaires better."
—*Under the Covers*

Never miss a new book from Lara Adrian!

Sign up for Lara's VIP Reader List at
LaraAdrian.com

Be the first to get notified of new releases,
plus be eligible for special VIPs-only exclusive content
and giveaways that you won't find
anywhere else.

Sign up today!

Have you read the entire 100 Series? Don't miss this sexy trilogy featuring alpha billionaire Dominic Baine and struggling artist Avery Ross!

For 100 Days

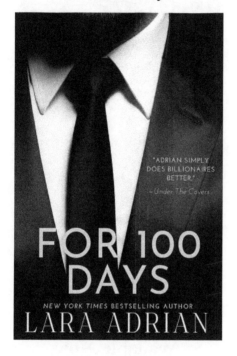

Available Now

eBook * Paperback * Unabridged audiobook

"Adrian simply does billionaires better."
—*Under the Covers*

Nick and Avery's story continues in the
suspenseful, scorchingly sensual second novel!

For 100 Nights

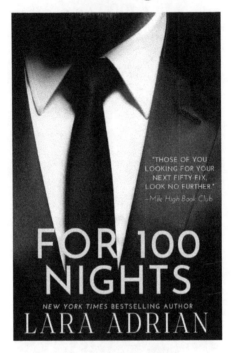

"THOSE OF YOU
LOOKING FOR YOUR
NEXT FIFTY FIX,
LOOK NO FURTHER."
—Mile High Book Club

FOR 100
NIGHTS
NEW YORK TIMES BESTSELLING AUTHOR
LARA ADRIAN

Available Now

eBook * Paperback * Unabridged audiobook

"PHENOMENAL."
—The Sub Club Books

Nick and Avery's story concludes in the
emotional, romantic third novel in the series!

For 100 Reasons

Available Now

eBook * Paperback * Unabridged audiobook

**"An emotional and powerful conclusion that
validated every word in this sensational series."
—*Smut Book Junkie Reviews***

Watch for an exciting new novel in Nick & Avery's steamy, suspenseful saga!

For 100 Forevers

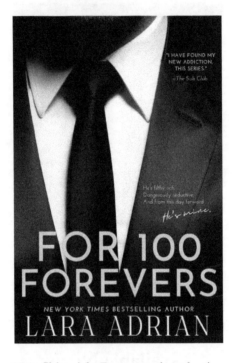

He's filthy rich. Dangerously seductive.
And from this day forward . . . *He's mine.*

Coming in 2025

Sign up at LaraAdrian.com to get notified of this release and other book news from the author.

Love paranormal romance?

Read the Midnight Breed vampire series

A Touch of Midnight (prequel novella)
Kiss of Midnight
Kiss of Crimson
Midnight Awakening
Midnight Rising
Veil of Midnight
Ashes of Midnight
Shades of Midnight
Taken by Midnight
Deeper Than Midnight
A Taste of Midnight (ebook novella)
Darker After Midnight
The Midnight Breed Series Companion
Edge of Dawn
Marked by Midnight (novella)
Crave the Night
Tempted by Midnight (novella)
Bound to Darkness
Stroke of Midnight (novella)
Defy the Dawn
Midnight Untamed (novella)
Midnight Unbound (novella)
Claimed in Shadows
Midnight Unleashed (novella)
Break The Day
Fall of Night
King of Midnight

Discover the Midnight Breed
with a FREE eBook

Get the series prequel novella
A Touch of Midnight
FREE in eBook at most major retailers

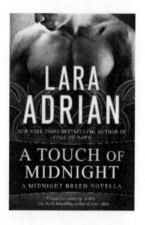

After you enjoy your free read, look for Book 1 at your
favorite bookseller in eBook, print, and audiobook!

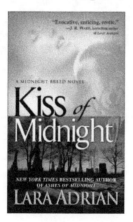

Watch for the epic conclusion of the bestselling
Midnight Breed Series from Lara Adrian!

King of Midnight

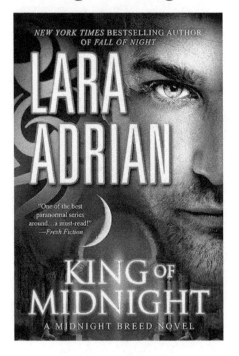

Available Now

eBook * Paperback * Unabridged audiobook

The Hunters are here!

Thrilling standalone vampire romances from Lara Adrian
set in the Midnight Breed story universe.

AVAILABLE NOW

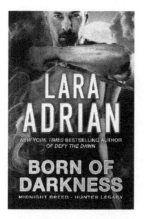

COMING IN 2019

Award-winning medieval romances from Lara Adrian!

Dragon Chalice Series
(Paranormal Medieval Romance)

"Brilliant . . . bewitching medieval paranormal series." –Booklist

Warrior Trilogy
(Medieval Romance)

"The romance is pure gold." –All About Romance

ABOUT THE AUTHOR

LARA ADRIAN is a *New York Times* and #1 international best-selling author, with nearly 4 million books in print and digital worldwide and translations licensed to more than 20 countries. Her books regularly appear in the top spots of all the major bestseller lists including the *New York Times*, USA Today, Publishers Weekly, Amazon.com, Barnes & Noble, etc. Reviewers have called Lara's books "addictively readable" (Chicago Tribune), "extraordinary" (Fresh Fiction), and "one of the consistently best" (Romance Novel News).

With an ancestry stretching back to the Mayflower and the court of King Henry VIII, the author lives with her husband in New England.

Visit the author's website at **LaraAdrian.com**.

Find Lara on Facebook at
www.facebook.com/LaraAdrianBooks

Connect with Lara online at:

www.LaraAdrian.com

www.facebook.com/LaraAdrianBooks

www.goodreads.com/lara_adrian

www.instagram.com/laraadrianbooks

www.pinterest.com/LaraAdrian

www.ingramcontent.com/pod-product-compliance
Lightning Source LLC
Chambersburg PA
CBHW031541090425
24719CB00075B/357